HELP LINE

A Portia McTeague
Novel of Suspense

DOUBLEDAY
New York
London
Toronto
Sydney
Auckland

HELP LINE

FAYE SULTAN
and
TERESA KENNEDY

PUBLISHED BY DOUBLEDAY
a division of Random House, Inc.
1540 Broadway, New York, New York 10036

DOUBLEDAY and the portrayal of an anchor with a dolphin are trademarks of Doubleday,
a division of Random House, Inc.

Library of Congress Cataloging-in-Publication Data

Sultan, Faye.
Help line : a Portia McTeague novel of suspense / Faye Sultan
and Teresa Kennedy.—1st ed.
    p.   cm.
I. Kennedy, Teresa, 1953–   II. Title.
PS3569.U3596H45   1999
813′.54—dc21   98-30253
CIP

ISBN 0-385-48526-3
Copyright © 1999 by Faye Sultan and Teresa Kennedy
All Rights Reserved
Printed in the United States of America
February 1999
First Edition

10 9 8 7 6 5 4 3 2 1

To Ken—everything is possible because of you.
—F.S.

For Andrew Early
in deepest appreciation of his dark and sinister side
—T.K.

HELP LINE

PROLOGUE

He wasn't anything like she'd expected. Not like most of her clients, at any rate. The ones who came to see her in the expensive suite in uptown Charlotte. Tamara Meredith's current offices were a far cry from the airless little room that had been her first place of business, back in the days when she did three-dollar readings out at the strip mall just past Gastonia. Yet, even back in Gastonia, Tamara had been able to pick out her clients as they hurried through the parking lot, to home in on their anxieties as she peered past those flyspecked windows and the neon sign. For all her customers, no matter what their reasons for coming, shared the same, almost embarrassed desperation, as if what had brought them was somehow shameful, an impulse they might have conquered had they only been stronger.

But this one was different; she could see it right away.

Even Angel, her part-time assistant, looked a little bewildered as she ushered him in from the reception area to a nearby chair. Tamara laced her long fingers together and assumed a distant, professional smile. It didn't matter, she thought. He was her last appointment of the day. Tamara allowed the edges of her vision to soften a little, waiting for some impression of him to take form. The man had no discernible aura, save a small darkening near his hip. An orthopedic accident, perhaps, she thought as she rose to greet him. Liver cancer.

Angel edged through the doorway, a perpetually apologetic expression in her dark eyes.

"I have to go," she said to Tamara. "I have a class. Shall I lock the outer office?"

Tamara nodded, still trying to read the client's energy patterns.

"We'll be fine," she said to the man. "Won't we?" She focused pale blue eyes on the client's face. "Thank you for coming." Meredith glanced surreptitiously at her appointment calendar. Paid cash—5:30. No name. Not unusual in her line of work. She assumed a faint smile of omniscient understanding and studied the man for another long moment. The jacket he wore over a collarless linen shirt and jeans wasn't new, but was nevertheless expensive and well made. He was heavily muscled. The man looked like everyone and no one. He sat carefully in his chair and she had the sudden notion that she was watching not the man, but only the image he wanted the world to see. Curious, she thought as she tried to read him. He didn't even look worried.

The worried ones were easy. They came to her when they wouldn't see a doctor or a psychologist or even a minister. They sat in her office and told her things they would say to no one else, confessing their fears and secrets with nearly identical expressions, nervous fingers twisting in their laps as they explained in muted tones about the spread of the cancer, or the mysterious pain, or the savage headaches that tortured them out of sleep. They told her so much without meaning to; their minds already linked intimately to their betraying flesh, their spirits tied to all their secrets with bonds of silent suffering. She would touch them and they would get better; or she would lay her hands upon them to no avail at all. Her clients came and went. Sometimes she was their last resort, sometimes their first. Either way, it was always, oddly, the same.

Cable television had made her something of a local celebrity. Four nights a month of public access brought more clients to

Tamara Meredith than she would have believed possible. The New Age had come to the New South. And here in Charlotte and its environs, the roots of belief ran deep in the psyches of a population given to salvation shows and tent revivals. Tamara offered a change from hell-mongering Bible thumpers with her benign message of healing and personal empowerment, and that message had been welcomed with open arms. In a few short months, she'd all but started her own religion, garnering a passionate following with her vague and reassuring doctrine of universal love. With her artfully blond, almost wraith-like good looks, she scorned a more flamboyant presentation for tailored suits and an uptown office suite. Tamara Meredith offered all the promise of a New Age wrapped in a neat, neo-Baptist package, and her live, call-in cable TV show had taken off immediately in this clean-cut city. Enough so that on top of the stack of papers on her desk were the final sponsorship proposals for a local weekend hour with Charlotte's NBC affiliate.

That step meant a great deal to Tamara, who in recent months had grown weary of the procession of souls who came through her office. Prime time could free her from private clients and their endless sorrows. She was kind enough to turn away no one who came seeking her help; yet she was sensitive enough to be all but overwhelmed by the constant pressure of their need. Finally, she was smart enough to know that, in the end, whatever miracles took place within the bright modern confines of her office were performed not by her hands, nor even by those who needed them, but according to the same capricious law that governed all miracles of healing and illumination. And that law worked always and only at random.

Now, the new client wore a preoccupied smile as he shifted easily in the deep leather chair on the opposite side of her desk, not looking at her, but rather out the window at the mauve-tinted shadows that pooled in the silhouettes of the Charlotte skyline.

"Nice view," he said.

Tamara shivered unexpectedly, though her smile never faltered. A dark, unbidden image rose up in her thoughts and part of her mind went racing after it, while another, more professional aspect began to conduct their interview.

"Tell me, what did you want to talk about today?" Her voice was low and soothing, inviting secrets.

He looked at her then, or rather at some point just above where their eyes should have met, and she saw that part of his confidence, at least, was feigned. The knowledge relaxed her. Perhaps this one was not so different.

Tamara tried another tack. "Where did you first learn about me? From a friend?"

The question appeared to confuse him. "TV, of course. On *Healing Hands, Healing Heart.* I watch you every Tuesday on channel 16."

Tamara folded her hands, long-fingered and startlingly pale on the desk. She noted how her client glanced at them, then dropped his eyes to the carpet, where a pattern of fine leaves curled around reproduction unicorns frolicking lazily in a cobalt-colored field.

"Have we spoken before? On the show? Did you ever call in?"

"I wanted to," he admitted. "But they put me on hold. I never got on. But I wanted to."

"I understand," Tamara said soothingly. Lately her calls had been backed up twenty minutes during the free call-in period. "So you are aware of my—gifts?"

He met her eyes for the first time. "I just want a healing. With your hands. I know you can—I want you to heal me."

And again, without meaning to, Tamara reacted to his tone. A dark and half-formed vision beat like wings against her thoughts and was gone. He must have read something in her face, because when he spoke again, a purplish blush crept around the tops of his ears and collar.

"I'm not a creep or anything."

"It's all right." Tamara fanned her bloodless fingers out against the surface of the desk and looked at them as if they belonged to someone else. "But I want you to understand something before we begin. I don't perform miracles. I wish I could. But I don't. The truth is, I'm not always sure myself why healing touch works, and I know for a fact that sometimes I can't help those who come to me. Even though I wish with all my heart and soul that I could. All I can promise you is that if you need me, I will do my best."

The client's handsome face contorted as he struggled to keep his composure. "What happens—when you—do it? When it works. Can you tell when you've been—successful?"

Tamara offered a delicate shrug. "Not always. Sometimes. You must understand, I am not the power here. All I'm able to do is to channel the energy of the universe. When I lay my hands on another, that energy comes through me to heal. My hands serve to focus a much larger force. And that force is the power of universal love."

He returned his gaze uncomfortably toward the view, the long shadows deepening to indigo in the dying light. "And if it doesn't work?" he asked with a desperate little edge to his voice. "What does that mean? That the universe doesn't love me?"

Now it was the psychic's turn to shift, almost imperceptibly, in her chair. "I'm not able to say," she answered smoothly. "When a healing fails to help the person for whom it was intended, it can mean any number of things. Sometimes it means the person isn't ready to accept the love of the universe. Or perhaps there is something that the soul must learn or experience from suffering. Sometimes," she finished wistfully, "it is only a question of karma."

The man recrossed his legs and looked at her. "Things are just—playing out. Faster and faster."

"What do you mean?" Tamara asked. Suddenly, almost desperately, she wanted to be home, playing with her cat. Away from her office and her clients, safe in her two-bedroom condo by the pool. She forced another, smaller smile, noting the strange excitement that played across the man's features.

His eyes flashed. "Don't you know?"

Oh Christ, Tamara thought. She should have expected as much. It was oddly childish, coming from this character, but it wasn't unexpected in encounters with her clients. Having made it this far, they always felt some need to protect their secrets, to play the game of having her guess.

"I can sometimes read people's auras and find certain problems," she answered evenly. "Sometimes I help them find the answers they seek by channeling their own spiritual guides. Or by using my own."

"Repthi," he interjected. "Your guide. You talk about him all the time. On TV."

"That's right," Tamara said, trying to regain control of the conversation. "But so far, I'm not able to tell why you've come. You don't appear to be physically sick, and you haven't asked any specific questions about the issues that concern you. I want you to understand that we are partners in this. The more information I have, the more I am able to give. The more I know about why you feel you need healing, the better I can direct the energy."

Though it hadn't been intended as such, her client appeared to absorb the comment as a kind of reprimand. He seemed suddenly to draw in on himself, and once again fixed his attention on the patterns in the carpet. In the few silent moments that followed, Tamara watched in astonishment as he began rocking, slowly at first, then more urgently as he wrestled with whatever internal demons had brought him there. Tamara could only wait, torn between regret and impatience as the last of his restless confidence drained away.

At last he looked into her pale eyes and the impact of his misery hit her finely tuned sensors so acutely that she caught her breath, and all her other impressions and emotions were engulfed by an overwhelming sympathy.

"Tell me. I can help you."

"I—don't—know," he managed at last. "It's—inside me somewhere."

"What?" Her voice was barely a whisper in the charged silence. "What's inside you?"

He lowered his eyes. "Blackness," he mumbled. "Just blackness. This—kind of—void. And I have these thoughts—crazy things."

Tamara rose somewhat unsteadily, smiling a little. "I can read your aura at this moment," she told him. "I don't see blackness. I don't see anything but light. I see a man who only needs to learn to love himself."

He gazed up at her. "Then you'll help me? Heal me?"

Her long white fingers rested lightly on the desk, sending an anticipatory tingle up her arms as she felt the power of healing come into her body. She smiled at him, genuinely this time, as she made her way around the desk, her back to the window, soft blond hair catching the last of the sunset's light like a halo. She looked like a spirit, or an angel. He stared at her wordlessly, straightening his back as she came closer.

"Close your eyes," she directed.

She rubbed her hands together, and it made a light rasping in the silent room, almost like whispering.

"Let us begin."

ONE

Portia McTeague elbowed her way through the glass double doors of her offices, arms full of thick case files, a well-used, overstuffed leather briefcase dangling precariously from one hand. Her assistant, Lori, glanced up and fixed her with an amused, slightly sardonic look, taking in her employer's wind-tossed hair and rumpled collar. From the looks of her, Portia had been up half the night. Lori watched as she unceremoniously dumped the files on the chest-high counter that divided them.

"Morning," Lori offered. "You look rested."

Portia squelched the sudden impulse to stick out her tongue in response to Lori's perpetually cheeky tone. Lori's eyes had already returned to the front page of Charlotte's *Star*, which was spread out over the appointment calendar. She propped her head on her hands and frowned over the printed columns as Portia came around and helped herself to morning coffee.

"That's supposed to cost you a quarter," Lori announced without looking up. "For the coffee fund."

Portia sighed, fumbling through her pockets for the necessary coin. The intractable Lori had been with her nearly three years, and never a day had gone by without some form of this good-natured verbal wrangling. "For heaven's sake. It's my office, isn't it?"

Lori half-swiveled on her chair and eyed her boss with wry amusement. "It's your policy, too."

Portia grinned. "I can't get away with anything anymore."

Lori's reply was low and all but unintelligible as she bent back over the paper. Portia swallowed gratefully and slid an adjoining chair from beneath the counter. "What's got you so enthralled?" she asked, peering over Lori's elbow. Her eye caught a photo of an ethereal-looking blonde, well groomed and smiling benignly out from the page.

"Who's that?" she asked. "Nice shot for a news photo. Pretty."

Lori sat up abruptly, snapping the newspaper back into its original folds with a threatening crackle. "The *Star*'s got a machine in the lobby," she said. "But that'll cost you two quarters. Lucky for you I'm done." She handed over the paper.

Portia was just about to offer an equally snappy reply when the phone rang an abrupt interruption. Lori grabbed for the receiver. Portia idly fingered the folds of the paper while she sipped coffee, eavesdropping on her assistant's half of the conversation.

"Is that right?" Lori asked with elaborate concern. "Well, that is inconvenient. What? Yes, ma'am, I'll see what I can do. She's just this minute come through the door. Can you hold for just a minute?" Lori's immaculately manicured finger jabbed at a button.

"It's Miz MacKenzie," she told Portia. "Claims she was so addled after reading about the murder she upended her brand-new bottle of Valium over the toilet bowl trying to get one out. She wants you to call the psychiatrist for a refill."

Portia glanced up, momentarily perplexed. "Doris MacKenzie?" she asked. Doris was a sometime patient with a history of changing therapists, disappearing prescription slips, and a number of gaps in her memory when it came to the use and misuse of mild tranquilizers. In their session two weeks before, Doris had claimed to be sharing her prescription with her Great Dane, Dukey, who had, according to Doris, required no little amount of calming down in the aftermath of a neutering operation. Last week, recalled Portia, she hadn't shown up at all.

"Down the toilet, my eye," she murmured to Lori, who was adroitly balancing the phone against her shoulder. Then, in the next instant: "What murder?"

Lori pointed in the direction of the *Star*. "That murder. Tamara Meredith. My Lord, don't you ever watch TV? It's been all over the news. They found her this morning."

Portia unfolded the paper, seeing again the delicate blonde smiling back at her from the front page.

"So what do I tell Doris?"

Portia thought about it. "Tell her she'll have to call Dr. Matheson herself. Tell her he'll probably want to schedule her for a regular med check before he prescribes anything else. He may want to run some lab work first. She'll have to wait and see."

"Okay, but she's gonna squawk." Lori's eyes held a trace of amusement, as though she were enjoying the prospect of being the bearer of such unpleasant news.

Portia smiled back. "Then tell her to get her butt in here for tomorrow's appointment. No cancellations."

"Yes, Madam Boss." Lori saluted vaguely. "What you said."

"That's Madam Doctor Boss to you—" Portia reached for the paper as Lori passed on the instructions.

Portia scanned the headline: TV HEALER FOUND SLAIN. Then, below that, *Police Report Grisly Scene.*

She began to read in earnest, a little frown of concentration between her brows.

> The body of thirty-three-year-old Tamara Meredith, well-known host of the public access network's television program *Healing Hands, Healing Heart,* seen locally on channel 16, was found murdered late Tuesday morning at her offices in the prestigious Wachovia building in uptown Charlotte. The body was discovered by her associate, Ms. Angel Tirado, when she arrived for work at the Meredith offices around 10:30 A.M.
>
> According to police sources, Meredith

had been brutally attacked with a knife or
similar instrument and may have been
stabbed "a hundred times or more." An
unconfirmed report has suggested the
remains may have been further "mutilated" after death. Police would not comment on whether or not Ms. Meredith
was sexually assaulted.

The last sentence in the paragraph made Portia grit her teeth.
Damn the press, she thought. And damn the public, too. It wasn't
enough the poor woman had been stabbed to death—and mutilated. What everybody couldn't wait to know was if she'd been
raped as well. Rage that resulted in a murder like this always had a
sexual connection. Whether the killer had spent his lust through
the stabbing, through a rape and then murder, or by masturbating
over the corpse would be critical to forming his profile. But all the
media ever wanted to play up was whether the victim had sex before
she died. As if being raped made a woman somehow more of a
victim even than dying. Irritated, she read on.

Ms. Tirado, a graduate student in nutri-
tion with a minor in world religions, has
been questioned and released and is not
considered a suspect at this time.
Police have, however, launched a full-
scale investigation into what one officer
has described as "the most savage and
sickening crime scene I have ever wit-
nessed." It has been speculated that local
authorities may call in experts from the
Federal Bureau of Investigation for forensic assistance.
Fans and devoted followers of Ms.
Meredith have expressed grief and out-
rage over the loss of what one former client described as "the most holy person I
have ever known." Funeral arrangements, yet to be announced by Meredith's family, are pending a completed
autopsy. Interested parties are encouraged
to make contributions in Ms. Meredith's
memory to the InterGroup Open Center
Foundation, a New Age alternative healing information resource library.

Portia glanced up to find Lori eyeballing her curiously. "Awful, isn't it?"

"Awful enough," agreed Portia. And it was disturbing. For all of her work in forensic psychology, for all the times she had testified at murder trials all over the country, she still preferred to think of Charlotte, North Carolina, as a place at least marginally insulated from violent crime. The idea that Meredith had been attacked in her offices made Portia a little uneasy.

"So what do you think?" Lori was asking.

Portia glanced at her. "Think of what?"

"You know, that forensics stuff. You ought to call the DA. Offer to do some profile or something."

Portia folded the paper, having finished the last of the article. "I do forensic *psychology*, remember? They have to have a suspect before I can talk to him. I can't come up with a why until they've rounded up a who. I'm not a cop."

"But the profiling thing is really happening," Lori insisted. "Getting shrinks involved right from the beginning."

Portia smiled thinly. "As you may recall, the Detective Division cops and myself aren't especially close. My testimony in court has a way of screwing up their plans to march somebody into the death house." The psychologist paused, scowling fiercely.

"Well," Lori answered. "You still could help them catch the guy."

"Thanks, but no thanks. I'm out of that stuff, anyway." Portia peered closely at her assistant's round, carefully made-up face. "Why're you so interested?"

Lori stared at her, exasperated. "Everybody's interested, for heaven's sake. Tamara Meredith was practically famous. The whole city's talking about it! Why, I spent half the night on the phone with my sister-in-law. She was so upset, you would have thought she'd lost a member of her own family."

A little perplexed, Portia rose and went for another cup of coffee, but not before writing and carefully dropping a signed IOU into the nearby basket. "But why? Who was she?"

Lori shook her head in disgust. "Man, you really don't get around much, do you?"

"I guess not," Portia admitted, still trying to place the face in the newspaper. Try as she might, the delicate blonde's features remained those of a stranger. An unfortunate one, certainly, but despite the seeming furor over the crime, Portia was sure she had never seen that face before.

Seeing her obvious confusion, Lori tried patiently to explain. "Tamara Meredith has—well—had—a television show. Like a psychic show. Where people would call in with their problems and she would help them. A lot of folks thought she was really good. Gifted. She even—"

"A psychic show?" Portia had to fight to hide her incredulous smile. "You mean like Dionne Warwick?"

Lori waved her silent. "No. Not like Dionne Warwick. From what I know, Tamara was—well—for real. At least, a lot of people said so. I used to watch her sometimes, and she was . . ." The young woman faltered, unsure of how to explain. "What I mean is—it always looked like she knew what she was talking about. Tamara was just so—real—normal. I mean, for somebody with special powers."

Portia bit her lip hard so as not to betray her amusement at this disclosure. "Lori," she chided gently. "Special powers?"

Her assistant nodded emphatically as she gulped the last dregs from her own mug. "That's why my sister-in-law was so upset. She went to her. And Tamara healed her."

Portia cocked an eyebrow, hiding a grin behind the rim of her cup. "Healed her?"

"Yeah. Her back. Corine messed it up bad when she had her last baby. Ruptured a disk or something. They said she needed surgery, but she went to Tamara and Tamara laid hands on her. And boom—cured! No surgery. No more painkillers. She just slings that baby around like it was nothing now."

Portia found herself thoroughly flummoxed. Though she'd certainly heard of psychics and even psychic healers, the notion went so utterly against her training and scientific background that she couldn't help herself. Here was Lori—levelheaded, cynical Lori, unflappable Lori—extolling the virtues of a cable television psychic. A breed that, despite all the quasi-mystical New Age palaver, Portia put in roughly the same category as snake oil salesmen and thieving gypsies. The idea of Lori in the ranks of a TV mystic's rapt audience seemed so completely preposterous, so utterly out of character, that McTeague couldn't have been more astonished if her assistant had chosen that particular moment to sprout a halo and wings.

"I guess you don't believe in any of this, do you?" Lori asked, clearly a little disappointed.

Portia shrugged, feeling suddenly, oddly ignorant under her assistant's bright-eyed scrutiny. "No, I guess I don't," she admitted. "Don't go for the woo-woo stuff. Never did. It's not my nature."

It wasn't, either. In her career as a forensic psychologist, Portia had already fallen witness to too much human misery to believe that it was something separate from the rest of existence, and she'd never convinced herself that goodness and wholeness could be anything so simple as "aligning oneself with the love of the universe." To her way of thinking, the personality's darker impulses might be acknowledged, managed, or even redirected, but they could never be entirely exorcised. Darkness was part of what it meant to be human.

Lori busied herself stacking and sorting the disarranged files. "Some people don't believe," she went on crisply. "And that's fine with me. But I know about my sister-in-law. And I tell you she was cured. By Tamara Meredith."

Portia glanced down at the paper, still unfurled on the countertop. "Too bad," she murmured.

"What?" Lori had already made her way to the row of filing cabinets at the far end of the room.

"Nothing," the psychologist answered mildly. "I was just thinking that it's too bad there's nobody around to cure Tamara."

"Ain't that the truth. But you'd better get back to your office. Phyllis Leech is due in about thirty seconds."

Portia hastily gathered her cup, culled an assortment of file folders from those prepared for the morning's appointments, grabbed her briefcase, and kneed open the door to the hallway that led to her private office. "Buzz me when she gets here," she said. "What's the rest of the day like?"

"Back to back this morning," said Lori, stooping over the appointment calendar and running a sharpened pencil point down a column written in her own cramped hand. "Lunch at one, and free the rest of the day."

Portia stopped in her tracks, a stray lock of auburn hair falling across her forehead. "Really? Free as in free time?"

"No," replied Lori simply. "Free as in not getting paid. You're on for a shift at the Help Line this afternoon. Remember? You still work—you're just not getting ninety dollars an hour."

"Very funny. I'm glad to volunteer down there and you know it."

"Whatever you say." Suddenly Lori's face brightened. "Hey, why don't you get your own talk show? Live, call-in shrink? That way, you could be a celebrity."

Portia could only gape at her in feigned horror. "Lori, are you trying to get me killed?"

Unexpectedly her assistant flushed, thoroughly offended. "Now what kind of a thing is that to say? You've got murderers on the brain."

"I do not—"

"You do, too. I swear, ever since you cut out your court cases, you've been psychoanalyzing the rest of us like we're all ready to go postal or something. For your information, I just thought TV'd be good for business."

Portia sighed heavily under the weight of the files and briefcase in her arms. "Thanks," she answered. "But I've got enough business, don't you think?"

Her assistant settled back down at her place near the phones, shaking her head. "You must be a Capricorn," she said. "You never want to try anything new."

Portia backed out into the hallway, grinning in spite of herself. First psychic healers, now astrology. "Nice try," she told her. "But as you well know, I'm a Sagittarius."

Still, Lori was right about one thing—all of Charlotte, it seemed, was abuzz with news of the murder. Phyllis Leech, her nine o'clock, was a local librarian with a theory about how Tamara Meredith had really been a devil worshipper; while her ten o'clock, Abel Delaney, a retired First Union executive, put forth his thoughts on how the crime was really the work of the federal government. Maxine Jenkins, a sixteen-year-old unwed mother, had been a regular caller on Meredith's show and confided how she had begun to develop her own psychic abilities and was trying to tune in on the killer's identity.

In short, Portia's therapeutic progress that morning was utterly overshadowed by two equally alarming revelations. The first was that whatever their specific and entirely individual reasons for seeking psychological counseling, her patients all seemed to know exactly who Tamara Meredith had been and what she was supposed to be able to do. And a number of them implied without meaning to that psychologists and psychics were more or less the same species. It seemed the consensus pointed to the idea that if psychics were outside the mainstream, it was only because their particular area of expertise had yet to be adequately explored by science. Or, as one patient pronounced: "Just because you can't get a Ph.D. in something doesn't mean you don't know what you're talking about."

And if all that weren't bad enough, the second, equally unnerving notion was that Portia, for all that she prided herself on awareness of her world and the workings of the human mind, was more or less completely ignorant on the subject of psychics in general and the now deceased Tamara Meredith in particular.

So the morning's sessions left her oddly out of sorts. As she waited for her final appointment of the day, she struggled to examine her own reactions. Something about the whole business made her feel positively narrow-minded. Though she was well aware of the spread of the so-called "alternative" therapies, she found herself a little resentful of how widely such philosophies were, if not accepted, then at least tolerated by the general public. If nothing else, she knew her patients represented a fair cross section of North Carolinians. It was like finding out that the New Age had become the First Church of Suburbia, a congregation to which everyone seemed to belong. Everyone, that is, but Portia McTeague.

As it turned out, her final appointment of the morning was a no-show, and after waiting fifteen minutes, she was only too glad to pack up and head out for a leisurely lunch. She scorned the quiche-

and-fern bars in the immediate neighborhood and headed for a simple coffee shop nearer the Help Line headquarters in an older, less distinguished area of the city.

The noisy bustle of the noontime rush was oddly comforting as she perched on a counter stool and, scorning her usual salad, treated herself to a huge cheeseburger with a side of onion rings. It meant that she'd have to skip supper, but she didn't especially care. Salads and sprouts and no-fat organics were, in her mind, tied too closely to New Age philosophy, so she opted for the least "spiritual" food she could think of. A number of the regulars (and it was a place that seemed to be populated almost entirely by regulars) took an interest in her presence and eyed her curiously as she munched, idly thumbing through a magazine.

"You're that psychologist, aren't you?"

Portia looked up to see the waitress refilling her glass with iced tea and blushing furiously. The waitress jerked a thumb at a gaggle of secretaries lined up a few seats away. "Margie said it was you. The one who was on TV last fall."

Portia nodded and plastered on what she hoped was a gracious smile. Ever since the Jimmy Weir trial, she'd come to be known around Charlotte as "that psychologist," or worse, "that lady shrink," because of her appearance at a number of television news conferences in the aftermath of the verdict. Even though the trial itself had taken place in South Carolina, the media in five surrounding states had jumped on the jury's choice of a life sentence over the death penalty as evidence of Weir's having somehow beaten the system. A sign, many locals believed, of society's ultimate and imminent moral decline. Public opinion had run high against the decision, and Portia had been dealing with the unwelcome notoriety ever since.

"That was me," she offered noncommittally, wishing the waitress away.

"I thought so," the woman went on. "What are you doing in this neck of the woods?"

"I work at the Help Line," Portia replied as civilly as she was able. "Down on Hawthorne, across from Presbyterian Hospital. I volunteer there a couple of afternoons a month."

The waitress met the comment with a blank look. "Oh," she went on. Then she nodded obliquely in the direction of the secretaries. "It was Evelyn thought you weren't. Evelyn said the one on TV was a lot younger."

And fuck you too, Evelyn, thought Portia. She made an effort to brighten her smile, directing it toward the women at the far end of the counter. Mentally she braced herself. What was next? Would they come over to offer an unsolicited opinion of her professional skills? One more of those tired eye-for-an-eye speeches? But, to Portia's relief, that was apparently the end of it. The group giggled like schoolgirls and went back to their lunches, whispering among themselves, while the waitress went to catch up with her orders.

Portia went for her pocketbook, already feeling the greasy burger begin to haunt her digestion. At her left elbow, another copy of the morning's paper was spread out over the counter, the headlines screaming their refrain: Tamara Meredith, slain celebrity. Television, Portia reflected bitterly, counting out money to pay the check and leave a stingier-than-usual tip. She glanced again at the fair-haired beauty in the newspaper photograph. A few simple answers at a few televised news conferences had garnered her more un-wanted notoriety than she would have dreamed possible. And yet it was the same medium that had made a celebrity of Tamara Meredith and her psychic sideshow, perhaps even part of the reason why she had been killed, the object of some starstruck stalker's revenge fantasy. One thing was for sure, the public was far too susceptible to the images and messages that came pouring at them from the idiot box.

Portia shook her head as she rose from the counter. She glanced at the stark black-and-white face of the old-style clock above the front door. If she hurried, she'd have a chance to walk around the block, maybe muster a better frame of mind before her shift at the Help Line began.

She was so wrapped up in her own irritated thoughts that she never noticed the man who'd been reading the newspaper, perched on the seat next to her own. She never saw his curious expression when he looked at her, or noted how he had eavesdropped on her conversation with the waitress. She was through the doors and back out into the sunshine, never once seeing how a kind of smile began to play around the corners of his mouth as he watched her leave.

Not Portia McTeague, nor indeed anyone else in the noisy, crowded luncheonette took particular note that day of the man who sat alone in front of a half-empty cup of cooling coffee with an odd, bemused little smile playing over his handsome features as he bent over the photo of Tamara Meredith and read again the details of her terrible fate. No one saw as he pressed his fingers first to his lips and then to her black-and-white image in a lingering farewell.

TWO

Kate Loveless sat in a scratchy, pistachio-colored designer suit, munching on the stalk of pale celery that had garnished her Bloody Mary and cursing to herself. She glanced at her watch and wished to God she were doing something productive instead of cooling her heels in this sun-drenched, relentlessly cheerful, and thoroughly pretentious little hellhole of a bistro, waiting for the latest godsend from Florida to show up for their lunch date.

Still, she thought sourly as she motioned to the waiter and ordered another drink, it was probably her own fault, having to eke out her afternoons in meetings like this, making nice with the new talent while the real newshounds were out there in the trenches. Her managing editorship at the Charlotte *Star* had sentenced her to at least three such luncheons a week, more often four or five. She met with the guys at corporate, she met with the big advertising accounts, and sometimes, like today, she met with a reporter. Her job demanded these endless, polite little meetings, and after four years they all ran together in a blur of business suits and insufferable conversation.

She gazed out miserably over the crowded restaurant, watching as the tense and falsely cheerful patrons got down to the business of lunch, making their deals and bargains, plotting their strategies. A line from *Prufrock* echoed in her head—"*I have measured out my life with coffee spoons . . .*" She felt as though she could measure out her own in goat cheese salads. Or breadsticks maybe, laid end to end.

Still, she had no one but herself to blame. It seemed this perpetual lunching was the price she paid for having landed a job she had wanted for more than twenty years. And now that she had it, all her dreams of real power had evaporated.

At fifty-three, Kate Loveless had gone from being one of the best news writers around to a closet full of expensive suits, a comfortable investment portfolio, and a calendar full of paralyzing lunch dates. She knew better than anyone that her title was little more than a joke; corporate called all the real shots.

The news of Tamara Meredith's murder had only made her situation more apparent. The call-in report had come from a kid working the police band, and from all the indications, the story promised to have some legs as far as real news went. Depending on the suspects, of course, depending on the details that any decent writer might ferret out in the course of the investigation—the autopsy results, the mourners at what would doubtless be a well-attended funeral. The angles of a murder like this one could be worked for weeks, maybe as long as a month.

But as Kate sipped her drink and peered disgustedly toward the restaurant's entrance, she knew in advance that whatever writers might be assigned to the story, she wouldn't and couldn't be one of them. For in her own mind, Kate Loveless had sold out; she was management now, and little more than a figurehead, thanks to the latest merger with their sister papers in Orlando. The merger was one of the reasons for today's meeting. John Campion, Orlando's ersatz wonder boy, was busy climbing the corporate ladder after a tiff with his editor down there. He'd been smart enough to lobby for a transfer before it really hit the fan, and his contract with the *Star* included limited syndication and a picture to run with his byline. What that meant to Kate Loveless was that she was being saddled with another shit-for-brains pretty boy whose photo sold papers, whose idea of social commentary was endless speculation on who was fucking whom in Hollywood or the impact of aromatherapy on stress levels. She held little hope that Campion would be any different. They were all princes and princesses these days. Little more than kids who thought their journalism degrees owed them some kind of living. None of them liked to get their hands dirty—not anymore.

Kate shifted uncomfortably and took care to put her drink down before she decided to finish it too quickly. It was just another lunch, she reminded herself. And Campion was apparently corporate's newest flavor-of-the-month. The new kid on the block, who'd no doubt try to impress her and take this meeting as an opportunity to pitch some lame story idea. He would be young and charming and clueless—they were all clueless in Kate's estimation. Her black eyes roamed the crowd restlessly.

Who knows? she thought with a small, grim smile. They might hit it off. Campion would be young and handsome and chock full of ambition. Maybe even savvy enough to drop a hint about finding her attractive. Maybe, if she were lucky.

She looked younger than she was, thanks to some fairly dominant steel magnolia genes on her mother's side and a grueling exercise program at the hands of a Swedish personal trainer. Naturally lean, her tough, youthful buoyance had mellowed to a kind of icy élan. Her white blond hair fell in a straight line to her jawbone, awesomely effective against a flawless olive complexion and those restless black eyes.

Over the years, she'd seen more than one young wonder boy come and go from her bed, though it was true the offers came less frequently than they once had. It wasn't that she missed the boy toys, or that she wanted them either. But she enjoyed their youth, their mindless enthusiasm, and their stamina for sex. Most especially she enjoyed her power over them. Power over their lives, their careers—she found it endlessly ironic that this was perhaps the only real power she still possessed. And though Kate wasn't especially proud of that quality in herself, she'd nevertheless found it a comfort often enough, curled in a pair of muscular arms in the light of some drunken dawn. In any event, sleeping with her employees had never caused her a moment's regret, for Kate Loveless had sold her own soul too long ago to suffer any pangs of conscience about what she did with her body after that.

But if a little pat-and-giggle was what she had in mind for the newest addition to her staff, Kate was curiously disappointed when, ten minutes later, John Campion finally showed up at her table, full of effusive apologies. She looked up to meet a pair of oddly soulful eyes that were a strange shade, somewhere between amber and olive green, the irises flecked with gold. He was stocky and square-jawed, shorter than she might have wished, and looked to be losing his hair, or more precisely, trying not to. A not-quite-invisible line of transplant plugs marked his hairline, and she found herself trying to avoid peering at them as he slid into an adjoining chair with a powerful, tightly controlled grace.

Kate nodded only perfunctorily at his too long story of getting lost in traffic, while she studied him with the practiced eye of a trainer sizing up horseflesh. He should have been attractive, but somehow his tan and his hair plugs and his stocky, thickly muscular build put her off. His camel hair jacket and trim, flawlessly pressed pleated trousers looked as if he were trying too hard, the subtle silk jacquard of his tie calculated to make an impression.

Campion, for his part, took careful note of her half-finished Bloody Mary and ordered himself a beer. For all his apologies, he didn't appear to be especially nervous, or particularly sorry either. As the waiter took down his order, and Campion met Kate's eyes once more, he flashed her a smile so confident it was almost a challenge.

"Another for Ms. Loveless," he said without asking.

"No, thanks," she interrupted coolly, and allowed herself a small smile at Campion's startled expression. "I'll get one if I want one."

He grinned again in answer, and she could see he had a generous mouth, lips full and inviting, teeth white and flawless. And still, the effect was strangely disconcerting, the smile so perfect it was like a disguise. Mentally she shook herself. In another moment, she'd be counting his fillings. She'd been prepared to hate him—that was all. Just as she'd hated everything since getting out of bed that morning, and the morning before that. It wasn't Campion's fault he was trying to look good in a world where everyone judged everyone else by exactly those criteria. Writers couldn't be just writers anymore—they had to be personalities too. Sincerity had ceased to be part of the job description.

"Sorry," Campion was saying. "I didn't mean to presume."

"Good reporters shouldn't," she commented evenly and returned his bright, phony smile in kind. "If you don't take anything for granted, you can't ever be disappointed, can you? So, tell me, what do you think of our little metropolis? Save for the fact that it's so difficult to find your way around?"

If he registered the snipe at all, it didn't show on his face. "Beautiful," he answered. "I've only just gotten settled, but so far I think I'm going to make out fine. I met some of the team down at the paper last night. They seem like a great bunch of people."

Bunch is right, the managing editor thought. Most days, her staff at the *Star* blurred together in her mind, their talents and enthusiasms as difficult to distinguish one from another as a number of grapes. "Oh," she went on politely, wondering how he'd managed it. "Already?"

Campion nodded with a single jerk of his squarish head. "Yeah, I decided to check out a few things on my own. So I hung around until the early shift was up and followed a few people after work. They all headed to a place called The Snug around the corner from the *Star* building, so I went up and introduced myself."

Kate nodded, flushing slightly with a mixture of annoyance and nostalgia. The Snug was a beer-and-burger joint nestled halfway between the *Star*'s offices and police headquarters. If she closed her eyes, she could still smell the mixture of beer and smoke and hamburger grease that hung over the place, hear the comforting uproar from the patrons. For years, it had been her place, an all-important source of information during her hectic days on the police beat, and an oasis from her cramped shotgun-style rental house on Tremont Street.

Once, she'd made regular jokes about buying stock in the joint, she spent so much time there. But lately, she'd been only once, shortly after her promotion. She'd shown up in a Chanel suit and heard the deafening silence as the ranks of reporters and copy boys and secretaries tried not to stare, watching as the off-duty cops closed ranks, silently resentful of her intrusion into their territory. She hadn't gone again, though she missed the place like an old friend. The run-down bar wasn't the last friend she'd lost in her climb to management, but it had been one of the first, and the memory still stung.

"Well," she went on, too brightly. "Did my employees all put you off by spinning terrible stories of unfair labor practices? Did they complain about being chained to their terminals day after merciless day?"

Campion shrugged. "Nothing so extreme, I'm afraid. We all just hung out. Swapped war stories. You know."

She did indeed.

His beer came and Campion poured it slowly, down the side so as not to bruise the head. He met her eyes again, and again she had the unsettling feeling that he was calculating something, sizing her up just as she was him. "I might mention one thing, though," he said after another moment. "Based on what some of your people told me?"

She returned his gaze warily, struck by the odd color of his eyes, those flecks of hidden gold. Christ, Kate, she chided herself. Get a grip.

"You are definitely the most beautiful dragon lady I've ever met."

Kate had to stare into her menu to keep from laughing out loud. Oh, this one was good, she thought, though she was in no danger of falling for his dressed-up, MTV version of the old "shucks ma'am" charm. She braced herself for a round of what promised to be some fun and games. If there were any falling to be done, she intended to make sure Campion fell first and on her terms. She looked him square in the eye.

"I'll have the cobb salad," she said, secretly relishing the momentary look of confusion that crossed his face. "And I'll skip the side of bullshit, if you don't mind."

Oddly enough, Campion refused to look down, or blush, or do anything else to offer some excuse for the remark. As if it would somehow be beneath his dignity to admit to flattery. "Touché," he answered simply. "I suppose I deserved that. What do you say we call it a draw?"

Kate smiled thinly. Maybe it was only the Bloody Marys, but she found herself warming up to John Campion, despite rather than because of his obvious and practiced charms. At least he wasn't stupid, and that alone came as something of a relief. Enough at least, that she found herself relenting a bit, willing to give him a chance.

Kate reached for the basket between them and cracked a bread-stick. "I've read some of your stuff. Some of it's decent. Not brilliant, in my own opinion. But decent. And," she said, pausing as the waiter reappeared to take their orders, "I am going to ask this next question just one time. I want you to answer it as honestly as you can. No kiss-up-to-the-editor party line crap, okay?"

He leaned back a little in his chair as if to distance himself from whatever was coming. Something hardened in his eyes as he spoke again. Something almost like hostility, though whether it was toward her or toward himself was impossible for her to fathom.

"Oh, spare me," he went on. "You're not going to ask why I haven't lived up to my potential, are you? Why I haven't gone after the big scoop? Or scored some bogus journalism prize?"

Kate found herself as close to blushing as she ever got. In fact, that was damn close to what she had been about to ask. Campion's writing had real potential, but his style, though eminently readable, seemed never to quite come to grips with what Kate perceived as the guts of any story—the issues behind the facts, all those nuances of reason that made a story a story in the first place. Campion's work was high on technique, to be sure—he adequately addressed the who, what, why, when, and where with style and confidence. But for all of that, she'd found, his material had an odd, almost half-finished quality, long on facts perhaps, but short on truth. Or at least what she thought of as truth—that passion good news writers have that isn't really about the facts at all, but about needing to know more than the facts. Digging deeper until they got at the real truth—the one with the capital "T."

She struggled to compose herself. When she was pretty sure her complexion had resumed its characteristic tone, she managed to meet Campion's gaze once more. His expression was utterly composed.

"Now who's bullshitting?" he asked.

Kate raised a carefully plucked eyebrow. "Meaning?"

"Meaning, you know the business," he replied evenly. "And the business demands a degree of fluff. Marshmallow cream. Fluff was what my editor wanted in Orlando, and Virginia before that. Though it wasn't so bad back in Virginia. Maybe because it was closer to D.C. Or maybe the world just got stupider, you know what I'm saying?"

Kate had to admit that she did.

Campion leaned closer, as if he were about to confide some secret, his eyes intent. "Look, I'm a decent enough writer, maybe someday I could even be a great one. But there's no law that says I have to be. I do a good job and meet my deadlines. I'm not a drunk and I don't do dope. I work for the *Star* now. And for you. But that doesn't mean you own me."

Kate sipped her drink, thoroughly taken aback.

Campion grinned again and his eyes softened a little, as if he both enjoyed and understood the effects of his statement. "The truth is, I took this job because back in Florida, I got sick of all the substantive stuff getting edited out. When all your best stuff gets shot down, you stop trying after a while. So I learned to do things their way."

"Campion, are you trying to make me feel sorry for you?" Kate interjected. What she didn't say was that she did, a little. The bitterness of his tone spoke to her own frustrations in a way she couldn't entirely ignore.

The reporter shook his head and swallowed more beer, never taking his eyes from her face. "No," he went on. "I'm just saying that I'm adaptable, okay? I'll work just as hard as you let me work, or I'll give you just as much junk as you want. It's all up to you."

Kate stared at him in some confusion, her untouched salad in front of her. Their conversation had hit a nerve or something very close to one, scratched an itch she was only half aware of having. If nothing else, she found her new reporter's forthrightness completely refreshing. At the same time, she was dimly aware of another thought taking shape in another corner of her mind: Maybe Campion was merely trying to set her up, trying to paint himself as some kind of victim of bad editors, so she would go easy on him. Lord only knew he wouldn't be the first writer to try that one. She studied him for a moment as he sat picking at a hangar steak and french fries, chewing slowly. When he glanced up again, his eyes held the same look they had when she'd caught him trying to flatter her. A look that told her she could make what she wanted of his remarks, but that he did not intend to further compromise his dignity with any half-assed excuses.

If that look was bait, in the end Kate Loveless was too much of a newswoman not to nibble. She speared a piece of avocado with her fork. "Sounds like you've got a story you want to pitch," she said offhandedly.

As if on cue, Campion flashed his bright smile. Jesus, thought Kate. He should have gone into television. Another month and the plugs wouldn't even show.

"Sure do," he told her. "Isn't that what we're here for?"

Kate raised an eyebrow. "Is it?" she asked with a trace of sarcasm. "I have been known to make some story assignments personally.

"Well, don't go sending me off to the Dogpatch tractor pull or some garden show before you've heard what I've got, okay?" Campion's smile never wavered. But something in his eyes dared her to listen.

"So—I'm listening. What have you got?" She waited, almost afraid to hear it. Afraid that it would turn out to be some lamebrained angle from Hillary Clinton's ex-secretary of lingerie. Or an in-depth interview with an animal therapist. Something that would make her ashamed of having been guilty of even a moment of confidence in the dandified egomaniac seated across from her.

The gold shone in the flecks of Campion's eyes. He leaned closer, as if to heighten the confidentiality of his next statement. "It's this Meredith murder," he said. "I was eavesdropping on some of the cops at the bar, and I think I've got an angle."

Kate didn't know she'd been holding her breath until she let it out. Careful, warned some inner voice, he could still screw it up.

She looked at him, eyes narrowed. "What angle?"

Campion placed his knife and fork carefully, crossing them at the top of his plate to signal he was done. When he looked at her again, his face was quiet, almost grave.

"I've got a lot of stuff that never made it to the page in Orlando. I've been working on it for a long time. I was going to put it all in a book, but I thought I'd come to a dead end. You can't publish a book without an ending, you know?"

Kate nodded, another red flag going up in the back of her mind. In her experience, reporters who wanted to be book authors almost always had some ax to grind, considered themselves closet poets, or were obsessed with fame and fortune, which was probably the worst of all.

Campion took a breath. "I'd pretty much bagged the whole idea of the book. Until this Meredith murder. When the story broke, I was still unpacking. I'd turned on the tube for some background noise. And it all started coming back. I don't know. Things started to make sense. Coming up here from Florida—this murder. All the research. It was like—kismet."

"What was?" Kate demanded impatiently.

He met her eyes calmly. "It's my hunch the Meredith murder is the work of a serial killer," he answered simply. "And unless I miss my guess, the authorities aren't going to put it together. Not until there's another one. The fact is, from what I managed to pick up the other night at The Snug, Charlotte's finest don't have a fucking clue."

A hundred objections bubbled to Kate's lips. A hunch doesn't make a story. Serial killers don't grow on trees. Bumbling cops don't make for feel-good copy and won't sell papers—and more. But Kate said none of those things. There was time enough for all that later. Instead she drained the last of her Bloody Mary and said, without a trace of cynicism, "I haven't heard the angle, Campion."

He smiled as though he'd just won something. "Okay, here it is. I worked the crime beat down in Orlando for a few months before they kicked me upstairs. I've got complete documentation on three other murder cases, all unsolved. One was a nurse, killed in a hospital parking lot. Same MO as Meredith—strangled, mutilated, multiple stab wounds. The guy cut off her ears. Another was a nun, across the state line over in Georgia, maybe eight months before the one in Orlando. I stumbled across it when I was going through the archives at the *Sentinel.* Same MO, more or less—strangulation, heavy knife work. He covered her face with her veil. Her tongue had been cut out. No sexual assault and still unsolved. The one before that was a doctor. Strangled, same as the others. But no cutting and no souvenirs."

Kate glanced at him skeptically. "So what? A similar MO on three unsolved murders doesn't make for a serial killer. Where's the connection?"

Campion shook his head slowly and went on to elaborate. "I didn't see it at first. I got into the whole thing by accident—just going through the open homicide files. I was planning to do a series of those Still Unsolved retrospectives for my column. Anyway, I came up with enough stuff for a year's worth of columns before my ME shot it down. Too gruesome. He thought it would make the readers paranoid." He shrugged vaguely at the memory and went on.

"So I thought, fuck him, and started to put together a book." Campion smiled ruefully. "For a while there, I guess I thought a book would be my ticket out of Disney World."

Kate understood. She'd been to Orlando.

"When I really got into it, I began to think there was a pattern in those three murders." Campion put up a hand when he caught Kate's skeptical expression. "I know, I know. Three cases doesn't make for much of a book. Hell, it doesn't make for much of a serial killer. But the pattern was still there if you looked." He began to tick off the items on his fingers.

"The first, strangulation, no assault, no cutting, no trophies. The second strangled and mutilated, but no sexual assault. The third was strangled, raped, knifed, and mutilated. You see? It would fit the serial pattern. As he's moving around, he's escalating. The ritual gets more complicated every time." Campion uttered a short, unpleasant laugh. "He's got to find ways to keep it interesting."

Kate allowed herself a tight nod. "What does that have to do with Meredith?"

"She was this healer, right? I think that's some kind of link. Maybe the guy keeps looking for help. Maybe there's something wrong with him. Something nobody can fix."

Kate turned the idea over in her mind, mentally grimacing. Part of her almost liked John Campion and was pleased to know that they shared enough curiosity about the world to go snooping after a story. At least Campion had looked for a pattern in these pet cases of his. That alone was more than she was able to say for most of the wet-behind-the-ears Jimmy Olsons in her employ. On the other hand, she knew just how easy and how treacherous it could be to find a pattern in random events simply because you were looking for one. And the last thing she wanted was to turn Campion loose to terrorize a sensation-hungry public with some half-baked, puffed-up crap about a serial killer. A tri-state serial killer no less, now stalking the magnolia-lined neighborhoods of Charlotte, North Carolina. Even the thought was somehow absurd to her. She knew the city well enough to realize that even its murders were of a more familiar variety—crimes of passion, mostly. Jealous lovers or stressed-out family members or the occasional downsized malcontent taking potshots at the post office.

The waiter appeared to clear their plates and Kate ordered coffee with a sudden, almost overwhelming sense of relief. In the end, she realized, she would prove herself the dragon lady and kill his story, despite Campion's obvious intensity, even despite her own instincts. If mere theories were stories, John Campion would be a hot item, the star reporter every newspaper longs for. But even the best theories need facts to make the story stick and even real stories need an angle to capture the attention of a capricious readership. Campion's pitch didn't have any of those things. She studied him intently as their coffee appeared, stirred in sweetener, and sipped politely. At the last moment she smiled and tried to look kind, moving in for the kill. She might have to play the dragon, but at least lunch would be over.

"Campion," she asked. "One obvious question occurs to me here."

He glanced up, not smiling for once. His olive eyes were alert, even wary, having caught something all too familiar in her tone. "Ask away."

"If you're right, how come the police haven't caught on? How come all of the authorities who've investigated these murders of yours didn't happen to notice what you think you've noticed? And if the Meredith murder is linked somehow to these other cases, what makes you think the authorities don't already know that?" Kate made herself continue, despite the flicker of surprise that played across Campion's features. Whatever the boy wonder had expected, it clearly hadn't been resistance. Kate raised her fingers and, in an unconscious imitation of Campion's earlier gesture, marked off the strikes against him with each melon-colored fingernail.

"You talk like you know a lot about serial killers. But face it, so does everybody else. Anybody who reads mystery novels knows the routine." She ticked off the attributes one by one. "The escalation of violence, the mutilation, ritual behavior. A guy who moves around a lot. A predator. Set the cat on fire as a kid, got Ds in school. All fine. But these days, the cops have profilers and psychologists and forensics people to figure this stuff out. They've got experts—the FBI, for Christ's sake. Are you trying to tell me they haven't noticed a pattern in these murders when you have? When every other guy who reads the papers can probably figure it out?"

Kate paused for breath, a fixed gaze directed at her fingernails, suddenly exasperated with both herself and with Campion. She wanted to look at anything but Campion's face, knowing in advance the betrayal she'd see in his eyes. She wanted to steel herself against the guilt of having put it there. "Besides," she finished lamely. "You're supposed to be writing commentary, not playing homicide newshound."

When she finally forced herself to look at him, ready to mumble the lip service about paying one's dues, Kate Loveless got one of the few surprises of her professional life, an experience she would later realize she found distinctly unpleasant. For John

Campion looked neither suitably chastised nor especially disappointed. Instead he appeared entirely calm, displaying that same shameless confidence he'd had at the beginning of their meal. He dabbed a little at the corners of his mouth with his napkin, looking satisfied, like the proverbial cat having dined on some canary. He folded it with the same meticulous precision he'd displayed with his knife and fork, and paused to brush a stray crumb from the white damask. Finally, when the table linen was arranged to his satisfaction, he glanced at his editor, his smile still wide and almost wicked.

"Oh, I know," he told her. "That's my whole angle. Everybody knows the profile, but nobody recognizes it. Not the cops, and especially not the experts. Remember what Dahmer's neighbors said about him? All that 'nice, quiet, kept to himself' stuff. And right here in Charlotte. Henry Wallace. Remember him? Eleven bodies in twenty months. All the victims knew him—worked with him. And the cops still can't figure it out."

Kate stared at him. The kid had done his homework, all right. She reckoned the Wallace case ranked somewhere in the crime fighters' "if only" Hall of Fame. Wallace knew each of his victims, most had worked at the two fast-food restaurants where he'd been employed. Yet the grisly series of murders had gone on and on, with nobody making the connection.

Seeing her expression, Campion moved in to drive home his point. "If everybody knows, why are serial killers so hard to catch? Everyone sees it, all the time. There are more and more of them out there. But nothing gets done about it because these so-called experts have everybody convinced they're smarter than we are. The cops don't do their jobs because they're supposed to consult with the experts, and the experts don't catch anybody because they don't know how. The system is a joke."

Despite herself, Kate was intrigued. She narrowed her eyes. "Cut to the chase, Campion."

The reporter leaned forward, his voice dropping to a more confidential tone. "I want to show the forensics experts up at their own game," he said. "I did a little research, and you've got one of them right here in Charlotte. Got a weird name—Portia something."

Kate nodded. "Portia McTeague. I think I met her at some benefit last spring."

Campion hurried on. "She calls herself a forensic psychologist.
She's supposed to be able to figure out why the murderers kill in
the first place, right?"

"Okay—" Kate prompted.

"She's pretty well known. Testifies all over the country." Campion's tone was derisive as he continued. "But what she really wants
is to make excuses. We're all supposed to feel sorry for these guys
because they had rotten childhoods. My own take on her is, she's
opposed to the death penalty and she's using the 'science' angle to
make her pitch."

"So?"

"So. What if I went to her for some therapy? What if I played
with her a bit, got her to admit to some of the holes in the system?"

"Campion—she's a psychologist. She's not going to spend session time pontificating about serial killers."

"If I pretended to need intervention, she might," Campion answered. "If it looked, for example, as though I might be violent."

"Are you nuts?" Kate blurted. "You're telling me you're going to
go in there pretending to be a killer?"

"Not quite," Campion answered. "I'd start therapy for some
other reason, and then pull her in—let her begin to believe I might
be violent. See what she does, how she'd help. It'd be interesting,
don't you think? Especially with the Meredith case wide open on
the books. I mean, what does a shrink do when she suspects she
might have a killer as a client? Can she actually help? That's commentary, isn't it?"

Kate was thinking hard, her eyes shining. "Oh, Campion," she
answered. "That's just evil."

"Is it? We're hog-tying the cops and the courts and the whole
system with new experts all the time. And what good does it do?
They're no smarter than the average person—they don't do any
good, and the killers are still out there."

Kate weighed the possibilities. The idea could work. The public
these days was positively neurotic on crime, and incensed over the
costs (both human and monetary) of too much bureaucracy. Then

there were the larger issues. The disconnectedness of people's lives—the apathy—how we all remained somehow invisible to one another. Victims who screamed out their windows while no one came to help. Killers who lived next door with nobody noticing until their grass got too long or the stench got too bad and somebody called the cops. All because we didn't like to get involved—all because we depended on experts to do our thinking for us. All because we didn't give a damn. Kate Loveless restrained herself from a sudden urge to fidget. Campion might indeed have something—something good. Good enough that Kate was beginning to wish she'd thought of it herself.

Campion's voice dropped another urgent notch, as if he'd been reading her mind. "There's something more important at stake here. Meredith's killer, whoever he is, is out there. He needs to be caught."

Kate eyed him, still uncertain. "And how does your story figure into that?"

Campion shook his head. "I can keep one eye on the cops," he said. "I'm willing to give them a chance to put it together, and work the McTeague angle at the same time."

"And?" Kate interjected. "What if they don't?"

"If there's another murder," he went on, "and I'm hoping to God there isn't, I'll put it together for them. By breaking the serial killer connection in my column. And the experts be damned."

The waiter appeared with a check encased in a small black vinyl portfolio. Kate slid gold plastic in his direction without bothering to open it up.

Instead, she looked at John Campion for a long, hard moment, feeling a strange mixture of things, grudging respect and a reluctant kind of hope among them. He had a real story, all right. Or at least the beginnings of one. The kind of story that went beyond the facts and tried at least to get at the truth behind them. Maybe he could even pull it off. Maybe together they both would. If she could get it past corporate, and if Campion was good enough to write it all down.

The check reappeared and she signed it. "Okay," she said at last. "I'll give you three weeks."

THREE

It had been a grindingly slow afternoon, now winding down toward evening as Portia glanced at her watch for the hundredth time and tried not to think about how bored she was. The small, cheerfully tacky office that housed the Help Line phones was little more than raw space, graced only by four large desks, about ten telephone consoles (half of which actually worked), and a lone, thoroughly tattered poster—a faded relic of seventies philosophy espousing white hyacinths for the soul.

She eyed the phone lines almost critically, as if willing them to light up. Not that she wished for someone to have a crisis specifically, it was just that she was beginning to long for someone to talk to. The only other volunteers that day were a woman named Nerida Rodriguez, whose broken English was on a par with Portia's equally broken Spanish, and a perpetually forlorn-looking social work intern named Dan Plumb, who was busy cramming for his certification exam and had barely looked up from his books since she'd walked in the door.

At the far end of the rather dingy room, Nerida was deeply in-

volved in a conversation with someone Portia could only assume
was a victim of Alzheimer's or some other grievous loss of short-
term memory, given the number of times Nerida had been forced
to repeat herself. So, her paperback finished, McTeague sidled over
to eavesdrop for lack of anything better to do. Though her Spanish
was rudimentary at best, Portia managed to glean after a few minutes that the saintly Nerida was reciting and repeating, with infinite
patience, the names and phone numbers for the Crisis Assistance
Ministry, the Legal Aid Office, and the Battered Women's Shelter.
She motioned with her cup in Nerida's direction, asking in panto-
mime if she wanted more coffee. The other woman looked up,
smiled, and shook her head no, and Portia crossed the expanse of
slightly sticky linoleum toward an ancient Braun burner to get herself a refill. The bulletin board above it was filled with a variety of
social service notices, tacked up with no particular thought to order
or even chronology, and after another moment, Portia wandered
back to her phone station, staring at the line of red lights as if she
could somehow make them blink.

This is really sick, you know that? an inner voice chided her. *You're
supposed to be a shrink and you're sitting here wanting somebody to have a
crisis, just so you can feel like a do-gooder. What the hell is that about?*

Boredom, she answered herself. What's it to you?

In truth, though, there was more to it than that. Ever since she'd
enjoyed the unwelcome notoriety of the Jimmy Weir trial, she'd cut
back on her forensics caseload as much as possible, partially by her
own choice and partially on the advice of the two people she trusted
most in the world: her own therapist Sophie Stransky and private
investigator and part-time boyfriend, Alan Simpson, both of whom
believed that her continued work in the courts was causing her
personal life a greater degree of damage than was healthy for her.
Even if she suspected Alan's reasons for wanting her to ease out of
forensics work were more self-serving than not, it meant she had
more time to spend with him as they explored their fledgling relationship. And she'd found that she had come to rely heavily on his
opinion these past few months. However imperfect Alan's check-
ered history with women, Portia trusted him, despite all her well-
established defenses. Trusted him on some deep and instinctual

level that had nothing to do with the easy, lighthearted bantering that comprised their usual conversation. And that alone was enough to take her by continual surprise.

Her confidence in Sophie's opinion, on the other hand, had nothing whatever to do with gut level feelings. Portia's respect for her elderly therapist, both personally and professionally, was so deeply ingrained, so beyond simple defense mechanism, that trusting Sophie was almost an involuntary response, like breathing. If Sophie had suggested she bag the whole profession and take up the priesthood, Portia would consider it seriously. Though she no longer saw her as regularly as she once had, they still met from time to time, and Portia felt that without the anchor of Sophie's wisdom, she would begin to drift in no time at all.

And so, on the strength of their mutual advice, in those confused, media-gorged days and weeks following Weir's sentencing, when scores of new patients had scheduled appointments merely for the dubious distinction of consulting with that "psychologist from TV," Portia had searched for some way out of the limelight, some way to reconnect with her reasons for becoming a therapist in the first place. She wanted to rediscover the roots of her profession, get back to the basics of helping others. When the Help Line volunteer center had solicited her for a shift at the phone lines, it had seemed the perfect solution. Once upon a time as a young intern, she had spent countless hours in a phone room much like this one, learning the nuts and bolts of being a therapist.

Which still doesn't mean you're not sitting there like some old buzzard, hoping someone goes bonkers before you get off shift.

Again, the inner voice disapproved of her.

Portia gulped the last of her lukewarm coffee, steadfastly refusing to check her watch. I just want to do my job, she mentally told the voice. It's what I'm here for.

Baloney. You're here because you love crises. Some poor anonymous schmuck calls you up and you get to pull out the bells and whistles. Ta-da! It's supershrink! Down there in the trenches, getting your ya-ya's off on triage therapy. Talking down the suicides, dealing with the overdoses, making the world a better place for humankind. Face it, kiddo, you just aren't happy unless you can rescue somebody. It makes you feel powerful.

That's what got you hooked on all those court cases, intensity, babe. Life and death. Can't get more intense than that.

Portia sighed softly. It was weird about that inner voice of hers. Twenty-two years of therapy and it still sounded suspiciously like her mother—disapproving, relentless, exasperating. And sometimes even right. Idly, she wondered about it. Did everyone have such a bitchy inner directive? Or did some people have inner voices that actually said nice things from time to time? Things like "great outfit" or "good for you" or "my heavens, aren't we smart today?"

The thought caused an unexpected little giggle to rise in her throat. Dan Plumb whirled around from his books to stare at her, his eyes huge and owlish behind his glasses. Portia flushed, the corners of her mouth twitching. "Just thought of something funny," she offered.

The thoroughly puzzled Mr. Plumb looked at her for another moment, as if expecting her to elaborate. When she didn't, he turned back around, sinking again into his private oblivion of concentration.

Funny ha-ha or funny peculiar? You know what they say about people who talk to themselves, don't you? You of all people should know. I mean, how much difference is there between people who do it just in their heads, and people who do it out loud?

Portia sighed. Oh shut up. There's hardly any difference, really. It just happens to amount to all the difference in the world.

At that moment, a red light on the phone panel in front of her began to blink, followed in the next instant by a chirping, insistent ring. Portia grabbed for the phone as if she thought someone would take it away from her.

"Good evening," she said to the caller. "This is the Help Line, Portia speaking."

A little rattle of static was the only response.

Oh shit—they hung up!

"Uhhh. Hi . . ." A hesitant male voice came over the wire. Portia felt an absurd and completely inappropriate rush of gratitude.

"Hi there," she said, a little more brightly than was necessary. "What can I do for you?"

There was a rush of air on the other end of the line. "Uhh—I'm not sure. Maybe nobody can do anything for me. But—I don't know. I just—need—to talk." The man broke off distractedly. There was a crackling sound, like cellophane, on the other end of the line.

"You still there?" asked Portia after the crackling ceased and another few moments of silence ensued.

"Huh? Oh, yeah. I was just thinking—you gotta start somewhere, right? Isn't that what they always say. You gotta start somewhere?"

A little tickle of anticipation went down Portia's spine.

Told you so.

Oh, knock it off. To the caller she said, "How about telling me your name? That's always a good place to start."

"Yeah . . ." he trailed off uncertainly.

"Just your first name is fine, if you want. Remember, I told you mine's Portia. Like the car." She always explained her name that way, especially to the callers on the Help Line. It had always proved far easier than giving a short course in Shakespeare.

"Uhhm. That's cool. It's—what do you call it? A coincidence."

"What is?"

"I got a kind of a weird name too. Ivan."

Portia carefully measured her response, encouraging but not pushy. People on a crisis line were already cornered. "What's on your mind, Ivan?" she went on steadily.

Over the wire came a sound that might have been a sort of laugh, Portia couldn't be sure.

"My mind's on my mind, lady. You get it? My mind. It's—well." The caller faltered again, as if unsure of how to go on.

"I'm not sure I understand, Ivan. But I'll try. You keep talking, okay? I promise as long as you keep talking, I'll listen."

There was a long pause, another deep inhalation. She wondered if her crisis caller was getting high, or just trying to hold himself together enough to keep from hanging up the phone. "I'm still here," she reassured him. "Take your time. Are you okay?"

The reply came with a choked, unexpected vehemence. "No! I—am—not—okay. I am all—fucked—up. Royally."

"Are you high? You can tell me. It's okay. No judgments here."

"No," he answered. "But I'm having—this—trouble."

"What kind of trouble?"

There was only a moment's hesitation. "I'm going fucking crazy, okay? I'm losing my shit. I can't—even—think."

"That must be very frightening. Don't worry. Just talk. Tell me about it, Ivan. What's going on?"

"I'm afraid—"

"It's okay. It's okay to be afraid sometimes," Portia reassured him. "You said you were going crazy. So tell me why you think that. Help me understand what's happening."

A short bark of laughter. "If I tell you, you're going to think I'm crazy."

Portia chewed her lip, thinking hard. "Ivan, people think all kinds of crazy things. That doesn't make them crazy. Maybe it would help to say it out loud. Sometimes keeping things bottled up just makes them seem bigger than they really are."

There was a silence. "I don't think I could stand to say it to you," Ivan blurted out.

Portia forced herself to be patient, making notes of their conversation on the record sheet in front of her. Male, probably white, possibly Hispanic. Ivan was a popular Hispanic name, for reasons that eluded her. Mid to late twenties from the sound of him. Some education. Possible user, though he'd claimed otherwise.

Portia was searching for some clue to his problem, a question that might prompt him further when, without warning, he spoke again, the words sending a shameful little thrill through her insides.

"See—the truth is, I think I'm going to hurt somebody. Pretty soon. A girl—or some woman maybe. I think I need to."

Instantly, her mind went on red alert, though her voice stayed calm, almost conversational. "Have you been thinking about hurting somebody, Ivan? Is that why you're afraid?"

He mumbled something she couldn't quite make out, then continued speaking, his tone once again detached, almost wistful. "I can see it happening—like a dream. Only it's more real than that. It's got all the details. She's lying down and I've got her tied up, with her stockings or something. I made her take off all her clothes so she's naked. And I'm hard and I'm so—ready. I can see it really clear in my mind. And it gets me off."

You asked for it, chided the voice. And Portia could only listen as Ivan rambled on.

"I feel bad that it's got to be like that. But it's good, too. You know what I mean?"

"Ivan—" Portia answered slowly. "Are you telling me about a fantasy? Or is this something . . ." She faltered a little. If this guy was close to the edge, she didn't want to be the one to push him off. Nonetheless, she had to know how far he'd deteriorated, if he in fact knew the difference between a fantasy and reality.

"Ivan—" she began again. "This—dream. Have you ever tried to act it out? In the real world?"

"No," he admitted. "But I want to. I need to."

Portia didn't miss a beat. "Do you have it a lot?"

The caller seemed to think it over. "More lately. Like at work. I'll be online or something and I'll start to see it in my head. I can see her eyes sometimes. And she's so afraid of me." Ivan's voice dropped a notch, low and urgent. "I know it's got to be bad, but I want to scare her some more. Make her really scream. And I get to thinking about all the things a guy could do. It's like I can't stop."

Mentally, Portia added to her list of information about the caller. He had a job, which meant he was still functioning, at least on some level. Online, he'd said. He worked with computers. And from what he'd been saying, it was a reasonably safe bet that his rape fantasies were still fantasies. More than likely augmented by a private pornography collection.

Her instincts told her Ivan probably wasn't in any immediate danger. Trouble yes, but not danger. His scenarios of rape and domination were clearly escalating to the point where he felt he couldn't manage them. And that was trouble by anybody's definition.

"Ivan," she went on. "When you see this woman in your head, what does she look like? Is it somebody you know? Your girlfriend maybe?" She was almost certain Ivan was single. And that his fantasies of rape hadn't developed out of the blue. Somewhere, somehow he'd developed a rage against women. The danger was that without intervention that rage might lead to an explosion.

Now, however, the question seemed to shock him, another relatively good sign. "No! Jesus, I told you. It's just a dream. I could never do something like that." Then in the next moment the caller sighed with resignation. "It means I'm sick, doesn't it?"

"It means you might feel better if you could talk to somebody, Ivan," Portia answered seriously. "You told me yourself you're afraid of what you want to do. Have you ever had a counselor? Do you see a therapist now?"

"I used to," Ivan admitted. "But I quit after a while. He helped me when my mom died. I called him, but his number's disconnected. I guess he left town or something."

"How long ago was that?"

Ivan's answer was curiously flat, devoid of emotion. "Few months. I took care of her. She was sick. Then she died."

Portia all but held her breath as she added these new items to Ivan's psychological inventory. Death of a parent was high on the list of principal stressors, especially if Ivan's relationship with his mother had been ambivalent. Which was quite possible, considering his lack of emotion. Again, a barrage of questions arose as Portia went after more information.

Slow down, the inner voice cautioned her. *You're not his damn therapist, just his date for the evening, okay?*

Okay.

Besides, the voice continued sarcastically. *It isn't like he's really killed somebody.*

Portia passed a distracted hand over her eyes. Maybe Lori was right, she'd spent so many years profiling killers that she had murder on the brain. And while Ivan's situation certainly called for some intervention, that's all it called for. Wishes weren't horses, and a fantasy, however vivid or even brutal, was still just that—a fantasy. Her responsibility now was to refer him to a decent therapist, not to try and cure him over the phone. Ivan's voice came back to her over the wire, interrupting her train of thought.

"So, am I nuts?"

Despite herself, Portia managed a weak smile. "No, Ivan," she told him. "I don't think you're nuts. You're having some trouble, and you did the right thing. You called here for some help and I'm going to see you get it, okay?"

"Okay," he answered.

Portia began flipping through the Rolodex at her elbow. "I'm going to give you the names of some doctors who can help you get through this. I want you to call one of them and set up an appointment as soon as you can. Have you got health insurance?"

Ivan's voice rose with sudden panic. "What if I can't get one? Sometimes you have to wait a long time."

Even though she was on the telephone, and couldn't be observed, Portia worked hard to hide a smile. "Just tell them what you've told me, Ivan. I guarantee you, you'll get an appointment. And if you do have any trouble, call back here. We'll straighten it out."

"Are you a doctor? A shrink, I mean."

"Yeah, Ivan. As a matter of fact I am—a psychologist."

"Then why can't I just come to you? For an appointment, I mean?"

"Because we're not allowed to do that, Ivan. I can't refer you to me as a new patient. It's a conflict of interest. You understand?"

There was a little pause. "Yeah, I guess."

"It's nothing personal, Ivan," Portia assured him. "Just the rules."

"Okay—" he answered after another moment. "Give me the numbers."

"You promise you'll call? Set up an appointment with one of these doctors and talk about the stuff that's bothering you?"

Ivan took a deep breath. "It's harder—in person. To say this stuff."

"But you can do it, Ivan," Portia said gently. "I know it's hard, but you've already got a head start because you've been in therapy before, right?"

"Right," he agreed.

Portia did smile this time. "Good. You've taken a very important step, Ivan. You started somewhere, looking for help. That's great. Now you've got to do the rest. There is help out there, Ivan. All you have to do is reach for it."

She rattled off the names and telephone numbers of five mental health professionals who were currently taking referrals, and made Ivan read the names and numbers back to her before concluding the call. And while she couldn't be sure he would make an appointment, at least she was sure he'd gotten the names and numbers right, and that he'd written them down. The rest, fortunately or not, was up to Ivan.

She hung up, more or less pleased with herself. This was, after all, the real point of therapy and of being a therapist, the point she'd been trying to return to all these months. And that was the ability to relinquish control—the realization that her true role as a mental health professional was only to help people help themselves. It was calls like Ivan's that reinforced that truth. The simple knowledge that, in the end, it was all she could do, and hard as it sometimes was, she'd learned to accept it. Even if she had been able to take him on as a patient, it was still Ivan who would dictate the success of his therapy. Ironically, it was her work here at the crisis center that brought that realization home. She couldn't save anyone, nor rescue them either. After twenty years as a therapist, she'd finally begun to absolve herself from the overwhelming sense of responsibility she'd always brought to her caseload—both in her private practice and in her forensic work. And with that sense of responsibility went the guilt that had crippled her for so long.

"You look chipper enough" came a voice from the doorway.

Portia glanced up to see that her volunteer replacement for the night shift had arrived. Bob Shade was a fortyish psychiatrist who worked out of the Carolinas Medical Center on Blythe Boulevard and donated his time a couple of nights a month. Though Portia had always rather liked him, she found him something of a mystery. Here was a great-looking, thoroughly personable and dedicated man who could have taken up a thriving private practice, yet seemed content with a chronically underpaid hospital staff position while devoting his spare hours to the Help Line. From what she'd been able to pick up from the other volunteers, Shade had no family, no significant other, and no discernible ties, save for his job. All of which had been enough to set Portia's investigative radar humming whenever they came in contact. She turned away from the telephone console, smiling broadly.

"Hey," she said by way of greeting. "Slow day. I hope you brought your knitting."

"Needlepoint, actually," Bob said, matching her bantering tone. "And no I didn't. Anything interesting come in?"

Portia handed him Ivan's record sheet. "Just a guy with some pretty vivid rape fantasies. I gave him the necessary referrals. Here's his info in case he calls back. But I would doubt it. Seemed like obsessive-compulsive rumination to me. I don't think he's a danger to anybody but himself."

Shade frowned over her notes. "He took the numbers?" he asked.

Portia nodded. "I made him read them back to me, just to make sure."

Shade passed a hand over his forehead as he slid into place in front of a nearby console and Portia could see suddenly how tired he was, his eyes defined by deep shadows. "Well, I hope he goes for it. I spent half the day with a guy the cops brought in for a competence evaluation. Attacked a woman near Dilworth. Tried to strangle her with the handle of her pocketbook. The cops were breathing down my neck on it too. They were hoping he might be responsible for that TV murder."

"You mean Tamara Meredith?"

Shade glanced up wearily. "That's the name," he answered. "But he wasn't the one. Not from what they told me, anyway. The one they brought in today was way too disorganized. The strangulation attempt was just a botched robbery. The kid figured out the woman could ID him."

Portia began to gather her briefcase and her own pocketbook, trying not to betray too much interest. "It happens," she offered. Then, in spite of herself, her next questions came tumbling out of her mouth before she could stop them. "What did the police say? To make you think the murderer was more organized?" Seeing Shade's startled expression, she could have bitten off her tongue. First because she knew perfectly well that as a consulting physician

he was not allowed to discuss an ongoing investigation, and sec-
ondly because she had no business asking in the first place.

But Shade was apparently too tired or too disinterested to quib-
ble over such a minor breach of confidentiality. Instead he only
looked at her a little sadly, his expression suggesting that he'd seen
entirely too much misery among the living to spare much in the
way of sympathy for the dead.

"Oh," he answered. "The killer took a trophy. He cut off her
hands. They're still missing."

Just then, the phone line lit up and Bob reached to answer it.
From his side of the ensuing conversation, it was clear he'd have no
more time to discuss the Meredith murder, even had she been indiscreet enough to ask. Frustrating as it was, there was nothing to
do but go on home, confident at least that Charlotte's Help Line
was in competent hands.

The apartment was lonely, almost, oddly quiet as he hung up the
phone. He'd liked it for that, tucked back behind a stand of bamboo
that created a sense of separateness from the rest of the city. There
were only three other units in the building, two above and one like
his, with a private entrance on the opposite side. The back window
opened onto a view of a culvert and the shadows of huge magnolia
trees that hid the complex's Dumpsters from view. It was quiet as
he hung up the phone. He could be alone now. Alone with her.

He fumbled with his fly against the explosive need, grasping his
swollen cock and stroking until he could hear her voice again,
soothing him over the wire. A little gasp escaped him and he found
the spot just underneath his balls and pressed it with his thumb,
trying not to come too quickly, trying to prolong the pleasure of
watching her smiling up at him from the newspaper photo spread
out on his knee. She had been so helpful, so willing. They were all
so helpful. A roar began in his head as the blood descended, stiffen-
ing him against his own fingers, and he pulled and fought with
himself while pictures of agony spun through his mind, urging him
on and on until at last the pictures flashed in a single explosion—
the sound of an echoing scream.

He wiped himself carefully, softening cock and fingers, making sure none of his semen had spilled on the face in the picture. He studied it again in the soft light of the lamp, noting how the camera had caught her expression, startled and a little confused as she'd stood on the courthouse steps, as though the flash had taken her by surprise.

Ivan zipped himself and smiled as he took up the clipping, holding it delicately as he went to replace it in the drawer of a nearby desk. He paused for a last long moment, then pressed his fingers to his lips, catching the scent of semen that lingered there. Then in the moment before he switched out the light, he pressed a solitary kiss to Portia's mouth, watching those frightened eyes.

FOUR

Less than a half-dozen blocks from home, Portia's car phone bleeped insistently. She started to answer it, but not before allowing herself a moment's wish that it were Alan Simpson, back from his latest investigative jaunt to god-knew-where. Though she was pretty sure each of them was doing no more than testing the waters of their future as a potential couple, between her schedule and his even that much had been difficult to do. He'd been out of town for less than two weeks, investigating a corporate spying case for Digital Controls Corporation, but she'd found herself missing him over the last few days especially, though whether she was truly missing Alan or merely missing the pleasure of Alan in her bed was difficult even for Portia to say for certain. Having gone for many years without anything resembling a regular sexual partner, Portia was feeling the need to make up for lost time.

"This is Portia McTeague," she said into the phone.

"Then I definitely have the right number."

Upon hearing Alan's voice, Portia felt her heart take an unexpected leap. She grinned wildly as she swung onto the broad tree-lined boulevard that was Dilworth.

"Hey!" she cried joyfully. "You must be psychic or something. I was just thinking about you. Are you back?"

"Almost," Alan answered.

"That doesn't sound good," Portia rejoined, pausing at a stop sign.

"It isn't," Alan admitted. "I thought I was going to be back tomorrow night for our dinner date, but I don't think it's going to happen."

Portia tried hard to keep the disappointment out of her voice and didn't succeed very well. "That's okay," she answered. "I'll take a rain check."

Oh nice, chided another part of her mind. *Play hard to get why don't you?*

Alan sighed heavily. "What can I tell you? Either I'm just losing my investigative touch, or these corporate guys are getting a lot better at covering their tracks. Whatever it is, I'm getting stone-walled. And I can't come back to Digital without something to show them."

"I understand, Alan. And you're not losing your touch." Her voice dropped a lustful little notch as she headed down the block toward home. "As I recall, your touch is just about perfect. As a matter of fact, I miss it."

Tramp.

Even over a distance of several hundred miles, his reply was enough to send a warm shiver through her insides.

"You keep talking like that and I'll have to do something about it."

"Hurry back," she told him.

"Friday for sure. Say, eight-thirty?"

"Fine." Portia's grin widened a little as she pulled into her own driveway.

"Hey," Alan said softly. "Don't start without me."

She hung up, still smiling a little as Alice came hurtling across the lawn from their next-door neighbor's, dark curls flying. Jessica, her best and inseparable friend, was close at her heels. Portia waved and scooped Alice up in her arms, managing a brief and passionate kiss on her cheek before Alice, screeching and giggling, wrestled her way to the ground.

Alice looked up at her, eyes bright and black as olives. "Jessica's grandma sent her an Angel Blossom Princess Barbie for her birthday next week," she announced. "And I need to get one, too."

Portia feigned surprise. "Now," she said. "Why in the world would you need something like that?"

"Because she's beautiful!" Alice turned and pointed, while Jessica, towheaded and shy in stark contrast to Portia's adopted daughter's dark beauty and boisterous disposition, pulled out the doll from behind her back for Portia to better inspect its merits.

"Oh my," breathed Portia. "She is beautiful," she said, though privately she found the combination of gossamer angel wings, glitter-covered blossoms, and shocking pink crinoline a bit much for one dress.

Alice fairly danced with urgency. "So can I have one, too? We could go to the mall right after dinner and buy one and then Jessica and me can play Angel Blossom Princesses who are twins."

"We'll see," answered Portia.

"Not we'll see!" Alice cried. "We'll see always means no!"

Jessica, always a little awestruck by her friend's more fearless approach to the adults of the world, drew back a ways, pretending to absorb herself in arranging the hot-glued blossoms on Barbie's skirt.

Portia frowned. Of all the things that truly bewildered her about being a parent, her daughter's rabid consumerism was high on the list. Though Portia would never have willingly denied Alice anything, the sheer scope of that childish combination of need and greed always left her a little amazed. She felt it unwise to give in to every one of Alice's demands on the one hand, and on the other she doubted the wisdom of haggling for what might turn out to be weeks over a $34.95 piece of plastic.

She took a deep breath. "Jessica got the Barbie for a birthday present, Alice," she explained. "Your birthday's not for another month."

Alice looked truly horrified. "I can't wait a whole month!" she cried.

"Look," Portia went on as patiently as she was able. "I haven't said no. All I've said is we'll see. I need to think about it, okay?"

"Okay—" mumbled Alice and scampered off to join Jessica in a whispered conference.

Another voice entered the conversation from somewhere to Portia's right.

"Do yourself a favor," intoned Aggie, Jessica's mother, softly. "Give in."

Portia turned to her neighbor and friend, smiling helplessly.

"Sorry about that," Aggie went on, gesturing in the direction of Jessica and her prize. "I never would have gotten her one. Personally, I think she's too young to get into fashion icons. Unfortunately my mother has no such principles."

Portia wrinkled up her nose. "I don't know," she said doubtfully. "The girls are so close. At this age they almost have to want what the other one has. But I don't want to create a consumer monster."

Aggie only shrugged and grinned. "Think of it as saving yourself some grief. If I know Alice, you'll get no peace until you cough up the doll."

Portia had to agree with that much. Even at seven Alice showed definite signs of the woman she would eventually become. Smart, beautiful, and stubborn as they made them. She gazed off at the two girls, now caught up in some secret discussion of the doll's merits. It was that same stubbornness that had served Alice so well in the earliest years of her life, when traits like determination had taught her to scavenge for food. As troublesome as it could sometimes be, Portia had never forgotten the trauma of Alice's early life, never failed to admire her sheer ability to survive. But that trauma, despite all of her efforts, had left its scars. And one of them was that Alice saw most things as issues of personal survival—even a doll.

Aggie interrupted her softly, as if somehow reading her thoughts. "She's just a little girl, Portia. And as mothers of little girls, we will all eventually be forced to worship at the altar of Barbie."

Portia couldn't help but smile. "What about your principles?"

"The hell with them," Aggie answered. "I guess I take after my mother. You want a beer?"

As a matter of fact, sitting over a beer in Aggie's bright yellow kitchen seemed like the best idea she'd heard all day. "Sure," she answered. "Tell you what, I'll trade you. A beer in exchange for taking the girls to the mall after dinner. Give you and Reg some time to yourselves."

Aggie nodded. "Excellent. As a matter of fact, Reg is off shift early tonight." Reg was a city police officer, and Portia had always marveled a little at Aggie's ability to handle the stress of sending her husband out among Charlotte's criminal population as though it were any other, more ordinary job. They began to cross the lawn toward Aggie's front door. All at once her neighbor shot Portia a knowing, sidelong look. "Promise me you won't buy Jessica anything?" It was more a question than a statement.

Portia crossed her heart and her fingers at the same time. "Promise," she replied. "One stop at the toy store. In and out. Guerrilla shopping."

Aggie opened the screen door to the neat, two-story brick house, the same skeptical expression playing across her features. "You're a better mom than I am, Gunga Din."

Once inside, with the girls safely installed in Jessica's room, Portia settled herself at Aggie's kitchen table, admiring all over again the welcome comfort of the place, the sheer homey quality that emanated from Aggie's well-used beechwood table and mismatched chairs, the simple muslin café curtains that graced the windows. Aggie was a homemaker in the truest and best sense of that word, with a natural talent for all the domestic arts that Portia herself had never quite mastered. Though her neighbors were more or less a single-income family (save for the hours Portia paid Aggie to watch Alice) and had far less in the way of monetary resources, Portia had always envied them a little. Not because she was a single mother, at times struggling to raise her adopted daughter, not even because she had had no regular man in her life until Alan, but because Aggie and Reg and Jessica made family life look easy. As far as Portia had ever been able to discern, their lives were almost miraculously free of the deep conflicts that had plagued her own family history. Though she was sure they had their share of squabbles, their love for one another had proved the overriding factor in their lives. And the result was that they were one of those rare and wonderful families that hadn't had to work very hard to stay happy.

She raised the glass that Aggie placed in front of her. "God bless us, every one."

"Cheers," Aggie replied, and clinked. "So what's new in the wide world of psychotherapy?"

Portia sipped gratefully at the cold beverage. "Not much," she admitted. "The truth is, I think I'm getting a little bored."

Aggie pretended to be horrified. "Bored? You? Help! You can't be bored. Your life is my principal source of entertainment. Interviewing serial killers, testifying on camera. Consulting with the ranks of Charlotte's depressed and disturbed. You've got the best gossip in the Carolinas—what do you mean you're bored?"

"I do not gossip," Portia corrected her. "Especially not about my patients."

Aggie grinned. "Oh, sometimes you let enough slip to get my imagination going."

"Do not," Portia chided.

"Do too. You just think you don't because you never give names. But this is just a small town, girlfriend. When you've lived here as long as I have, you get to know practically everybody. At least to look at. And that means I get to guess at who you might be talking about."

Portia grinned. This was a familiar conversation, one that had been played out in various ways over the years. Speculating on some of the more interesting psychological quirks of Charlotte's population was one of Aggie's favorite pastimes, as she tried to match up the names and faces of PTA board members or her daughter's dentist or the stock boy at the grocery store with a preference for women's undergarments, a drinking problem, or an illicit affair. Once or twice, her neighbor's guesses about people had proved uncomfortably near the truth. So finely honed were her instincts about people, Aggie might have made a fine psychologist herself.

Portia took another swallow, and slowly shook her head. "Nope," she said. "The world of shrinkdom has been pretty slow lately. D-U-double hockey sticks. I'm starting to think I should get back into forensics consulting."

Aggie sipped her own beer and raised an eyebrow. "Missing prison, are you?"

Portia shook her head slowly. "No. But I'm missing something. Maybe it's just the sense that what I'm doing really matters. That I'm doing more as a shrink than just seeing the same old patients with the same old problems." She looked into her friend's face. "I guess I should be ashamed of myself. Maybe it just doesn't seem like anybody's life ever really changes."

Aggie shrugged. "Not necessarily. Most people's problems are boring. Relationships, money, fears. It must get dull, getting an earful of the same old unhappiness. I suppose the real question is, why did you give up on the forensics when it's so much more interesting?"

Aggie shot her a quizzical glance when Portia didn't answer. "You know you make some kind of difference to your clients," she went on. "Maybe it's just not dramatic enough or something."

Portia smiled a little. She could always count on the more practical Aggie to cut through all of her intellectualizing and analyzing and get straight to the point. While anyone else might have been honestly horrified at hearing a psychologist confess to simply being bored by the problems of her patients, Aggie never so much as blinked. Instead, she simply addressed the problem as Portia had stated it and gone to the next, far more relevant level of discussion. It was an ability Portia wished she had more of. The psychologist sighed reflectively, watching the stream of amber bubbles rise from the depths to the surface of her glass. Sometimes she couldn't help but feel that her training got in the way of being human.

"I hate it because it takes me away from Alice," she said quite honestly. "And I really hate the publicity. But I don't know, maybe it is the drama—the life and death stuff. But God help me, I guess you're right. I do miss it."

Aggie reflected for a moment. "I hear there's a nice fresh murder on the books down at police headquarters," she suggested. "Still unsolved. What's that thing where you look at the crime and go backward to find the killer? What do they call it? You ever do that?"

"Profiling," Portia answered. "And no. At least, not much. You always have to familiarize yourself with the specifics of the crimes. It's really the only way to approach the psychology of the perpetrator. Find out why they had to do what they did."

Aggie rose from her chair and began rummaging through the refrigerator in preparation for the family's dinner. "Well, correct me if I'm wrong, but it's pretty much the same thing, isn't it? Only up till now, you've been interviewing the killers after they were arrested. Why not use what you know to help crack the case?"

Portia giggled in spite of herself. "Crack the case? Aggie, don't you think you've been watching a little too much TV?"

"You know what I mean—" Aggie grumbled, rinsing spinach in the sink. "And if you want my opinion, it might be one solution. You could get into a new area of your job, using stuff you already know, get a little excitement, and avoid all that whipping boy publicity at the same time. You wouldn't be trying to save somebody's sorry ass that nobody cares about."

"I suppose." Portia considered the idea with new interest. "I've never worked like that before, so I don't know the procedure. But there's some real differences between what I do and what a profiler does. I start with the personality and infer behavior from what I know about the person. They do just the opposite."

Aggie began chopping onions. She turned to her friend. "It still means getting inside somebody else's head. Empathy. And you know how to do that."

Portia shook her head. "I don't know, Aggie. It would mean teaming up with the authorities. Who knows if they'd even have me? Up until now, I've always been working for the defense." She grinned ruefully. "I'm the bleeding heart, remember?"

Aggie grinned. "From what Reg has told me, I don't think anybody at headquarters would turn you down. They're all in a regular lather over this one. Charlotte's worst murder in decades—all that stuff. Makes poor old Henry Wallace look real polite by comparison. The mayor and the DA are joining forces to set up some sort of task force to see if they can catch whoever did it."

"But I can't just waltz in there and offer to solve the crime for them—I'm no detective."

Aggie turned off the faucet and shook her head. "Honey, that's the point! You don't have to be! You'd be part of a team. And you can't honestly believe those old boys in homicide would give you the credit if you did solve it, do you? That's the beauty of it. You don't get all the glory, but you don't take all the heat. Everybody wins."

Portia nodded, a little chagrined. "Wow," she said after another moment. "You're right, of course. That was pretty narcissistic."

Aggie began peppering a couple of steaks. "Narcissistic?" she asked.

Catching herself, Portia hastened to explain. "A shrink word. It means self-involved—sort of."

"Hmm." Aggie considered it, turning around. "Well, I wouldn't know about that. But tell me something—"

Portia looked up. "What?"

"What's the shrink word for always thinking you have to do everything alone? That's what you've got."

Portia blushed in spite of herself. Once again, her friend had proved her knack for taking the shortcut to the real issue.

Aggie bent deep into the refrigerator, pulling out an assortment of things. "People need to share the burden, Portia," she went on. "They ought to share the work, too."

Portia rose. "Hey, Aggie, thanks. I need to think about this."

Aggie turned and faced her, trying to look stern. "You think too damn much, if you ask me. And I should be thanking you. Me and Reg haven't had dinner alone since I can remember." Aggie paused, seeing Portia standing rooted to the spot, as if trying to decide what to do next.

"Oh, for heaven's sake, go home," she said more gently. "It's not like you have to decide this minute. I'll send Jessica by in a while."

FIVE

Over the next few days, the Meredith murder headlines gave way to some far less interesting scandal over the misappropriation of school board funds and Portia resolutely pushed the idea of working with the authorities to some mental back burner as she headed for the office each morning, determined to go through at least the motions of fulfilling her role as a competent, if more ordinary sort of therapist. Despite her more concentrated efforts to silence it, though, her nagging inner taskmaster wasn't quite so willing to let the matter drop.

After driving Alice to school Thursday morning, Portia pulled up at the intersection of East Boulevard and Euclid Avenue, waiting for the interminable red light to change, when an announcer came on the all-news station with an item about the ongoing murder investigation.

"Local authorities appear to have few leads in the murder of Tamara Meredith, cable television psychic and alternative healer. A spokesman for Charlotte police this morning made a public appeal for anyone who has information about the crime to come forward.

The mayor's office has now joined forces with the district attorney and the police in the formation of a special task force, and this morning's press conference revealed that authorities have once again interviewed Angel Tirado, who worked with Ms. Meredith, in an attempt to identify the principal suspect, but they have not as yet come up with a positive identification. Again, police have appealed to anyone who may have information about the case to contact—"

Suddenly annoyed, Portia switched off the radio. But the voice of the announcer was soon replaced in her mind by another, more familiar one, all but chortling at her discomfort.

You junkie, it sneered. *You think if you stay clean for a few months you're not addicted anymore? C'mon, Portia, old girl. Turning off the radio doesn't quite scratch the old itch, does it?*

Portia scowled through the windshield. The light remained stubbornly red. Think about something else, she scolded herself. She glanced at the telephone near her elbow. Call somebody.

Do they have sponsors for murder addicts?

Oh, dry up.

So why don't you call the cops? the voice insisted. *They want information, and you've got it.*

I do not. I don't know anything about this.

You've stuck your head in the sand and you're choking on it, you mean.

Portia sighed with exasperation. Sand was right. The day's appointments stretched out before her like an expanse of empty desert. Despite the fact that she'd taken on more new patients than even an overachiever like herself could reasonably be expected to handle, the sheer predictability of her day was enough to make her mouth go positively dry with distaste. Marital conflicts, unmanageable children, the odd sexual dysfunction, depression. Especially depression. Sometimes it seemed to her that three quarters of the population was depressed. She'd wondered more than once if it wasn't something in the water supply.

It wasn't that she felt any of those problems were insignificant, it was simply that she was tired of listening, and manufacturing enough patience to allow her clients to arrive at their own discoveries. As proactive as she tried to be, there was only so much any therapist could do. Some problems, she had come to realize, were part and parcel of the human condition. And some things about the human condition were incurable. They went with the territory.

No wonder you can't stand it, the voice continued. *Look at you. Here you are, trying to help all these people have happy, normal lives. For the first time in your own life you've actually got that. A happy, normal life. Only it's driving you crazy. No wonder you feel like a hypocrite.*

Or maybe, Portia thought wearily, I'm just a bad therapist. A horn blared in back of her, making her jump. She saw with a shock that the light had turned green, and accelerated her Volvo across the intersection to catch up with the flow of traffic. The niggling suspicion that there might be something to all this was troubling enough. More troublesome still, she felt somehow compelled to continue her inner argument.

It isn't that simple, she assured herself. Even if she volunteered to help in the investigation, there was no guarantee she'd come up with anything.

Like that stopped you before. You get up on the stand and give your psychological opinion. Maybe that helps keep some crazy off death row and maybe it doesn't. Since when did you get entitled to a guarantee? Was it when you got to be such an expert or when you got to be so damned normal? You want my opinion, I think you're scared. Scared that maybe you don't know as much as you think you do. Hell, maybe you're just scared to be yourself.

Portia shook her head. Shit, she thought, you're the one who keeps calling me a murder addict. Pick a side, why don't you?

I have, the inner voice answered her.

Yours.

Fifteen minutes into her first appointment she made her decision. Unfortunately, she still had thirty minutes of what amounted to something very close to torture to get through as her patient, Sandra Mahoney, regaled her with a nonstop diatribe against her ex-husband. How he'd never been sensitive, how he'd been unable to get in touch with his real feelings, how he'd never thrown his dirty underwear in the hamper or swept the kitchen floor. Never, that is, until he'd discovered Tiffany, the young MBA he'd run off with to New Jersey four months previous. Tiffany had apparently put him in touch with a whole range of emotions. Portia had been trying unsuccessfully for months to get this woman to focus on herself, rather than endlessly berating her ex. But reluctant Sandra had proved less than cooperative, showing little interest in assuming responsibility for her own circumstances or for her future.

Now, Sandra shifted restlessly from her position on the chintz-covered sofa in the corner of Portia's office.

"I'd just like to get my hands on that sonofabitch," Sandra went on. "Just get him alone in a room for ten minutes. That's all—ten little minutes. I'd take his no-good balls and—"

Portia struggled to intervene. "You're allowed to be angry, Sandra. As long as you understand—"

"I don't understand!" Sandra insisted bitterly, interrupting. "I had the perfect marriage! How could he have done this to me?"

The perfect marriage. Right. Portia considered the remark. "There's no such thing as a perfect relationship," she interjected quietly. "You yourself have just admitted as much."

Oh, brilliant. The silent accusation rode up from another part of her mind. *Fifteen years of clinical practice and you sound like a cartoon.*

Signaling the end of their session, Portia rose to her feet, thoroughly relieved not to have to listen to either her patient or her own thoughts for the moment. She felt like dancing on the desktop. Instead, she managed a small smile.

"Why don't you think about that? For next time."

Sandra sniffed a little. "Well, if you say so. But if me and Pete had problems, I sure didn't know anything about them."

"See Lori and set something up for next week, okay?" Portia ushered Sandra out to the hall, watching her rangy figure disappear into the outer office. Therapeutically speaking, Sandra had a ways to go.

Portia resumed her usual chair and tried to rub the knots of tension from her neck, trying to quiet her own restless uncertainty. It wasn't just Sandra, she knew. And it wasn't just boredom either. When she was fairly sure Sandra was safely out of the office and released back into the unsuspecting world, she punched the button that opened the interoffice intercom.

"Who's up next?" she asked Lori.

Lori made a sound like she was cracking gum. "Somebody new. John Campion. He said he's relocated from Florida and is having adjustment problems."

Portia closed her eyes. Just what she needed, adjustment problems. She took a deep breath. Why in the name of heaven had she ever given Lori permission to book new patients?

So you'd have someone to blame your frustrations on? Or so you wouldn't have to look too closely at your own adjustment problems? Heal thyself, shrink. Isn't that the deal?

"Listen, Lori. I want you to track down the number for the mayor's task force on the Meredith murder."

"What?" Even unflappable Lori could barely keep the excitement from her tone.

"Tell them you're calling for me," Portia went on. "That I heard the announcement this morning and that I want to volunteer my services. As a forensic profiler."

"Cool!"

"Never mind cool. Just tell them I'm willing to come down and talk about it. When do I have time?"

"Tomorrow," answered Lori. "After two." Then, in the next breath, "God, I can't wait to call my sister-in-law!"

"You do and I'll fire your butt," Portia answered calmly. "No one, and that means no one, including your sister-in-law, is going to know anything about this. I'm going to talk to them only on the condition that there will be no publicity attached to my coming on the case. And that's assuming they'll even let me."

"You're nuts," insisted Lori. "Of course they'll let you!"

"There's no guarantee of that," Portia answered sternly. "And either way, my name is to be kept strictly out of it. Got it?"

"I get it," Lori answered sulkily. "But that doesn't mean I like it."

"You don't have to," Portia continued. "Just make sure they know it down at headquarters, too. I mean it. Otherwise, I don't show for so much as an interview."

"Whatever you say," Lori answered. "But I swear I don't know why you've got such a thing about getting your name in the paper."

"It's an old Southern thing," Portia answered wryly. "You're only supposed to get your name in the paper twice in your life—the day you're born and the day you die. Anything else means you're not a lady."

Lori's response was a disapproving sniff. "Tell that to Princess Di."

Portia ended the connection and sat with her hands locked behind her head, smiling at the ceiling as she awaited the arrival of her newest patient, John Campion.

For once, even her inner voice had nothing to say.

SIX

The new patient smiled cautiously as he entered the room, and, buoyed by the prospect, however remote, of working on a murder case again, Portia smiled back.

"Hi," she said, extending a hand in his direction. "I'm Portia McTeague."

"John Campion," the man answered. "I'm glad you could see me."

"Sit anywhere you like, Mr. Campion," she answered. "Or may I call you John?"

Avoiding some of the more comfortable pieces of furniture, Campion took a chair opposite her desk. Not wanting to begin a session with a new patient at such a confrontational angle, Portia eased around and sat in a nearby armchair. Campion was forced to move, and swiveled his chair from its original angle until they were facing each other, nearly eye to eye across the coffee table. Since they were of similar height, the result was an oddly formal arrangement, him on one side, her on the other.

Portia mentally took note of his posture. From his expression and choice of seating it was almost as if he had come there for some other reason, like a job interview or applying for a loan. Whatever Campion's reasons for wanting therapy, clearly he was less than comfortable with the idea.

Once settled, he flashed a huge, inappropriate smile without actually looking at her, and began to pick surreptitiously at some imaginary piece of lint on his trousers. Then, quite suddenly, he stopped, looked up, and met her eyes full on.

"Oh, of course, call me John."

"Fine," she answered. "John it is. Now, before we really get started—have you ever been in therapy before, John?"

Campion's smile faded to a vague uneasiness. "Why? Do I look crazy?"

Portia suppressed a little sigh. Oh, wonderful, she thought, one of those. "Not at all," she answered smoothly. "It just helps me find a starting point for some of the things we'll be talking about, okay?"

Campion nodded. "Okay, so yeah. I've had therapy. Lots, actually. Well, not lots, but off and on. You know. I mean, it's pretty much what people do these days, isn't it?"

Portia considered the remark, a little unsure of how to respond. "I think people are seeking help in greater numbers than they once did," she answered carefully. "But then perhaps people are more aware of how getting the right kind of help can affect the quality of their lives."

Campion smiled again, as if on cue. "I guess what I meant was, we can probably skip some of the preliminary stuff. You know, the part where you ask me if I take medication, if I'm married, did I ever wet the bed—that kind of stuff." Restlessly, his fingers moved toward the imaginary lint, but stilled again when he saw that she had noticed and was watching him closely. He smiled suddenly once more, revealing the sheer cosmetic perfection of his teeth. "The answer to all of those questions is no," he assured her.

Portia meanwhile was trying to form an initial impression of the man. He was of average height, but powerfully built, somewhere in his early to mid-thirties. She suspected that under the well-cut sports jacket he wore was a thickly muscled physique. Perhaps he was an ex-athlete or had a history of bodybuilding. The latter might prove significant. A compulsion to perfect and control the body generally meant that the person felt out of control in other areas of his life.

She smiled graciously, again trying to put him at his ease. "My assistant said you mentioned some difficulties with a job transfer? You want to tell me about that?"

Campion looked at her with a curious expression, and for the first time, she noticed that his eyes were an odd shade, khaki almost, and astonishingly clear. They might have been arresting save for the fact that the eyes somehow seemed at odds with the rest of his face. They seemed older than the smooth, tanned cheeks would suggest, sadder than Campion's flashy, perfect smile. He was clearly making an effort to keep from fidgeting as he found words to reply. He glanced up, almost embarrassed.

"Yeah, okay. That's what I told her. I moved to Charlotte a couple of weeks ago. You can even call the paper if you don't believe me. The *Star*."

Portia's expression never wavered, though inwardly she was a little taken aback. "I believe you," she assured him.

Campion reached up restlessly and patted his hair, as if to make sure it was still in place. "Can I smoke?" he inquired. "I feel like I could talk better if I could smoke."

Portia shook her head. "Sorry. Not here. Just take a deep breath. Try and relax. I'm not in a hurry."

Campion obeyed, taking several deep breaths and blowing them out again, then dropping his head down on his chest and rolling it from side to side. She could almost hear his neck cracking. When he had finished, Campion straightened up and looked at her. "Sorry," he said. "I guess I'm just nervous." All at once he leaned forward, hands on his knees, as if to impress her with the veracity of what he was about to say.

"Okay. Yeah, I've got adjustment problems—with moving. The new job—I'm a reporter, did I say that?"

Portia nodded, wondering what was to come. Then, just as suddenly as he'd leaned closer, Campion sat back in his chair, so abruptly it rocked a little on its back legs. His eyes were jittery now, the odd, uncomfortable smile still plastered across his features.

"The truth is, I'm not even really sure why I'm here. Moving is only sort of the reason I'm here. I guess it's the pressure and everything. A principal stressor, isn't that what you shrinks call it?"

Portia interrupted him gently. "I don't think it really matters, John. The point is, you are here. So why don't you tell me what's on your mind?"

And still he evaded the question. "The last guy, down in Florida, he thought I wouldn't be able to handle it. Moving to Charlotte, I mean. He was pretty sure I was going to screw it up."

Portia studied him for a long moment. Either this guy was the victim of some kind of psychological malpractice or he was revealing some deep insecurities. "Is that what your psychologist really told you?" she probed gently. "Or was that what you heard, because you were already anxious about coming here?"

John Campion looked at her curiously. "What's the difference?"

Abruptly, he got to his feet, reaching around one side of his chair to retrieve a battered briefcase. "I brought you my file," he replied, rummaging through its contents. "It's all in there."

Portia frowned a little as he handed her a manila folder, his name and a patient number typed neatly on the tab. She was a little startled to see he'd had a recent manicure, the nails even and quite highly polished. Then, as if the movement itself had cost him considerable effort, Campion sank back down in his chair, as though he were suddenly exhausted. He sat perfectly still for another moment, waiting for her to open the folder. When she did not, it seemed to disappoint him.

"Aren't you going to read it?" he asked.

She smiled. "I can read it later. Right now, I just think we should talk. Get to know each other a little bit."

Campion blushed furiously. "Shrinks," he said contemptuously. "You can't fool me with that stuff. You've already formed some opinion, haven't you?"

Portia remained calm. "Not really—"

But John Campion, whoever he was, was clearly unconvinced.

"You think you know so much. Sitting there taking your little notes. You meet a person and five minutes later you think you've got them all scoped out. Well, let me tell you something. I'm a reporter, okay? I know something about sizing people up, too. And I've got your number—don't think I don't."

Portia glanced at him, surprised at the confrontation. "Well, good," she replied emphatically, forcing a small smile. "Now that I think I know everything about you, and you think you know everything about me, why don't we cut to the chase?"

He stared at her in amazement, and from his expression, Portia could see that he was in fact younger than she'd thought him at first, that it was only the eyes that had made her think otherwise. Now, in his astonishment, he appeared almost adolescent. Her smile broadened encouragingly.

"I thought you wanted to skip the preliminaries," she added evenly.

Campion's derisive laugh exploded, harsh and false-sounding in the quiet room. "Oh, touché, Doctor," he answered. "I guess you got me there, didn't you?"

Though her smile never wavered, Portia nevertheless had to fight back a little flutter of annoyance. It was clear that whatever Campion's problem, he was reluctant to talk about it. Reluctant enough, anyway, that he preferred to try and establish a cat-and-mouse game of projection and retreat. She sighed inwardly; she had more than one patient like John Campion. They knew they needed help all right, they even went so far as to show up for their appointments. Yet, once they got there, they'd spend their forty-five minutes evading the issues, busily projecting their anger onto their psychologist, anxiously insisting they knew what she thought.

Now, Campion was playing the cat, eyeing her carefully, awaiting her next move, trying to see if she would continue the contest. When she simply returned his look without comment, he backed down, his anger dissipating as suddenly as it had flared. Clearly, her strategy worked.

"Fine," Portia said. "Let's continue. You mentioned you're from Florida?"

Campion slouched deeply into his chair. He framed a triangle with his fingers and stared through it. "Fucking Disney World Orlando," he answered sullenly.

"You sound like you didn't like it much," she prompted.

Campion grunted a little. "Oh, it was okay," he went on. "If you happen to like being a hack writer in a land of whores. I was just one more. Churning out bullshit for the bucks. And getting royally fucked by my editors in return."

Portia made a note. "I take it your relationships with your co-workers were part of the reason for coming up here?"

Campion chuckled. "You know what they say about one bad apple," he replied. "I guess they thought my continued presence there would taint the precious psyches of all their little drones."

"Was that what you thought?" Portia inquired, getting into the rhythm of a question and answer exploration. This Campion might be peculiar, and hostile as hell, but at least the chip on his shoulder was proving more therapeutically promising than Sandra's marital woes.

"Let's just say I had other plans." He glanced at her. "I've got what you call a bad attitude. Poor work habits. Check my chart— I'm your basic chronic underachiever. At least that's what they say. The shrinks, the bosses. My own version of it is a little different."

"And what's that?" Portia asked him. "Your version?"

Campion faced her with a fearless sort of expression. "Christ," he said. "You must be bored out of your mind."

Portia glanced up from her notes. "Pardon?"

Campion shrugged. "I said, you must be bored out of your fucking skull. Sitting here—hour after hour—day after day—listening to the same old people with their same old problems. Is it rough, Doctor? You ever get sick of it?"

Portia recrossed her legs, while somewhere inside that insistent little inner voice demanded: *How could he have known that?*

"I'm not sure what you mean," she answered evenly.

Campion's eyes glittered. "Oh," he replied. "You know what I mean."

Portia felt herself begin to blush and tried desperately to stop it. "John," she went on coolly. "We're here to talk about you. Not about me."

Campion's teeth shone white as he smiled again. "Yeah," he said. "I can almost see it. How crazy it makes you—listening to the same old crap about Mrs. So-and-so's sex life and Mr. Dumb-ass's divorce. Their so-called issues. All those symptoms and syndromes—"

"John," Portia interrupted firmly. "Is there a point to any of this?"

"Sure there is—" Campion chuckled. "I believe you shrinks refer to this part of the process as establishing empathy. How about it, Doc?"

Good god—who is this guy?

"I can empathize with you, Doctor, that's all. 'Cause we're so much alike."

"How do you mean?"

"I mean we chase the same old stories—we listen to all the same old lines. Think about it. Is news really so different from delving into the personality? Truth isn't about truth anymore. It's about staying functional. It's about survival, okay? Neither one of us can tell people the truth, at least until they're ready to face it. And since we live here in the land of the bland and the home of the tabloid, I'm giving all those folks out there in newspaper land just what they're asking for. Just enough to make them feel a little bit better about their lousy lives. Just enough to keep 'em going through one more lousy day."

He leaned forward, hands on his knees, while his voice dropped to a low, almost stagy whisper.

"And so, I suspect, are you."

Portia glanced at him, at once fascinated and skeptical. Listening to Campion talk was like watching some awful car accident. She didn't want to look, but at the same time, she didn't quite feel she could turn away.

"I want a cigarette," Campion said suddenly.

Portia eyed him quizzically. A moment ago, he had been challenging her. Now he had shrunk into himself to such an extent it was almost visible. He looked smaller somehow, more helpless than when he'd first walked in.

"Sorry again. Regulations," she answered.

Campion's knotty fingers strayed again to that imaginary lint.

"It's okay—" she told him. "You're only here for a little while, longer. You'll make it."

Campion nodded. "Sorry," he said again. "I—I'm nervous."

"You said that," Portia commented. From the look of this guy, she reckoned, nervous had to be both the understatement and overstatement of the decade. Mentally, she was still taken aback by the acuity of his perception. But now, her new patient sat fidgeting in his chair, looking for all the world as if he was losing air somewhere, as if his challenge had left him the one defeated, deflated like some used-up balloon.

"But you don't need to be nervous," she intervened. "This is just talking, right? Just a conversation."

Campion nodded silently.

"You mentioned your work," she prompted. "You don't feel good about it?"

Campion stared at her in a way that made Portia suddenly uncomfortable. "Do you?" he demanded. "My readers want drivel," he continued. "The highest level of thrills at the lowest level of vocabulary. And I give it to them. And no, since you asked, I don't feel good doing that."

Campion stubbornly refused to look at her. Instead his gaze drifted to a corner of the room, as though contemplating some great mystery she might only guess at. "I'm spoon-feeding thrills to the sensation-starved, Doctor," he answered after a moment. "I'm surviving by adding some spicy and supposedly controversial columns to their otherwise deprived lives." Campion paused, sighing heavily. "Guts and gossip, Doctor. That's the name of the game. And I play the game very well. I'm a frigging master of the damn game. Only—"

Portia noticed a light blinking silently on the phone panel. She couldn't help thinking it might be Lori, on the phone with police headquarters.

"Only what?" she asked, turning her attention back to her patient.

Campion leaned forward once more, his eyes bright, his voice taking on an earnestness he'd not displayed before. "Only I've just got to get over this spot. Once I do, things are going to change. Everything is going to be sorted out. I'm going to be right where I want to be. I can feel it."

Portia wrestled with the vagueness of the statement. Whatever the central issue, he had spoken of it as a "spot." Once he got over it, whatever it was, "things" were going to "change." The generality of it disturbed her. Campion professed to be a reporter, and though she'd certainly experienced the confusion of dealing with patients who communicated poorly, that obviously wasn't Campion's problem. Which meant he had chosen his terms as another sort of smoke screen, while at the same time his earnest expression begged for understanding. And help. Yet encouraging him to further define his problems had only generated anger, to say nothing of a high level of anxiety. So she chose yet another tack.

"You seem to have a pretty good handle on your situation, John," she began. "It's pretty clear you've done a lot of work on yourself. So, tell me something—"

"What?"

"Why are you here?"

Once more, the question took him by surprise. "Don't you know?"

She met his bewildered look with one of her own. The guy was so locked into his projections, he probably didn't even realize he hadn't told her anything. She lifted up the yellow legal pad with the notes she'd made for him to see, perhaps a half-dozen lines on an otherwise blank page.

"That's what I know, John. I know that I see a lot of anger in you—in how you talk about your work. But I see sadness, too. And I wonder how we're going to work your sessions with me to a point where you feel you can talk about those things. But that's all I know. I'm just a psychologist—not a mind reader. Okay?"

He sat back in his chair, studying her, as if he might read somewhere in her face what he ought to say next. There was a long moment of silence.

All at once, he broke into another of his broad, flashy grins. Yet his eyes remained remote and sad, as if fixed on some inner landscape—one that she could only guess at.

"Oh," he said finally. "That. The reason."

"Yes. The reason."

He shrugged and slouched deeper in his chair, as if trying to disappear from under her scrutiny. When he spoke again it was more to himself than to her, as if he were recollecting some long-ago memory rather than speaking of the thing that was causing him pain.

"I can't write anymore," he said. "I managed to get transferred from Orlando before anybody could find out. I would get by pulling out paragraphs from my old columns. All I had to do was change the names. Mix them around a little." Campion gave a soft, contemptuous little snort and passed a weary hand over his eyes. "Nobody even noticed." He paused then and looked at her, the smile gone, his mouth sunk into a grim line.

"I haven't written anything in six months."

After ushering John Campion out into the hall, Portia leaned against the doorjamb for a few long moments, thinking hard. Then she turned and plucked the file folder from her desk and headed toward reception, where she was startled to find Lori wearing a wistful sort of look, staring off into space.

Portia tapped her gently on the shoulder. "Make copies of this for me, will you, Lori? I need to read up on Mr. Campion."

Lori glanced up. "Sure," she answered. Then, unable to contain herself, she went on. "Was he gorgeous or what?"

"Huh?" Portia looked up as she searched a small refrigerator in the corner for something to drink. "Who?"

Lori rose to her feet, "Mr. Campion, of course. I about fell through the floor when he walked in here." She took up the file folder and opened it, idly scanning the top document. "Is he married?"

Portia popped the top of a can of diet soda. "Hey, you know the rules. No reading the files." It was a protest without conviction, though. As far as she knew, Lori had more information on her patients than she did. "And no," she went on as Lori obediently snapped the folder closed. "He isn't. Not likely to be either."

"Oh hell, I knew it." Lori's voice was rife with disappointment. "He's gay, right?"

Portia shrugged doubtfully. "Don't know. Let's just say definitely not a hotbed of mental health—"

"So gorgeous," interjected Lori.

"Believe me, you don't want to go there." Portia tossed the now empty can into the recycling bin. "Hey, I almost forgot, what'd you find out from headquarters?"

Lori edged back over to her desk, where she checked her notes. "Well, I got good news and bad news," she began.

Portia frowned a little, trying to quell a little flutter of anxiety. "Meaning?"

"Meaning they are very interested in your input as—" Here, Lori squinted at the pink message slip in her hand. "And I quote, 'an interim expert' on the investigation."

Portia wrinkled her forehead. "Interim?" she asked.

"That's what the man said," replied Lori. "But don't ask me what it means. Bottom line is, you've got an appointment tomorrow at three. The DA's office. The task force is having some big powwow over there and somebody's going to talk to you after they're done."

Portia considered this, mulling over the prospect of having to appear down at the state office building. From the sound of it, she might be speaking with anyone from the DA to a beat cop. And the knowledge that her offer to volunteer as a profiler wasn't being met with more enthusiasm stung a little. Less than six months ago, she'd been the best-known psychologist in North Carolina. Now, she was being treated as if she were going on a job interview. "Well," she said. "I guess I'm not as well known as I thought down there."

Lori managed a small, sympathetic smile. "You know how it is," she said. "Folks have short memories."

SEVEN

John Campion sat late in his cubicle, busily typing, watching his words displayed on the monitor screen, his amber eyes picking up the glare from the monitor as a little smile played around the corners of his mouth. The day staff was slowly but surely giving way to the night shift, as reporters and secretaries and gophers gathered up their belongings, calling their farewells to one another. Campion sat back and read again the few paragraphs displayed on the screen.

So far, so perfect, he thought.

A hand on his shoulder interrupted him. "Hey, Campion" came a voice from behind him.

In a single movement, Campion hit a key to save his file then another to close it. He smiled and turned around to face Sam Barton, a financial reporter who worked in the cubicle adjoining Campion's. Sam grinned foolishly behind his glasses as a bevy of *Baywatch* babes popped onto Campion's screen, giggling and beckoning.

"Some screensaver—be still my loins," he said. "Pamela Anderson."

Campion's smile was bright. "Pulled it off the Net," he said to Barton. "Beats the hell out of staring at flying windows. Tell you what, I'll download you a copy."

Barton blushed a little and continued to grin. "Ah, thanks, but no thanks," he said. "If Lucy ever got a load of that, I'd be doing domestic hard time for a month."

Campion shrugged. Lucy, from what he'd been able to glean from around the watercooler, was Sam's wife, a redhead whose fits of jealousy were legendary. Now, with their first child due in November, Sam's wife was keeping him on an increasingly short leash. Showing up unannounced at the *Star*'s offices for lunch and beeping her good-natured husband at all hours.

"Whatever you say," Campion continued. "But I'd invoke the First Amendment if I were you. Freedom of the press and all that."

Sam hung his head and winked good-naturedly. "I'll take the Fifth instead," he said. "Marriage does that to you. Say, speaking of fifths, what do you say you give it a rest for a minute and come on down to The Snug? Tomorrow's edition's pretty much wrapped. A bunch of us are going to hang for a while."

Campion's smile evaporated all at once, as though the other man had reached across and wiped it from his face. His yellowish eyes glinted. "What about Lucy?" he asked without a trace of sarcasm.

Sam smiled, privately wondering at Campion's abrupt change of attitude. In the few days they'd been working together, Sam had wondered more than once just what the guy's story was. For all the hype that surrounded Campion's coming, there seemed nothing to especially recommend him as the wonder writer they'd all been expecting. Of course, he wasn't due to debut his column for another two weeks, either.

Then, with a little inward shrug, Sam's curiosity vanished as suddenly as it had come. He supposed that was why he worked the financials; human interest had never been a strong point with him.

"Oh, I'm safe for the moment," he replied. "Lucy just beeped. Said she was going to her mom's." He slung a battered leather knapsack over his shoulder. "You coming?"

Campion shook his head. "Next time," he promised. "I've got to keep at this column, and then I've got a meeting with Lady Love-less."

Sam eyed him curiously. "First the big mystery debut, now the dubious privilege of an audience with the dragon. I got to hand it to you, boy. You're a fast mover. Enough to leave this country boy in the dust."

Again, Campion displayed his teeth. "Oh, you know Loveless—she's just keeping me after school so she can chew on somebody's balls before dinner."

Sam grinned. "Lucky you," he called as he entered the elevator.

When he had gone, Campion turned back to his monitor and stared for a long minute at the endless, undulating beach party unfolding on the screen, smiling a little as he waited for the call from the managing editor's office upstairs.

Lucky me is right.

The next day, at exactly two minutes of three, Portia McTeague took a deep breath as she headed up the steps that led to the district attorney's headquarters.

You can still back out, you know.

She caught a glimpse of her own image reflected in the glass doors to the building, unruly auburn hair flying in the insistent breeze, her face half hidden behind a pair of tortoise-framed sun-glasses, her mouth pressed into a tense line. Resolutely, she pulled open the door and headed inside.

The fact was, she had no intention of backing out of her offer to become part of the task force investigating the Meredith murder. She knew herself well enough to realize that her sudden attack of misgiving was the legacy of old wounds inflicted in this building, battle scars she'd worn proudly since her first fledgling days as a forensic psychologist, when she'd gone traipsing through endless hearings and appeals for her clients, being interviewed by attorneys and other authorities, all of whom had seemed uniformly insensi-tive to her causes. Though the actual battle for the recognition of psychological evidence in the courts was being won by slow degrees all over the nation, she was only too aware that all the old preju-dices still lingered. Whatever the current veneer of understanding of severe personality damage and its impact on criminal behavior, there lurked just underneath the far more simplistic notion of treating offenders like so much human refuse, as if cleaning up the streets were something just that easy.

Once inside, the flow of people hurrying through the lobby reassured her in some way that was hard for her to define, the echo of their shoes on the terrazzo tiles like the melody of a long-remembered song. The very scent of the halls excited her, sending some signal of affirmation deep into her brain and bloodstream.

She found the correct elevator bank and, when a pair of doors slid open before her, she pressed the button for the fifth floor. The doors slid silently closed and she stared fixedly upward at the progress of orange numbers as the floors went by, trying very hard not to think about anything at all.

Detective Sergeant David Goodman wasn't a beat cop, but he wasn't exactly the mayor, either. When she found her way to the room number Lori had written down, she was surprised to find herself in a conference room, the chairs disarranged, the Formica table littered with paper coffee cups and sandwich wrappers. Near to the door was a man of about her own age, slumped wearily in a chair, wearing a plain tropical-weight worsted jacket and a colorful, loosely knotted necktie depicting the straw man from *The Wizard of Oz* dancing down the yellow brick road.

Portia surveyed the room. "I feel like I missed the party," she offered.

The man glanced up and she caught the sharp intelligence in his eyes, despite his obvious fatigue. "Don't worry about it," he answered with a sigh. "Believe me, the food stank and the band was lousy."

She liked him immediately. "I'm Portia McTeague," she said, extending a hand in his direction.

"Dave Goodman," he answered. "Homicide. Please, make yourself comfortable. As far as that's possible anyhow."

Portia took a chair near the one he'd been using. Goodman resumed his own seat heavily, as though his knees had buckled. Portia observed him carefully. More than anything, the homicide detective looked as if he needed about three days' worth of sleep.

"Must have been some meeting," she said after another moment.

Goodman leaned back in his chair and shoved his hands deep into his pockets. "Oh, it was a beaut," he replied. "I haven't seen the DA that red in the face since the Hornets made the play-offs." Goodman paused, fixing his attention on the place at his waistline where his shirt buttons had just begun to strain across his middle. "Problem is," he continued, "all that shouting is going to mean exactly shit when it comes to catching this guy. That's one of the reasons I wanted to talk to you. I know some of your work. And I figure we got nothing to lose."

Portia studied him silently. The statement seemed meant to be taken at face value, with no tone of voice or change in his expression to color its meaning—no unspoken even-though-I-think-it's-a-bunch-of-horseshit left hanging in the air.

"Then you probably know I usually work the other end of things," she offered. "Forensic psychologists work from a different perspective than profilers do."

Goodman's eyes narrowed slightly. "Can you explain how?"

Portia shrugged. "Sure. At least, I think I can. I'm usually called in to evaluate suspects, do the standard psychological tests and some interviews—that kind of thing. I try to reconstruct an individual's state of mind at the time of the offense and to discover—if I can—why they did what they did—if they knew what they were doing—all those things. Then," she went on with a rueful smile, "I bring my findings to court. And we all know what happens then."

Goodman failed to pick up on her implication. "Go on," he said.

Portia swallowed hard as she tried to further delineate the differences. "Profilers work with the authorities right from the beginning. They start with the crime. They look at how it was committed, what happened at the scene—any specific rituals or signatures that were used—and then use standard psychological information to construct a picture of the type of individual who would commit that particular crime."

All at once she paused and peered at Goodman, a little uncertainly. "Excuse me," she said quietly. "But you already know all this, right?"

Goodman nodded. "Most of it," he answered without a trace of irony. "A person picks up a fair amount of psychology in my line of work. But I don't pretend to know it all, Doctor." He gazed at her, a little sadly. "That's why I wanted to talk to you. I wanted to see if you could come up with anything new. Despite all the politicians," he finished, gesturing lamely around at the empty room.

"My assistant said something," Portia prompted him, "about my being an 'interim' investigator?"

Goodman sighed again and studied her for another long moment while he seemed to consider whether or not to tell her the rest. "I need all the help I can get, okay? And I'm taking you on for a trial because it's my own opinion that you might be able to offer a fresh perspective." Goodman paused, rubbing his eyes. "I had a teacher once—criminology—back in college. She told me that when you're exactly sure you know everything there is to know about a case, turn around and look at the opposite—you'll find things there, too." Goodman smiled wearily. "That's why you're here. You know the opposite of what I'm supposed to know."

Portia studied him intently, with new respect forming in her mind. Whoever Dave Goodman was, it was becoming increasingly clear he was no ordinary redneck cop.

"Problem is," he went on, "the mayor and the boys already contacted Quantico before you called yesterday. They want to get some FBI hotshot down here. Makes for good press, lots of photo ops. Crime fighters on the rampage—all that crap. You know what I mean?"

Portia nodded assent. She knew only too well what the detective was talking about.

Goodman stared around him at the empty chairs. "Before they formed this fuc—sorry. Anyway, before they formed this so-called task force of theirs, I happened to be heading up this particular investigation. I was at the scene—"

Here Goodman paused. She saw something darken in his face as he reached for a cup near his elbow and gulped the last dregs of coffee from the bottom.

"But it so happens they've got all their boys tied up on cases around the country and have put the Meredith thing on the back burner until they can free up some personnel. Or so they say, anyway. My own feeling is, the case just isn't big-time enough to suit them. So when you called, I asked to bring you on in the interim. Simply because I thought you might be able to offer some new angle—some fresh perspective we haven't thought of before."

"Sounds fair enough," Portia offered.

Goodman chuckled a little. "Tell that to the DA. I've got to say, Doctor, you're not real popular down here."

Portia smiled ruefully. "I can believe that. What have you heard? That I was a bleeding heart? A do-gooder? How about a godless, wild-eyed liberal?"

For the first time, Goodman grinned, and all at once she saw underneath the layers of cynicism and fatigue a trace of the man who'd bought a *Wizard of Oz* necktie. At the same time she felt herself relax, tension she hadn't even been aware of leaving the muscles of her neck and shoulders.

"Oh, worse," he told her. "Much, much worse."

Portia eyed him with new interest. "And you still wanted to talk to me? Okay. I mean, forgive me, but what's wrong with this picture? I know I volunteered, but Carolina cops aren't usually quite so broad-minded."

Goodman leaned forward and met her eyes. His own were quite suddenly serious. "My job right now is to jump-start a murder investigation that is going precisely nowhere—task force or no task force. Look, I want you to know exactly how I feel about the Feds coming in on this one. I've worked with them before. Sometimes they have some insight, most times they don't. And the reason they don't is because they're too locked into their own system, okay? Despite all the crap you see on TV and in the movies, most of those guys don't have enough gut instinct to fill the average tooth. They're doing it by the numbers. By rote. And believe me—" Goodman reached across the table in front of him and slid a manila envelope in her direction. From the open flap Portia could see that it contained crime scene photos, already a little worn at their edges from all the sets of hands they had passed through. She glanced at the detective, suddenly unsure of herself.

Goodman's mouth compressed into a grim, unyielding line. "I've got to find this guy," he said. "Because this one is definitely not doing it by the numbers. And because," he went on, "unless I'm wrong, he's going to do it again. Soon." Goodman's eyes were filled with frustration and something else too. Something almost like fear.

"And he'll do it for sport."

Portia swallowed hard. Then, with trembling fingers, she reached toward the envelope.

The naked body of Tamara Meredith had been photographed from at least a dozen different angles, and it took Portia a moment to fight back a wave of nausea as she reviewed the pictures, silently cursing the need for color photographs. The light from the huge windows of the office had tinged the interior shots with a glassy eeriness that was hard to ignore. It was as though the light itself were some further invasion of Tamara Meredith, as if such tortures as the ones endured by that fragile body better belonged in some everlasting darkness, not illumined by the morning sun.

The first thought that managed to register in Portia's mind was that the victim's many wounds were neither savage nor especially brutal. She knew enough anatomy to see that the killer's knife had been placed very deliberately, the deeper cuts running along major arteries, some more superficial ones over the breasts and neck. There were small x's etched over her eyelids, nicks taken from her earlobes. Her navel had been oddly enlarged, with small cuts going outward, like the rays of the sun. Longer, yet relatively shallow cuts ran from deeper wounds at her pubis and navel, up through the diaphragm toward the heart, the throat, and finally the mass of golden hair, where the scalp had been cut away near the top of the skull.

"These wounds," she said, glancing at Goodman for some confirmation. "It looks like—I don't know—a pattern of some kind."

Goodman shrugged. "Forensics thought the same thing. The arterial cuts assured that she would bleed to death. The rest were apparently made both before and after death. They can't call it. There was evidence of probable sexual assault in the bruising around her pubic area, but no semen, no hairs, nothing to take to a lab."

"Defense wounds?" Portia asked.

Goodman managed a tight smile. "Since her hands are missing, it's hard to say. Other than that, there's almost nothing. Our best guess is, he took her by surprise, knocked her unconscious, and went to work. We know she wasn't dead when he started cutting. But she sure as hell is now."

Portia continued to study the photos. Now that her initial revulsion had passed, she found herself drawn to the arrangement of the body. There was something odd about it. Like the pattern of the wounds, she found herself straining to identify what it was. Meredith had been placed carefully in the center of a reproduction unicorn carpet, almost as though she were the grisly medallion, the gory center of the otherwise pastoral scene. It was all so careful, so deliberate that she had to suppress a little inward shudder. Whoever had murdered Tamara Meredith had not done so in any uncontrolled fit of passion. He'd taken his time; each of the cuts indicated to her a thoughtfulness and planning, an almost sinister playfulness as he'd added the finishing touches. When she managed to speak again, her own voice sounded oddly out of place in the strained silence.

"What have you got so far?"

"Just what you see here," Goodman answered. "He paid cash. No name recorded in the appointment book. We're still trying to get the assistant who booked him to come up with a name. But even if she does, it's no guarantee—probably a phony."

"But the assistant—she saw the guy, right?"

Goodman's air came from his lungs in a rush. "Angel Tirado," he answered. "And God help us there."

"Why?"

"She's so indoctrinated into this New Age stuff, she's totally unreliable as a witness. She gave us a description of an average-looking white male with the eyes of a beast. She claims she had a psychic impression of the numbers 666 written in blood on his forehead."

"Oh my—" Portia began.

"Of course, that was after the fact," Goodman went on. "I guess finding your boss like that when you come to work in the morning is enough to knock anybody's screws loose. But you can understand how her eyewitness description is, uhh, shall we say, less than succinct?"

"Maybe I could talk to her," Portia suggested. "The imagery could just be some kind of displacement due to trauma. Have you got a phone number?"

"It's here somewhere," agreed Goodman, taking a small notebook from his breast pocket and flipping through the pages. He read off the number as she copied it down. "But I don't know how far you'll get. Believe me, I've already tried. According to Ms. Tirado, the devil himself came in for a reading. You can imagine how well that's going to go over down at the courthouse. I've had her down to the precinct three times to go over the mug books. Nothing." Goodman managed a thin smile. "Apparently, the devil has yet to be apprehended by the Charlotte PD."

Portia chewed her lip thoughtfully. "I see your point," she answered. "It's certainly a new twist on the eyewitness problem."

Goodman's eyelids all but drooped. "Even if we could ID him, we can't be sure this character is the killer. It may have been somebody else—someone who came in after he'd gone."

"I hadn't thought of that—" Portia admitted. Suddenly, she was struck by a new realization. "It's funny," she went on.

"What's funny?"

"The way people have a tendency to form conclusions without even being aware of it. The last appointment is a natural enough suspect certainly, but it really doesn't follow that Meredith was killed by one of her clients. Sure, it's opportunity, but it's not motive." Portia paused, glancing again through the photos. "Yet, because her work was, well, outside the norm, we naturally assume that her clients, or whatever they were, are automatically dysfunctional."

Goodman studied her appreciatively. "Keep talking," he said. "This is what I need. Fresh perspective."

Portia gestured helplessly. "I'm not entirely sure what I'm talking about just yet," she admitted. "I guess I'm saying that we can't afford to take anything for granted. The New Age aspect might be irrelevant in the killer's mind, a kind of—I don't know—window dressing." Portia met Goodman's eyes. "I'm a psychologist, right?

If I were found dead in my office, there would be an assumption that the crime was committed by one of my patients. Because people who see psychologists are presumed, at least on some level, to be, well, crazy."

"But that doesn't make it so," Goodman interjected doubtfully. "Okay, fine. But you know what they say—if it looks like a duck and it walks like a duck. Dot, dot, dot."

Portia smiled. "Point taken. But I still want to talk to the assistant. Maybe I can get past her symbolism long enough to get a real description."

"Give it a shot," the detective conceded. "The best we can do for the moment is to keep her under twenty-four-hour surveillance. If the killer and the mystery client are the same man, he knows she can identify him. And that means Tirado's troubles haven't even begun."

Portia studied the photos for another few moments. It was all so very deliberate, almost as though he'd visualized the scene in advance, down to its smallest detail. Enough at least to produce the very images she was staring at—these silent tableaux of a fragile bloodless form, minus her hands, arranged like some broken statue on the floor.

And then another thought, more disturbing still, followed upon the heels of the first. It was as if the murderer were an artist and this flesh his canvas, this murder a necessary destruction from which arose his terrible creation.

Goodman was watching her with a troubled expression, his eyes sad and thoughtful. "He left the weapon," he continued quietly. "It's a chef's knife. All-purpose, standard brand. Well sharpened. Could have been purchased anywhere. We'll never know. The thing was clean—no prints, no traces—*nada*. He even bagged it for us, if you can believe it. Left it right out on the desk where we couldn't miss it. His little gift to the homicide division."

Portia's mind absorbed this new piece of information. "You think he's playing with you?"

This time, Goodman's grin was decidedly strained. "Well, Doctor, what do *you* think?"

Portia blushed a little. Ask a stupid question, she thought. "I think you're right," she said aloud. "You do need all the help you can get. This guy is highly organized. The placement of the wounds indicates a kind of ritual. He left this knife for you to find. And that means his fantasy, whatever it is, is highly developed. He's been working on it for a while." She paused, then began to gather up the photos. "Can I take these with me? I need to think about this."

Goodman rose heavily and again Portia was struck by his immense fatigue. For a relatively young man, he moved as if he were a hundred. "Whatever you need," he answered. "I've got lots of copies."

Portia rose as well. "I'll need the police and coroner's reports too. Anything."

Goodman nodded assent. The man was practically asleep on his feet. "I'll fax them over this evening. You have a machine at home?"

Portia swung her handbag over her shoulder, groping for a card. "The numbers are here," she told him.

Goodman met her eyes as they made their way to the door. "We'll use your machine at home, if you don't mind. I don't want any details of this case leaking out from any source whatever. The press is crazy enough as it is."

Portia could see the wisdom of this, knowing Lori's predilections. Though she trusted her assistant implicitly, even Portia couldn't predict her reaction to the wealth of bizarre details attached to the Meredith murder. "Good idea," she agreed. "When can I get a look at the scene?"

Goodman swung the door inward, allowing Portia to pass through before him. "Day after tomorrow the earliest," he said. "I have the day off tomorrow, and I don't come back on until four the following day. I want to be there when you see it," he said sincerely. "But I got to tell you, right now I need some space away from this case. I need to go home. See my kids. Kiss my wife."

"No problem," said Portia, eyeing him kindly. "And for heaven's sake, get some sleep. You look like you're about to drop."

Goodman managed a wan smile. "Oh, I am," he assured her. "But I have to warn you, sleep doesn't help much. I always look this way."

EIGHT

John Campion stretched luxuriously, listening to his lover, now making a sound somewhere between a snore and a kind of contented purr as she slept beside him. The beginning was always the best time, he reckoned silently. The first few days and weeks when the lust ran pure, unadulterated by all the tiresome refrains that were supposed to constitute couplehood. Lust had always seemed to him so much purer than love in that respect. Lust was real; love was the illusion. It was a shame people felt such a compulsion to make it otherwise.

That was why Kate had so appealed to him, right from that first day. She was so beyond the usual insecurities he'd come to expect from women. She liked to fuck with an abandon that matched his own. He'd found it breathtaking. More breathtaking still was her well-honed body, sinewy and hard as a man's underneath the silk fabrics and designer lines, tough and tanned and adaptable to more sexual antics than were described in the Kama Sutra.

Campion smiled benignly at the ceiling, seeing his own reflection grinning back at him from the mirrored ceiling tiles. They'd star-

tled him at first, those tiles, then delighted him. He found it exciting to observe their follies, so much so that he discovered he was
even fond of being on the bottom, allowing Kate to straddle him as
she humped them both into sweet oblivion, fucking him with a
violent hunger that both astonished and intrigued him. In the two
short weeks he'd been in town, bedding Kate Loveless had become
a more or less regular arrangement, as satisfactory to them both as
a good workout. He knew, with a tinge of regret, that one or the
other of them would eventually grow tired of these games, that
even well-toned flesh like Kate's lost its novelty. Even now, he
could see it in her profile as she lay splayed out on the bed next to
him. There was a little sagging around the neck, a trace of age in
the flesh of her upper arms that forecast the bony old woman she
would become. So it would end, sooner or later. Even the purest
lust ran out of nourishment after a time. But thus far, she'd made
none of the usual noises, and that too pleased him, because it meant
he had some time to plan.

Pleasure, Campion knew, always exerted influence, and lust was
its own kind of power, mysterious and pure and utterly necessary.
He sensed Kate knew as much, and had agreed, at least for the
moment, to their unspoken bargain. She was willing to trade the
pleasure of his body for a portion of her power. And that pleased
him. It pleased him very much.

He hadn't pressed the issue, of course. That would have been
indiscreet. But he could see it in the way her eyes flicked over him
as they passed one another at the office, he could feel it in the heat
that came off her body as they stood close in the elevator or on the
stairs. She was using him and he was using her, and for the moment
it was absolutely right. That she could turn on him at any moment
only heightened his pleasure. As long as she didn't, he was still in
control.

He felt a sudden burst of pleasure as a hot, sleepy hand reached
across the expanse of sheet between them, grabbing his member
with surprising force. Campion smiled lazily at the ceiling, feeling
the blood rush to his groin. Sweet, insatiable Kate. Always so hungry, so ready. She'd already granted him enough of an extension on
his column to insure he'd have time to plant his profile with

McTeague. He smiled again, feeling that hand and thinking of McTeague. He hadn't expected her to be so self-assured. But he must have made a fair presentation, mixing just the right measure of truth with just the right measure of lies. A little inner torment here, a little anger there. It had been so easy. She'd believed him right away, even without his records. She'd been so anxious to help that she'd scheduled him for three appointments a week. He'd get his story all right, and then some. Campion grinned at his reflection. Things were finally going right.

And last night Kate, his ever so sexy managing editor, had surprised him with his own office space—a small room away from the prying curiosity of the other staff. Some expert fucking had been neatly traded for a chance to do his story right—the way he wanted. Pleasure for power, he thought with a little gasp as those insistent fingers tickled toward his scrotum.

It was like money in the bank.

An hour later, on the other side of town, Angel Tirado sat in the light of morning, practicing her meditations. Nude, her skin still glowing and damp from the shower, she assumed the standard lotus position, perched on a worn prayer rug in her two-room apartment, arms slightly extended, the tops of her palms resting lightly on her knees. A rainbow candle dedicated to Santa Barbara burned fitfully on a small makeshift altar in the corner, adorned with a few white flowers. Barbara was her protector, her *patrona*. Barbara was her guide now, the patron saint of prisoners. "For she escaped the snares of the enemy and rose like a sparrow to heaven."

The air was thick with incense and Angel sucked it deeply into her lungs. She closed her eyes. It was important to meditate at the same time every day, she knew. The strength of the ritual came from the ritual itself. Her spiritual progress depended upon it. And so she had chosen this time—the hour of her birth. The hour of her power. She drew in another deep breath through her nostrils, held it, and let it out again.

Nothing.

The absence of any vision or thought comforted her. It had been so difficult to clear her field of the terrible memory of Tamara's

corpse lying so profaned on the carpet. She could still feel the
blackness of that memory lingering at the edges of her aura, trying
to sap her strength. The *cabrón* with the eyes of a beast had stolen
her hands, those frail instruments of Tamara's gift. But the hands
would not help him now, Angel thought with a certain resignation.
Even God could not help a soul such as that.

"I am surrounded by the light," she began, her voice little more
than a whisper. "I am made of light."

The police didn't understand the laws of the spirit—of karma.
They knew only the laws of men. She had done her best, but it was
beyond her power to help their investigation. She knew that now. It
had become so clear. The lords of karma would not be cheated.
Tamara had tried to stay on the path of goodness, but even she
could not conquer her karma, her destiny. She had taken a life in
some other time, some other place. And she'd had her own life
taken in return. It was the law of the universe. It was the only
justice that could be. All that remained was to offer prayers for her
spirit. And to pray for enlightenment. Angel could not help the
police. The laws of men had no control over the destinies of souls.

Angel struggled to return her thoughts to her breathing, to visu-
alize only the light. The heart must be kept humble and free. She
reached for some image. Sunlight, yes, that was it. This was better.
She looked inward and saw brilliant sunlight and blue, blue water.
Light that spilled like diamonds across the waves. In her mind she
could almost hear the ocean, little waves lapping gently at the
shore. And there was only light and peace and deep relaxation and
she felt the warm sand between her toes and heard the endless
secret music of the water. And she breathed the sounds of the
ocean, in and out. Angel Tirado aligned herself with the universal
rhythms; she bathed in the light and the water and she heard a
voice then, rising up from the song of the ocean. She heard it and
struggled to listen, just making out the words above the eternal sigh
of wave and breath. And she knew then who it was. And deep in her
meditations, she smiled. For it was her guide and her teacher. Santa
Barbara called softly to her across the reaches of water and sky and
her words struck deep into Angel's soul.

"*Mira, Angel,*" she sighed. "*Viene la bestia.*"

There was a knock at the door, so far away, so soft she did not understand at first what it was. Then, the metallic turning of the knob and lock, strange and unfamiliar—some animal scratching there, fevered and insistent. Something gave way, screws protesting, metal torn from flimsy wood.

And deep in her meditations, Angel Tirado began to scream.

It had been so easy. That part of it troubled him, almost. It was as though she'd been waiting. Bathed and ready, posed like some dark goddess on the floor, her caramel-colored skin smelling of roses, that midnight hair like silk against her spine. It had been so quick, so easy. And when he was done he wondered at it. It seemed so strange to him. The way she died. So easy. Too easy. A single scream, so easily silenced—weak arms, so powerless against him— the mindless animal terror in her clear brown eyes. It was so easy. Like hitting some fawn on the highway. The bones of her neck had snapped like twigs in his hands.

It disappointed him a little. He'd felt nothing when it happened, none of the sweet thrill as their souls passed through his body and into the darkness inside. He looked down at her and touched himself. He hadn't even gotten hard.

And then, in a moment, it came to him. He understood. This one did not belong to him. Not like the rest. The Angel was simply necessary to the game, a simple pawn sacrifice. She'd understood that somehow. That's why she'd been so easy to kill. So willing to die. She'd known her life was nothing. Only her death mattered now. It was necessary to the game.

He glanced up, startled. Someone upstairs was stirring; footsteps scuffed softly on the floorboards above him. He froze for a long moment, listening, his nerve endings alert for any sound, any threat. And there was nothing. No one had heard, no one had seen. And still he lingered, amazed at himself. It was done, he should leave now, disappear the way he had come, out into the oblivious world. No one would know. No one would see anything.

But no, not yet. He ought to give them something, some clue to his presence there. So they would know him. The thought made him smile. It would fool them if he did that. They would think this ruined meat meant something. They would think she was part of it. And they would be wrong. Just like always. They would find her and believe that she mattered to him. And they would be wrong.

His eyes darted sharply around the room, then came to rest. An old kitchen chair was placed on some newspapers near the sink; a can of spray paint nearby. He walked over to it, his mind working through the possibilities. He would have to be cautious; he would have to take that can with him, dispose of it somehow. Explode it somewhere.

He carried the paint back to the place where she lay, smiling a little. He leaned over and carefully extinguished the flame of the rainbow candle. It wouldn't do to ignite any fumes. It wouldn't serve the purpose. He wanted them to find her now. Mixing marbles clattered as he shook the can. He would take it with him when he left, though even that would probably not make a difference. They wouldn't be looking for a can. Not when they found what he would leave them.

The telephone rang, once, then twice. He froze, the long skein of Angel's hair caught tight in one hand as he jerked the body upright. The machine picked up, and a woman's voice echoed in the stillness as the caller left her message.

"Uh, hi—Angel Tirado? My name is Portia McTeague. I know you've been having some trouble. And I wondered if we could talk. I'm a doctor—a psychologist. And I'm working with the police. We want to try and find the man who killed Tamara, Angel, but we need your help. Will you call me? I'm at 555-2222."

He smiled dreamily, wonderingly, at the voice that rang like low bells into the silence of the room. He closed his eyes, letting the perfection of the moment course through him like some forbidden drug. It was all real, then. He could see that now. The dream was coming true. Even down to the smallest details—the voice on the phone. His breath came in little gasps as he yanked viciously at the mane of hair now twisted around his fist. He felt a rush of needy fire surge through his thighs and gut, pooling in the middle as he began to throb with excitement. He looked into that dead face, saw the tiny scar above one eyebrow, the dark hairs of her nostrils, a tiny blemish on her lip. She was so empty, so devoid of meaning. A tool, nothing more—used up now, she lay like an empty candy wrapper, all the sweetness gone. He jerked the body clumsily to its feet. He thought again of the voice on the phone.

And he laughed as he began to work.

NINE

The next afternoon, Portia arrived at the rambling Victorian mansion that housed the offices and living quarters of her therapist and friend Sophie Stransky. Though she was in better shape, mentally and emotionally, than perhaps she'd ever been before in her life, Portia refused to give up her private therapy sessions with Sophie, even though the older woman had all but retired. Over the years, they had formed a unique relationship, part therapist and client, part mentor and protégé, and part trusted friends.

So she was smiling as she rang the bell that sunny afternoon, excited as a child returning from school, full of news of the day's discoveries. Complaining of the ravages of advanced age, Sophie had recently had a security buzzer installed to save herself the many trips through the huge house's halls and stairs. When Portia identified herself through the small speaker, her therapist released the door. Portia knew her way to the gracious back parlor that served as Sophie's consultation room. Filled with the relics and souvenirs of Sophie's many travels, the place had only grown more endearing over time. A little dustier, perhaps, but still awash in the broad afternoon light that filtered through high bay windows, still stuffed with books and artifacts of every possible description. After greeting her diminutive therapist with a quick embrace, Portia settled into her usual wing chair. She met Sophie's bright birdlike eyes and smiled.

"You're looking good, my dear," Sophie began. "Life must be agreeing with you."

"It is," Portia conceded. "Well, mostly, anyway. You know me. I'm still superstitious. When things go too well, I start waiting for the other shoe to drop."

Sophie's smile was oddly distant. "Never borrow trouble, Portia. Be content when it leaves you alone."

"Well, I'm working at it. Actually, I'm having some fun for a change." Portia smiled shyly. "Alan's coming back tonight, and I can't wait. Honestly, Sophie, I don't know, my relationship with him, it's like being fifteen again. You know what I mean?"

Seeing the excitement in Portia's face, Sophie nodded, and though she was smiling, there was doubt in her eyes. "As I recall," she began kindly, "being fifteen was not the happiest time in your life," she interjected softly.

"That's what I mean," Portia went on. "This infatuation—I guess you'd call it that—between Alan and me, it's like—I don't know. I feel like somebody finally gave me permission to enjoy myself. All of the things that used to drive me so crazy in my relationships with men. They're just not happening. I'm not worrying about our commitment, or what he thinks of me, or anything really. He's introduced me to this really carefree part of myself." Portia's smile broadened to a wide grin. "It is like being a schoolgirl. Only it's the part I never got to experience before."

"The fun part?" suggested Sophie kindly.

"Yes," Portia answered earnestly. "But it's even more than the fun. It's sex and—"

"Sex?" prompted the older woman. "Let's stay on that a moment."

Portia paused almost guiltily, her eyes shining. "Wonderful," she admitted. "Absolutely great. Honestly, Sophie, you know my background, the rapes, the abuse. I never would have believed I could enjoy sex this much. Until Alan came along, I thought it was pretty much ruined for me. That I would always have all these issues about it—this guilt. Only this time I don't. It's really weird."

Sophie chuckled. "Rather than weird, I would say it's mysterious. Attraction between people can never entirely be explained by psychology, and perhaps that is as it should be. There is always an element of mystery in why one pair of eyes meets another across a room, or why one person's touch fills us with warmth while another's leaves us cold. Sex is a powerful human drive, Portia. Surely you realize that. But it's wise to remember that most of it takes place between your ears."

In spite of herself Portia blushed. "You haven't met Alan."

Sophie winked wickedly. "Oh, I've met an Alan or two in my time," she assured her. Her expression turned more serious as she continued. "My point is that you have given yourself permission to enjoy this relationship, whatever Alan's talents as a lover. That is what is so significant. It is little wonder that you liken your feelings to being fifteen again. As an adolescent you were cheated out of the normal discovery of sex. Sexually at least, you were old before your time. And I would say that with Alan, you have begun to reclaim what was taken from you. Your innocence, your passion, your sense of play."

Portia considered this last statement in silence, her thoughts in a turmoil. On the one hand, Sophie's insight was formidable. On the other, her assessment of the situation seemed to Portia to bode ill for the future of her relationship. She'd seen enough of her own patients working through their issues with various partners to know how impermanent such arrangements could be. And caught up as she was in her pursuit of pleasure, Portia wasn't ready to face that—not yet.

She met Sophie's eyes uncertainly. "I honestly believe my relationship with Alan is more than just some sort of regression," she began hesitantly.

The older woman shook her head, chuckling. "Don't put

words in my mouth, my dear. You are a very competent psychologist, but that doesn't mean you are allowed to project." Sophie leaned across the cluttered expanse of her antique desk and met Portia's eyes, fixing her with an expression both intense and a little amused. "No, what I was trying to do was simply to make you realize that you are at least partially responsible for the happiness you experience with him. Like I told you at the beginning of our talk today, don't borrow trouble. Enjoy yourself. Alan is meeting some very real needs in a woman who for a very long time could not admit to anyone that she had needs, especially emotional and sexual needs. And that is truly important. For you." She paused and leaned back, flattening her palms against the desktop as though the movement cost her some effort. But Portia, momentarily lost in thought, missed the little wince of pain that crossed the older woman's features.

"Okay," she said, rousing herself from her reverie and running a restless hand through her hair. "You're right as always, Sophie. Like the song says—let it be, right?"

Sophie smiled. "Right," she agreed. "Let it be."

Portia glanced at the small silver watch on her wrist. Her sessions with Sophie were somewhat casually arranged these days. Though she would never have admitted it, Sophie's stamina had decreased somewhat in the past few months, and Portia didn't want to tax the older woman's limited energy. She looked up uncertainly. Sophie did indeed look tired this afternoon. It was as though the spidery network of lines in her face had somehow deepened. Nonetheless, Sophie's eyes were as bright as ever, studying her with the same expectant expression that had always put Portia in mind of nothing so much as some enormously intelligent bird.

"There's just one more thing," she began. "If I'm not keeping you?" She knew Sophie well enough to know that any reference to her fatigue or frailty would be resoundingly silenced, so she'd always chosen the more indirect route, implying only that the venerable Sophie might have some more pressing engagement.

Sophie smiled gently. "Not at all."

Portia relaxed a bit, her earlier enthusiasm returning in force.

"I'm working on the Meredith case," she continued, as though she were confiding some delicious secret. "As a profiler."

Careful, the inner voice warned.

For one of the few times in their acquaintance, Sophie looked genuinely surprised. Then, just as quickly, her expression changed to one of genuine concern. "Are you sure that's wise?" she asked. "Isn't that a bit like Daniel in the lion's den?"

Portia took a deep breath. "I thought so too. At first. But so far—I don't know. I feel, I don't know, validated." She went on to explain her conversation with Aggie and the subsequent call for anyone with any information on the crime to contact the task force and her subsequent meeting with Detective Goodman.

"This is a cop—yes—but I have to tell you, Sophie, he's a real human being. Smart, compassionate. I can tell we're not going to agree on everything. But he's somebody I really feel I can work with. At least, after our meeting, I didn't feel like I was volunteering for the same old punishment. I didn't have the sense that I was going to be beating my head against the same old walls." She paused for breath, noting again how exhausted Sophie looked. "I'm sorry, I don't mean to be running on about it. But I did want your opinion."

Sophie smiled gently. "My opinion is that you seem very enthusiastic about this," she answered wryly.

Portia shot her a glance, then relented and returned the smile. "Okay," she went on. "I guess what I'm feeling is that this profiling thing might be a way to continue some of what I do best without all the conflict that's attached to the court work."

Sophie raised an eyebrow. "A murder investigation?" she asked. "Free of conflict? I'm sorry, my dear, but I cannot agree with you. I'm not a criminal investigator, but I'm quite certain that anxieties, not to mention conflict, run very high."

Portia flashed suddenly on Dave Goodman's bloodshot eyes, the tense lines around his mouth, the tone in his voice as he'd filled her in on the politics of the task force. Of course, Sophie was right—perhaps she was viewing profiling through rose-colored glasses.

Or maybe she doesn't know what she's talking about. Portia flinched a little at the sheer disloyalty of the thought.

"The conflicts will be there, I know that," she continued aloud. "But they will be different from the ones I've been dealing with over the years. And I think I'll learn a lot, working on a case from the beginning and—who knows? The police might even learn something from me. If psychology is introduced right from the beginning of the process, maybe everyone will be a little bit more sensitized to the things that cause criminal behavior, not just the results."

Sophie nodded agreement. "But won't it be even more difficult for you? From a personal point of view?"

Portia stared at her in surprise, trying to quell the little flutter of annoyance that Sophie's comment provoked. "How do you mean?" she asked coolly.

Sophie hesitated, as if trying to decide how to break the news. "In your court work, you were frustrated because you felt yourself under attack because of your status as an expert in criminal psychology, correct?"

Portia nodded.

"I am simply asking if you are ready to endure the scrutiny of being a novice once more. Because in this particular area, this profiling—you are."

Portia sighed. "The new kid on the block—"

"Exactly," Sophie replied. "And please understand me, Portia. I am not saying that you should not do this. It may be an excellent choice for you right now. What I am saying is that you are putting yourself in a position that will require you to prove yourself. To take a few lumps, maybe even more than that. I am only wondering why it is that you feel that necessity."

Portia met the older woman's eyes. "Sophie. I want to do this. And I don't think I'm trying to prove anything."

Signaling that their session had come to an end, Sophie stood up a little stiffly. "There's nothing wrong with following your heart, my dear. The trick is to keep your head on straight at the same time." The old woman paused, searching Portia's eyes. "The phoenix rises from its own ashes, time and again in a continual process of reinvention."

Portia glanced away. "What's that got to do with profiling?"

Sophie offered a shrug. "Maybe nothing. I'm only reminding you that there are ways to fly without all those heaps of ashes."

Following her lead, Portia also rose. She took both of Sophie's hands in her own and squeezed them gently. "Ain't that the truth?" she replied a bit too brightly. "But don't worry, Sophie. I promise not to burn anything down."

After Sophie walked her to the door, they said their goodbyes under the heavily carved entrance. Portia made her way down the steps toward her car. As she drove away, the older woman watched her for a long moment before she turned, a little reluctantly, and headed back inside.

A little after seven, Portia pulled her Volvo into the parking lot of a quiet little Italian restaurant called Castaldi's on East Boulevard. The night was ready-made for romance, not too warm, with low humidity and a restless, exciting little breeze that felt as soft as a touch on her skin. She glanced around hopefully as she locked the car, trying to pick out Alan's vintage Triumph XR5. But he hadn't arrived as yet, so she made her way to the door and stepped inside.

She loved this place, one of many she'd discovered while dating Alan Simpson. It was small and intimate, the decor a mixture of old-world élan and mom-and-pop kitsch. And the food was truly a discovery, rich and authentic and redolent of garlic and wine. The first time they'd gone there for dinner, Alan had laughed heartily at her appetite and teased her by insisting that if she continued such gluttony he'd be forced to find a slimmer woman. But Portia hadn't cared. It was as if being with Alan had awakened a whole new range of sensual frontiers to be explored. As if, with the profound reawakening of her sexuality, all her other senses had awakened as well. Food tasted better, music was sweeter—even the night air was filled with a heady, anticipatory perfume.

It was also decidedly off the beaten path, far removed from Charlotte's regular restaurant circuit, another factor Portia cherished about the place. She and Alan had always been able to sit for hours over their dinners without having to be concerned about greeting colleagues or even friends at adjoining tables, or feeling as if they were being rushed through their evening by a bevy of anxious waitpersons. In short, she'd joked to him once, it was exactly the kind of place where a private investigator might choose to spend his time, a secret sort of haven, safe from the prospect of unwanted discovery.

Portia moved up to the quiet bar, where the soft, final strains of an aria from *La Traviata* echoed to a heartrending close. The dark-eyed bartender poured her a generous glass of wine and she sat easily, as relaxed as if she were in her own living room.

Several minutes later, Alan appeared in the doorway. She saw him before he saw her, and she watched him as his eyes hastily scanned the room, enjoying a moment of sheer appreciation of those broad, well-muscled shoulders, the shock of curly blond hair, and the strong-jawed, clean lines of his profile. When he caught sight of her, his face broke into a wide smile. He made it to her side in four long strides and took both her hands in his.

"What have you been up to?" he demanded in a teasing, light-hearted tone. "You look far too good to have been pining away in my absence."

She planted a soft kiss on his cheek. "Hey you," she said softly, tugging a little at his earlobe with her teeth. "Welcome back."

His blue eyes sparkled as they met hers. "Good to be back. I didn't think I was going to make it. Did anyone ever tell you your eyes are the color of swamp water?"

She glanced up at him, feigning offense. "Swamp water?"

"Absolutely," he assured her, linking fingers with hers and tugging her gently toward the dining room. "Murky green with brown in it, covered with an overlay of new algae. It's gorgeous."

"Thanks," she said, laughing. "I'll remember that the next time they ask me my eye color for my driver's license."

They made their way to a small table by the only window that didn't face the parking lot. Outside was an open stretch of land that fell away to a small pond where some white swans glided like so many visions across the moonlit water.

Portia met Alan's eyes. She felt as though she would never be able to stop smiling. "Missed you," she said.

Alan nodded. "Missed you too," he replied. "Hardly had time to, but I did." He paused and signaled the waiter to bring him a duplicate of Portia's glass of wine. She flipped open her menu but did not look at it. Instead she studied Alan's face for a long moment, seeing for the first time since he'd come in that there was an indefinable uncertainty about him that evening, his natural confidence and overflowing charm replaced by some quality she was not yet familiar with in him—an edginess or fatigue that was hard to define. Some alarm went off in the back of her mind: that his nervousness was the harbinger of some awful decision he'd come to in their absence from one another, that he'd fallen in love with someone or decided never to see Portia again. Then, in the next instant, her misgivings were squashed by a stern inner reminder.

He has a life, you know. Apart from you. Why don't you just ask him what's wrong?

I don't want to be pushy, she protested inwardly. I'm trying to respect his boundaries.

Oh, for crying out loud. You're not respecting anyone's boundaries but your own. You're chicken, that's all. You don't want to ask because you don't want anything to screw up tonight's plan for getting him in the sack.

Am not.

Are too. Is this the same woman who told her shrink not four hours ago that she wasn't worried about this relationship?

Okay, okay, I'll ask, Portia relented silently, and sighed.

Alan sipped his wine reflectively. "Hmm?" he said, glancing at her. "Did you say something?"

Portia's long fingers gripped the stem of her wineglass protectively. "Uhh—no. I was just thinking. You look . . . tired. Is everything okay?"

Alan's tanned face creased in a collection of smile lines around his deep blue eyes. "Yeah," he admitted. "I guess I am tired. This job, down in Georgia, it got me thinking. I spent most of last night pacing around my hotel room."

Now Portia's hesitancy was replaced by genuine concern. "Why?"

Alan settled back against his chair and sighed heavily. "I don't know for sure. Maybe I'm having some sort of midlife crisis."

Immediately all her psychologist's programming came to the

front of her brain. But that small insistent voice inside her stopped all the usual responses before she could give them voice.

Don't be his shrink, be his friend. Hell, be his girlfriend, why don't you?

"Tell me," she said aloud.

Alan drained the last of his wine and signaled for another. "I was finally able to dig up some stuff on the corporate spying they thought was going on," he replied. "But it took longer, it was more difficult, and I got less than I should have gotten going under-cover."

Portia tried to make sense of this cursory explanation. "So?" she asked. "I mean, I'm sorry it didn't go as well as you'd hoped, Alan. But every case is different."

They paused in their discussion as the waiter reappeared with more wine and a pad to take their orders. That completed, Alan leaned across the table earnestly. "See, that's the thing. This case was just like a hundred others I've worked on. I can't say that I handled it any differently. But the business itself has changed, Por-tia. It's all this Internet stuff. Any nerd with a computer can do what I do and never leave his chair."

"Oh, Alan," she began gently. "Don't you think that's overreact-ing just a little?"

Alan tore a piece of warm garlic bread from the basket on the table, took a bite, and began to chew slowly. "I went undercover on this job. And it was crazy. Here I am, waltzing around playing a suit, when everything I need is in the damned computers. The guys who are stealing the information are doing it from home, okay? No one suspected them because they weren't operating out of the of-fice. They didn't need to." He paused, his face morose. "I worked from my experience," he went on after another moment. "But I'm feeling like my experience doesn't count for much anymore. It's like I'm this dinosaur in my own profession well on my way to becoming extinct."

Salads appeared and Portia looked longingly at the bright greens and reds of radishes and romaine while she considered how to re-spond. On the one hand, she felt Alan was simply being too hard on himself. Some people, she knew, especially smart, good-looking people like Alan Simpson, were always a little surprised when things failed to run smoothly. On the other hand, he was right about one thing. He was starting to sound an awful lot like a person heading for a midlife crisis.

"Well," she began carefully. "If you're feeling like that, why don't you check out what's happening in computers. I mean, aren't there some courses you could take? Some training?"

"I'm well enough versed in the database technologies and the search engine stuff, Portia," he said bitterly. "That's not really the point."

"Then what is?" she asked. "I mean, I'm not trying to be unsympathetic, but it seems to me that if your industry is changing, you need to take some steps to change along with it."

Alan fixed his gaze outside the window, momentarily lost in the sight of white swans floating on the silvery, moonlit waters. "The point is, I really don't think I want to." He turned and looked into her eyes, his own face etched in a mixture of anger and sadness she had never seen there before. "I'm not cut out to be some computer hacker who sits behind a desk and crunches numbers. That's not who I am. I need to be out there, where the action is. Only the action has moved. The action is behind those desks now. The crack investigators in the world aren't Sam Spade anymore. Or Magnum, P.I. They're a bunch of guys in thick glasses wearing plastic pocket protectors."

Steaming plates of pasta arrived, his swimming in chunky tomatoes and clams, hers in prosciutto and cream. Portia pushed her plate to one side for a moment, despite the fact that her mouth was watering. Mentally she reviewed her own recent career choices. She'd wanted to share with Alan her excitement over profiling, the way her blood was up at the prospect of working on a murder case again. But this was definitely not the right moment. She watched him fondly as Alan grated Parmesan over his pasta. He glanced up to her eyes and managed a weak smile.

"So," he went on. "What do you think? Is it too late for a forty-four-year-old gumshoe to take up another line of work?"

There was a long moment before she answered. In the interim, she reached across the table and laid a hand lightly on his arm, noting how the golden hairs curled over prominent bones of his wrist.

"I think you're right," she said softly, smiling a little. "You'd make a terrible nerd."

TEN

After dinner, they drove back to Portia's house in Dilworth. She preceded him into the driveway, and he parked behind her under the shade of an enormous holly tree. Alice had been invited to a pajama party in the neighborhood, and as she and Alan made their way through the garage and into the kitchen, Portia welcomed the cool silence of her house, its interior strangely enchanted by the silver-blue moonlight that poured through the windows, transforming familiar things into objects of wonder. She drew a shuddery little breath and smiled, turning to her lover and taking him by the hand.

"I want to make love to you," she said simply.

Alan's eyes deepened to match the blue shadows that gathered in the corners and he bent his mouth to hers in a lingering kiss, his tongue probing her mouth gently, rhythmically, full of exploration and desire. And they tasted one another, their kisses ripe with hints of wine. Alan moaned softly and Portia felt a twist of response rise up from her belly to her breasts. She wrapped one long leg around his thigh as his lips traveled down her neck and over her collarbone, his tongue tracing a hot trail back to her face, where he sucked gently, urgently, on her chin.

She grinned, giggling. "God," she managed after a moment. "You're the first man I was ever with who managed to turn my chin into an erogenous zone."

Alan's teeth shone white. "You're the only woman I know with such a sexy chin."

They faced each other for a moment, their smiles full of happiness and the unexpected reverence of desire as they stood together in the moonlight, each savoring the heat and sweetness of the other's nearness. Then, as if responding to some secret command, they moved together again. She scattered a hundred little kisses, soft as petals, over his face and neck and eyelids. He ran his hands across her thighs, hiking her skirt over her buttocks with one swift, expert movement that made her gasp with pleasure. He tickled her cheek with the soft hairs of his mustache, his tongue flicking in and out more hungrily now, as she felt the hardness of him press closer. His restless hands moved downward as hasty fingers undid her blouse to expose high full breasts, nipples already hard. His breath was hot and insistent on her skin as his tongue moved to her cleavage, licking away the trace of talcum just above her heart.

"Oh, God, Alan—" Portia breathed, then gasped again. Her knees turned to water and she fell against him as he slid an urgent finger into the elastic of her panties, reaching for the place he knew she yearned for him to touch.

Her fingers fumbled toward his fly, struggling to unzip him as the fabric strained against the throbbing inside. His breath came in hot little pants as she bent to kiss his chest and belly, reveling in the downy hairs that covered him, the taut muscles straining beneath his skin. She raised her face to him, laughing.

"Hey," she whispered, "we'd better get upstairs."

The fingers of one hand clutched in the tangle of Portia's hair, Alan pulled her gently up to face him. He bit her bottom lip softly, teasingly, as the fingers of his other hand went exploring, and he began to stroke between her legs until she was weak and slick with desire. He buried his face in her neck, murmuring softly.

"No," he whispered. "Here. Now."

And he pulled her roughly down beside him on the floor.

She lay for a long time afterward, their bodies bathed white in the moonlight, making a bed of the bright rag rug that lay between them and the cool tile beneath. Alan dozed, snoring softly beside her, and Portia reveled in the sound of it, still a little amazed at this miracle of longing and fulfillment that happened between them, trying to form some thought or reason for it. Her more logical side struggled to make sense of the torrent of sensation that had just passed through her body—trying to find some word for the way she'd felt when he called her darling at the moment of his climax, repeating it over and over with each powerful thrust, as though she were something precious to him. Someone adored.

She turned lazily to one side, watching Alan's profile, still etched in moonlight. Somewhere a sound began to echo at the edge of her hearing, some rhythmic background noise muffled by Alan's soft, regular snores. Portia sat up languidly, her limbs still heavy. The phone was ringing. She listened. Again. The phone. Her private line in the study. She braced herself and started to get up. Alan stirred and propped himself on one elbow, beautiful and naked in the moonlight, smiling up at her and looking for all the world like some lazy god. His fingers encircled one of her ankles.

"Where you goin'?" he whispered.

"Alan, it's the phone. I have to answer it," she protested.

"Let it ring," he said, yawning a little.

She smiled down at him fondly. "I can't, Alan, it's the private line. It might be a patient. Or something with Alice."

"Okay, okay," he said, releasing her and struggling to rouse himself. "But this is the last time I fall for such a busy woman," he called as she disappeared through the door.

In the study, Portia snatched up the phone. "Hello?"

An unfamiliar voice came over the line. "Oh, you're there. I was just about to hang up."

"Who is this?" asked Portia, suddenly uneasy, knowing instinctively that the call boded trouble in some way she could not identify.

"Oh, sorry. Forgot." The voice answered tiredly. "It's me. Dave Goodman. I hope I'm not disturbing you."

Portia made an effort to clear the muddle of her thoughts. "No," she answered. "I was just—well. How can I help you, Detective?" Then in the next instant she remembered and asked, "Aren't you off duty?"

"In the ideal universe, yes," he answered. "But not tonight. I had to call and see if you can come and view the crime scene."

Portia swept the hair from her face in confusion. "I thought we weren't doing that until tomorrow," she began.

"Oh," the detective replied. "That's right. You don't know."

"Know what?"

Portia heard the sound of what she was coming to recognize as a characteristic sigh over the wire.

"Looks like our guy has struck again," Goodman said flatly. "Angel Tirado. She's dead. A cousin of hers found her a few minutes ago. When she didn't show up for dinner, he went over and got the surveillance cop to bust down the door."

"Oh God," breathed Portia. "But she was under watch—how could he have—"

Goodman's answer was full of a harsh resignation. "We don't know any of that. At least, not yet. I'm on my way over there now. I thought you should be there. Get a firsthand look."

Portia grabbed for a pen. "Where?"

He gave her the address and, after agreeing to meet in twenty minutes, Portia hung up the phone. She glanced uneasily back toward the kitchen, trying to quell the flutter of anticipation coursing through her innards. She had to go meet Goodman. It meant everything that she could be at the scene while it was still fresh— relatively untouched by the army of cops and forensic people that would follow. But she hadn't yet told Alan anything at all about working with the task force. And judging from his mood earlier in the evening, she was not at all sure he'd react favorably to the idea. Worse yet, he might feel compelled to tag along. And the last thing she needed was to have Dave Goodman and the rest of the cops thinking their new profiler couldn't show up at a murder scene without some man tagging along in case she got the vapors.

Resolutely she padded across the room back toward the kitchen, her bare feet slapping against the floorboards. Alan lay more or less where she'd left him, stretched out languidly in the moonlight, his hands behind his head.

"Alan," she announced. "I'm sorry. I've got to go. I'm going to need you to move your car. So get dressed." She snatched up pieces of his clothing and began tossing them in his direction.

He sat up and cocked an eyebrow, clearly a little put out. "Talk about seduced and abandoned," he offered wryly. "What's up?"

Already headed toward the door, Portia turned to him reluctantly, not wanting to lie, yet not having either the energy or the inclination to go into the whole issue at that particular moment. She walked back and took him by the hands, tugging him to his feet. She kissed him softly, her eyes begging for understanding. "I have to, Alan—please. Just get dressed, okay?"

He gazed at her in some confusion as he yanked on his shirt. "But what is it? Hey, Portia?"

She turned to him from the doorway as she headed upstairs.

"Was it a patient on the phone?" Alan asked. "Some emergency?"

Portia looked at him, her expression a mixture of impatience and fondness and something like regret.

"Yes," she told him. "It's an emergency."

She found her way to the address just off Seventh Street in a little under half an hour. The area near the front of the modest run-down building was choked with police cars and emergency vehicles while a smattering of spectators and neighbors hung behind the lines of yellow police tape, straining for some look at the proceedings.

Portia flashed the temporary ID Goodman had given her in front of a sleepy-looking rookie and gained entrance.

"Three floors up," he told her, jerking a thumb toward the staircase. "In the back."

The building was old, but reasonably well kept and clean. Portia climbed the stairs easily, keenly aware of the people who lived behind each of the closed doors she passed on the way up. Everyone in the building seemed to have been jarred out of bed, and low, anxious voices came from behind the closed doors, occasionally punctuated by the sounds of television news.

The door to Tirado's apartment was partially open, guarded by a uniform who spared barely a glance at her identification. She saw the wood was splintered along one side.

"I'm looking for Dave Goodman. Is he here?"

The cop blinked as if surprised by the question. "Inside somewhere," he answered. "Help yourself. Don't touch the door, they haven't dusted it yet."

Using the toe of her shoe, Portia pushed the door wide, not knowing what to expect and trying to prepare herself for the worst.

She found herself in a minuscule alcove covered in dusky old-fashioned wallpaper, an expanse of no more than three feet that opened on the living room beyond. Her eyes were drawn to what appeared to be a small shrine set up in one corner, where a multicolored candle stood, adorned with the face of some sad-eyed saint. A bouquet of flowers sat near it, along with a profusion of textbooks and papers stacked up on the floor a little to the left. From Portia's first impression, it was the only idiosyncratic touch in an otherwise rather generic-looking student apartment. A futon couch done in plain fabric was pushed against one wall, next to an overflowing bookcase. A small stereo sound system perched on top of that, next to a telephone answering machine, which was blinking forlornly. The sight of it brought unexpected tears to Portia's eyes. She'd left a message on Tirado's machine. And now this young woman, little more than a teenager, was dead. From her position in the alcove, that much was all she could see of the room. Whatever horror awaited her was around a corner, beyond the wall.

Dave Goodman saw her then and extricated himself from the center of a group of four or five police officers gathered in a corner near the futon.

"Glad you could get here," he said, grasping her hand.

One look at the detective's tired face spoke volumes. If he indeed had gotten some sleep since their last encounter, the good it had done him had already been consumed by what he'd seen so far that night. "Me, too," she answered in a steady voice.

But he must have read the worry in her eyes. "You okay?" he asked.

"Sure. It's just that—well. Let's just say the last dead body I saw was in church," she answered nervously.

"They took her away a few minutes ago," Goodman assured her. "After they got the pictures."

Portia nodded, her mouth suddenly dry. "So. What are we looking at?"

Goodman fixed her with an odd yet understanding look. "She was still pretty much in one piece, anyway. Coroner says he thinks her neck was broken. She wasn't cut like Meredith and he's not sure about rape. Doesn't think so, based on his first look. My best guess is, the guy gained access through one of the porches here in the back. Every one of the rear apartments has one. He probably hid out till he saw the cop outside go take a leak and busted in."

Portia considered this, frowning. "He didn't use a knife?" she asked in some confusion.

"Nope. Came up behind and snapped her neck. Kaboom—she's dead. Afterward he strung her up on the curtain rod, arms outstretched. Like a sort of crucifix."

Portia absorbed this statement in shocked silence. Then, in the next instant her mind started working again, percolating with questions. She gazed intently into Goodman's tired face. "Based on what I saw of the Meredith photos, I can't believe he didn't cut her. This guy's rage level almost demands it."

Goodman gave a casual shrug. "You're the shrink, but the facts are still the facts. Meredith was cut to ribbons. This time he didn't use anything. Bare hands."

Portia ran a distracted hand through her hair, sweeping it from her neck. The night had turned humid and the throng of police in this small space made the air close and uncomfortable. "Look," she said after a minute. "I know how this is going to sound. But can we be sure that the same man killed both women?"

Goodman nodded and looked at the tops of his shoes. "We're checking some leads, McTeague. But I know it was the same guy. I just wish I'd been the one on surveillance, that's all. Maybe she'd still be alive."

Portia stared at him. "Look," she went on. "I just don't want to go down any rabbit holes, that's all. I don't think you can jump to conclusions. From what you're telling me, there's a difference in MO, a difference in sexual assault, mutilation. Serial killers always escalate. It doesn't make sense." She looked a little anxiously into Goodman's eyes. He managed a small smile.

"You're starting to sound like the inside of my own head," he told her. "Welcome to homicide, Doctor. But you see, I asked myself all those same questions before you got here."

Portia shook her head, a little embarrassed as she followed Goodman into the living room. "Sorry," she said. "I keep forgetting you do this for a living."

"Never mind," Goodman answered. "I had fifteen minutes on you when you walked in. You'll catch up."

The rest of the room revealed little about what had gone on there. The rug was rumpled and tossed to one side. A little cart full of houseplants and herb pots teetered in another corner near a line of windows all but obscured by uniforms. She caught, but could not immediately identify, a familiar odor in the room, something chemical, a scent that hung heavily in the humid air.

All at once Goodman paused, with a strange distracted expression, his hand fumbling over his breast. Portia stared at him. "Detective?" she asked. "Are you all right?"

He looked at her as if just remembering she was there. "Huh? Oh, yeah," he said, fumbling in his breast pocket. "It's this damn vibrational beeper. Freaks me out every time."

He took the thing in his hand and frowned at the numbers. "No," he continued after another moment. "It's the same guy as did Meredith, never mind the discrepancy in the MO." He met her eyes intently. "And he wanted to make sure we didn't miss the connection. You see, it was just like last time. At least in one thing. He left us a little present."

"A weapon?" Portia asked bewildered. "You said he used his bare hands."

Goodman shook his head slowly. "Nope, just a little something to let us know he'd been here. To let us cops know how frigging stupid he thinks we are."

Portia glanced around the room, straining to pick up some detail, some aspect of the layout or arrangement of things she had not seen before.

"Hey!" Goodman shouted, making her jump. "Get your butts out of the way, will ya. The doctor here needs a look."

The uniforms near the window parted like some navy sea, and when they did Portia saw what had drawn them to the spot, saw it clearly and completely. And her mouth fell open in surprise. Because the thing she saw was unimaginable somehow—so unreal and perfect and so obscenely mocking of their presence in that place.

She could see now how the killer had hung his victim, not in the manner of a crucifixion, as Goodman had suggested, but more that of some angel, her arms spread wide and head hung down as she ascended to heaven and made her farewells to the unfortunates left here in the world.

A perfect outline of Angel Tirado's final tableau was left on the window, the place where her form had hung outlined in golden spray paint upon the glass, augmented only by the addition of two small and perfect renderings of wings.

ELEVEN

Twenty minutes later, Portia followed Goodman down the narrow flight of steps and into the street, where the gathering of reporters and curious neighbors had tripled in size. They were all vying for position behind the newly erected police barriers, hollering questions into the night as the detective and the psychologist made their way to their cars. Portia hastily yanked up the hood of her jacket as she all but ran for the curb, while Goodman did his best to block their view of her. Even in the pre-morning darkness, the thought of being recognized by any one of those reporters sent a chill of apprehension down her spine. That was the last thing this case needed, she reckoned silently. The semifamous advocate of criminal rights and forensic psychology changing her stripes and working with the cops. It was enough to send the tide of public opinion against the authorities all by itself.

Goodman escorted her to the Volvo, and after promising to meet him down at headquarters, Portia turned the ignition key and paused for a long moment trying to quiet the fluttering in her belly, even as the attention of the spectators turned toward some other member of the investigating team now emerging from the run-down building that Angel Tirado had so recently called home.

Portia turned on the lights and swung away from the curb, only to hit her brakes savagely as the broad-shouldered figure of a man jaywalked across the street toward the building's entrance, then froze in his tracks at the squeal of brakes, staring blindly into the glare of her headlights as the Volvo skidded to a stop less than two feet away. The man blinked once, then waved offhandedly as if to apologize for his thoughtlessness, before striding gracefully toward the police barriers, his trench coat flapping around his knees.

Portia gripped the steering wheel with icy fingers, her terrified heart pounding in her chest. She took a deep breath and put her foot cautiously on the accelerator, still watching the man disappear into the crowd. She hadn't been going fast enough to do him any serious injury, but it wasn't the near miss that plagued her, only the memory of his eager face, clear as any mug shot in the glare of her headlights. For it wasn't just another reporter she'd seen heading for the scene of Charlotte's latest murder. It was her patient, John Campion.

Small fucking world, isn't it?

Too small, agreed Portia silently as she pulled into the intersection and made the turn toward police headquarters. Way too small.

Nothing like picking off your patients, is there?

Never mind, she told herself. Besides, he didn't even see me. He was blind in the headlights.

Very charitable of you. Here you almost run the guy down and all you're worried about is whether or not he recognized you.

It's not that—I just didn't expect—

It is that. Getting awfully worried about protecting your involvement in this case, aren't you? Campion has as much right to show up at a murder scene as you do. He's a reporter, remember?

"I just don't want to blow this." Portia startled herself by speaking aloud, then glanced sheepishly into the rearview mirror, as if to reassure herself that there was no one in the backseat. Then, help-lessly, she finished her own thought.

I started this and I'm going to see it through, that's all. Reporters or no reporters.

□ □ □ □

Three hours later, Portia and Goodman were still sitting on either side of the detective's littered desktop, wrangling over the seemingly infinite possibilities of the killer's profile. Scattered between them was an overflowing ashtray, crime scene photos and autopsy reports on the Meredith murder, a soggy paper coffee cup, and three almost empty cans of Diet Pepsi. Goodman stared at her through bottomless bloodshot eyes. "Tell me again," he said tiredly.

Portia felt like screaming. Dave Goodman might prove a brilliant interrogator, but at the moment, his unflappable insistence on fitting every possible shred of information into a working profile was downright maddening. The man was like a dog with a bone, forcing her to go over the same facts again and again. It was almost as if he were questioning some suspect, looking for those little details that would either glue the story together or cause it to fall to pieces. She drained the last of a Pepsi and steeled herself before she spoke again.

"The manner in which any murderer acts reveals a lot about the man behind the crime. So, in order to understand the act itself, we've got to break that crime down into four distinct phases of behavior." She paused, counting on the fingers of one hand as she continued.

"Phase one. Antecedent behavior and planning. Planning the crime is a huge part of the thrill—the fantasy. Phase two is the act itself. Murder is the way a killer reinforces his fantasies of ultimate domination and control. Meredith was raped and successfully so. So we know that his rage is sexually based. The third thing we have to look at is how the bodies are disposed of. Both the victims were left in fairly typical states of sexual disarray, and the ritualized arrangement of the corpses will turn out to mean something—though it's anybody's guess just what. Meredith was left as a kind of centerpiece, and Tirado was strung up like an angel. I'm not seeing any overt similarities there."

"Me neither," Goodman agreed sadly.

Portia rose and began to pace restlessly around the desk. "The last phase is the post-crime behavior. And that's the hardest to predict of anything. Some killers report falling into a deep sleep, while others run for their lives. But whatever a killer's initial reaction is, the important thing to remember is that, in a sense, the murder completes the fantasy, only the fantasy needs to go on. And since the killer's primary motivation is to sustain his fantasy, my guess is he's already planning another murder." Portia paused and glanced at Goodman, a haunted look in her eyes. "He already knows who his next victim is going to be," she finished quietly.

But Goodman was either too tired or too numbed by the evening's events to offer much in the way of reaction. "So what do we know?" he asked.

Portia resumed her chair and stared for a long moment at the pile of photos before going on. "Meredith's killer had it planned to the nth degree. He probably stalked her for some time after forming a fantasy about her and seeing her on television. There's an incredible degree of organization in his behavior. He thought about this, worked it out in his mind, down to the patterns he cut into her skin. Everything we see here means something. And even some stuff we don't see—like the absence of fibers, prints. And the hands—especially the hands."

"He isn't the first killer to take a trophy," Goodman reminded her.

"No, but they all take trophies for the same reason. To sustain the fantasy. Maybe he'll use them to relive the murder. I don't know. But if we can figure out why her hands were taken instead of her hair or a foot or a breast, then we know something more about our guy."

"Hands," mumbled Goodman. "What does it mean?"

"I wish to God I knew," replied Portia. "The point is, everything we're looking at is indicative of planning. It's carefully thought out, very intelligent. And not just as a highly developed fantasy, either. He took a lot of pains to protect himself—his identity. Why else did he pay in cash? Why wasn't there any record of his name anywhere?"

"So you don't think he's insane?" Goodman asked.

Portia threw up her hands. Amateurs, she thought bitterly. Aloud she said, "We've been over that, Goodman. Of course I think he's insane. Do you know anybody who goes around carving up blondes with a kitchen knife who isn't insane? By definition, this is a very crazy thing to do. I just need to understand his behavior on his terms. Because if I can do that," she leaned across the desktop and fixed Goodman with glittering eyes, "then we can predict his actions."

Goodman peered at her. "Back up a minute. How could you predict the Tirado murder from the Meredith stuff? Psychologically speaking?"

Portia sucked air. "We've got two options there. If it's the same guy, and I think we've got to concede that it is, it might mean that he's deteriorating, becoming more disorganized as he becomes more worried about getting caught, maintaining control—all that stuff. Though personally, I don't think we're going to get that lucky here."

Goodman scratched a note in the small worn notebook that lay open in front of him. "How do you mean? Lucky?"

"You see, all that really matters to somebody this far over the edge is that they can find ways not only to act out their fantasies of control and domination by killing, but also to sustain that fantasy— to keep it going. To keep elaborating on it. That means more deaths, more bodies. Psychologically, our killer will deteriorate if he can't do that, or feels he can't because the risk is too great. The anxiety will make him even crazier, he'll make mistakes. A few mistakes would be lucky for us." Portia paused. Her eyelids felt like sandpaper. "But so far, I'm not seeing any, are you?"

Goodman tapped his ballpoint on the edge of his desk. "Still doesn't explain Tirado."

"It does if it was a convenience killing," Portia argued. "If she could identify him, her presence put him and his fantasy in danger. Killing her was necessary to restore his sense of control. So even though the crime itself appears more disorganized and spontaneous, the advantages to having Tirado dead far outweigh the risks. At least in his mind. Think about it, Goodman—this was a blitz attack; he killed her with his bare hands. But even though the conventional wisdom indicates this was an impulse killing, I can't read it that way." Portia stopped abruptly as a new idea took reluctant shape in her mind. "You could interpret that to mean he was supremely confident about taking out Tirado. So confident, he didn't even need a weapon."

"I am become death," murmured Goodman. Meeting her glance, he elaborated. "Oppenheimer said that. After the bomb."

"Quoting the Bhagavad Gita," she replied without irony. " 'I am become death. The shatterer of Worlds.' " Portia nodded a solemn agreement. "Something like that. That's why he did his thing with the spray paint. To show us just how in control he really feels himself to be. That's why he left the knife at the first scene. Showing control is his signature—the thing he has to do. He wants us to know he can control more than just his victims—he can control us. Because he really believes he's smarter than anybody else."

"Shit," said Goodman, rubbing his face. "Are you trying to cheer me up?"

It was almost dawn when she returned home, though Portia was hardly aware that she hadn't slept, her mind preoccupied with the haunting image on the window glass in Angel Tirado's apartment. Even now, if she closed her eyes, she could still see it burned in a kind of negative behind her eyelids. As she pulled into her own driveway with the first wan light of morning edging over the eastern horizon, her exhausted thoughts went picking once more over the possibilities.

Nothing she had ever been taught about the psychology of murder seemed to provide any conclusive answers. As insightful as her theories might be, it seemed the more she knew, the less she knew.

Portia scowled with concentration as she fumbled to turn off the ignition. As the engine sputtered and died, Portia sat staring through the windshield as the world around her lightened by degrees. Was the killer really playing out a kind of "catch me if you can" scenario? Or was it something else, something she'd missed? Part of the standard profile dictated that serial killers, if, in fact, that was what they were looking at, tended to insinuate themselves into police investigations. All the statistics dictated that they wanted simultaneously to be caught and not to be caught. But they weren't dealing with statistics now. And all her instincts were telling her that the killer's behavior meant something more than a patched-together collection of motives, means, and opportunities. He was trying to tell them something. And it wasn't that he wanted to be caught.

She stared unseeingly forward as she got out of the car and made her way down the driveway and into the garage, trying to assimilate the wealth of new information she'd received in the past hours. Meredith's murder had involved rape, yet the initial postmortem exam on Tirado's body had yielded no indication of sexual assault. This despite the fact that everyone at the scene had concluded from the condition of the apartment and the body itself that Tirado was probably nude when the killer had burst in, probably just out of a shower. So, if sexual domination was part of the killer's fantasy (as it always was), why hadn't Tirado been raped? Her nudity alone should have proved provocative. Yet there was no evidence of sexual assault and no blood anywhere. If he'd killed Tirado to protect himself from possible identification, why had he taken the time and the risk to hang her from the curtain rod and spray-paint the outline of her body?

Sighing, Portia shivered a little in the dewy chill. One murder was bloody and slow, the other fast and comparatively clean. All her training as a psychologist told her there was only one thing on which to depend in human behavior. And that thing was its consistency. Even the oddest, most aberrant behavior was somehow consistent. Even the craziest people had some method to their madness. And if a thing was consistent, it could be predicted. The key, then, was to discover not the differences between these two crimes, but the similarities. If she could do that much for this investigation, she would be able to place in Dave Goodman's capable hands the means to solve the mystery of the killer's identity.

She heard her own shoes echoing a little on the concrete floor as she crossed through her garage toward the kitchen, and wished suddenly that she'd asked Alan to stay last night, if only so she'd have someone to greet her inside. Nervously, she fumbled her house key into the lock, chiding herself for her sudden attack of nerves, now that last night's horrors had passed and she was safe at home. Once inside, though, she felt calmer. She flicked on the kitchen lights and stood for a moment, staring at the rumpled rag rug in the center of the floor, remembering the events of the previous night and all that had transpired since. Lying with Alan felt like something that had happened years instead of mere hours before, and the recollected image of those two distant, moonlit bodies failed to conjure its usual mystic fire. She reached out with the toe of her shoe and pulled the rug abruptly into its usual place.

If walls could only talk, she thought wryly. I'd have so many damn questions.

But despite her fatigue, that thought only returned her to still another restless mental inventory of the Tirado apartment as she crossed to the sink and began filling the coffeepot. She recalled the small altar in one corner of the place, the rainbow-colored candle with its sad-eyed saint. Goodman had said the body was strung up like a crucifixion, but the stunted wings were unmistakably those of an angel. Portia watched as brown liquid gurgled through the filter, trickling into the glass carafe below. Was there some religious connection? Or had he simply known her name?

Had he gone in with the relatively simple idea of ridding himself of a possible witness and subsequently seen or heard something that changed his mind? Why had he painted the window?

Her mind circled around a whole range of possibilities—the candle, the altar, even the victim herself. What had happened in that small, spare room? What had Angel Tirado said or done—there at the hour of her death—to trigger the killer's fantasy to the point where merely killing her had not been enough? The painted figure was a message, but what that message meant was anyone's guess.

Portia poured a steaming mug of coffee and wandered toward the study. She plucked a cordless telephone from her desk and opened the doors to a small stone patio as she dialed the number of her office. Lori wouldn't be in for hours, but Portia wanted to leave her a message to cancel her first two appointments, a third if she could swing it. Half her library was devoted to works on criminal personality and she wanted to review what she could. She needed time to work through the details of what she'd seen that night. She needed to be alone, to think.

The air was deliciously cool and the first pink light of dawn showed hesitantly on the horizon, hitting her tired eyes like a balm. The phone rang mournfully as she waited for the machine to pick up.

It was going to be a very long day.

Lieutenant Kevin Ryan closed his eyes against the monstrous glare of the noontime traffic. His eyes felt too large for their sockets, sending pulses of agony spiraling through his skull. He would have run the siren, but the mere thought of any sound louder than a whisper made him queasy. He glanced at his own reflection in the rearview mirror as the light changed and he made the turn back toward headquarters from the lab. He was greenish around the jowls and his tortured eyes were violently bloodshot against the pallor of his skin.

Goddamn hangover, he thought bitterly. Goddamn last night. He should have known better. He did know better. But there was a difference between knowing what was good for you and doing it, and somewhere in between had always lain the road to Ryan's private hell. And when it came to alcohol, Lieutenant Kevin Ryan had a history longer even than his years on the force, longer than his marriage and the ages of his three kids put together. It hadn't been a problem by Kevin's own definition until lately. But lately Kevin's definition had started to break down.

He belched and squinted as the light changed. Despite the squad car's air conditioning, he had started to sweat. He allowed himself to wonder just how much the muckety-mucks down at headquarters knew. There had been an incident or two, things that mercifully faded into the fog of his memory in the face of his headache. Something about failing to respond to a call, something else about excessive force, each resulting in a reprimand. He'd been quietly shuffled off to desk work—gofer errands like the one he was on now. "Pick up the photos from the lab, Ryan. Get 'em back downtown before one."

Not that he cared, especially. Ryan had come to believe they were doing him a favor. He had less than three years before retirement, and he was far too old to be shagging his ass after crack dealers and armed robbers. He knew the world well enough to understand how it was going. The cops went down and the bad guys rose up and if there was, indeed, a war on crime, everyone was losing as far as he could see.

He glanced at his dashboard clock as a crackle of unendurable static came over the radio. It was only a little past twelve. The lab had had the photos ready for once, and they lay on the seat beside him now, neatly labeled, encased in an orangish envelope. Ryan sighed. Some murder, they'd said. He hadn't looked. He hadn't cared.

All at once The Snug beckoned him, rising up on the right with an almost mystical appeal. He could have taken another route, he supposed, but he hadn't. It was as if the car had driven itself, as though Ryan had relinquished the power to choose and was simply a bit player in this larger, siren's drama of drink. And in his present state, sweating behind the wheel of a squad car and nursing the devil's own hangover, it was a role that suited Kevin Ryan just fine. He pulled up slowly to the curb, already anticipating the soft, cool beeriness of the interior.

Ryan calculated his chances. It was early. The place wouldn't have filled up yet. More than likely it was empty except for a silent, understanding bartender who would assess his pitiable condition and slide a beer in his direction without Kevin's having to ask.

Ryan glanced uneasily at the photos on the seat beside him. He would take them along, to remind him that time was passing. He would keep them at his elbow, to make sure he didn't fuck up. He smiled weakly as he glanced again in the rearview mirror. He had almost an hour. Just a couple of beers. Something to steady him. Maybe a sandwich, and then back to headquarters. He could manage that much, he knew. A couple of beers, was all. He smiled a little as he took up the envelope in trembling fingers. No way they could say he wasn't on top of it. Kevin Ryan was a cop, after all. One of the best, if you asked around. Liked his beer, but so what?

He was in control.

True to his predictions, the place was almost empty. A lone woman sat staring into space at a corner table, an untouched glass of red wine in front of her, and a man in a sports jacket and tie was telling secrets to the pay phone on the far wall. Ryan smiled a little, feeling the welcome cool of the interior against his perspiring face. As he slid heavily onto a nearby barstool, Mike, the day bartender, was sloshing glasses in and out of the washer at the other end of the bar. Ryan waited another moment before catching his eye.

The bartender trudged in his direction, and Ryan had only to nod before he jerked on the handle of a nearby tap, filling a frosty pilsner glass with amber and foam. He set it in front of the cop with no expression. Ryan took a long draw off his beer, so grateful his eyes watered.

Mike cocked an eyebrow. "You want a shot?"

Ryan, his beer halfway gone, nodded. "Bourbon," he answered. "And a coupla aspirin, if you've got 'em."

The bartender fulfilled his request without comment. The man who had been on the phone sidled up to the bar a few seats away from Ryan and motioned Mike over with a wave of his hand.

Ryan took care to sip at the bourbon, feeling the welcome burn as it traveled down his chest and into his gut. A few more minutes and he'd be back on track. Another beer and he'd be right as rain. The monstrous headache had begun to recede a little, enough to allow him to study his companion for a moment as Mike set him up with a beer. He looked familiar, but Ryan, in his present condition, could not precisely identify what it was about the stocky body and expensive tweed jacket that rang a bell. The man took no immediate notice of him, but kept glancing over at the pay phone, as if he were expecting it to ring.

Ryan squinted in the soft light, amusing himself by trying to fathom who it was the man so resembled. Some actor, maybe. Or maybe, he thought, as the haze of drink began to mellow him, he was a regular, too. Somebody he saw all the time, but had never really looked at before. As he drained the first, vigilant Mike placed another beer in front of Ryan.

The man at the end of the bar, as if sensing Ryan's eyes upon him, turned his eyes in that direction. His glance seemed to swallow Ryan whole—the uniform, the envelope, the beer, and the tell-tale pouches under his eyes. Ryan felt a kind of rebellion rise up in him at the implied dismissal as the man's glance once more drifted back toward the telephone. He slid two seats nearer, taking care to slide the envelope of the photos along with him.

"You look like somebody," he began, his voice rising a little more loudly than was necessary in the silence. The man turned toward him, as if surprised by the challenge of the policeman's tone. Then he flashed an odd, welcoming sort of grin, as out of place in that dim bar as neon in a nursery.

"Lots of people say that," he replied. "But nobody knows just who."

Ryan eased back, squinting. "You on TV?"

The other man's grin widened, and Ryan saw suddenly that his eyes were a peculiar shade, almost yellow in the half-light.

"Not yet," the man answered. "Maybe soon, though. I'm a reporter. Got a job over at the paper."

Ryan shook his head slowly, chuckling tipsily. "Reporter. Shit. I thought you were somebody from TV."

The man continued to smile, bright and somehow oblique. "People see what they want to see," he answered. "You're a cop. You already know that."

"Shit, yes," Ryan replied. "That's the goddamn truth all right. You take one fucking car wreck, five eyewitnesses, and fuck! All of a sudden you got five different accidents. Never seen it fucking fail." He drained the last of his second beer and hesitated, glancing at his watch. Twelve-thirty. He had plenty of time.

The reporter eyed him curiously. "You on a lunch break or something?"

"Naw," Ryan blustered. "I'm on a—personal break. That's it." He grinned foolishly, his face flushed. "A personal break. Headquarters got me shagging my ass all over town for these goddamn things." He plucked up the envelope and brandished it.

"Oh yeah?" the reporter asked casually. "What's that?"

"Pitchers," Ryan slurred. "Some goddamn murder. Some Latino kid—I don't know. Don't give a shit, either, if you want to know the truth. The world's going to hell on a handcart. I just hope I can get my goddamn pension before it does."

The reporter wet his lips. "Work is for the working man," he commented idly. "Buy you another?"

Ryan paused, smiling a little. He was feeling so much better. "Just one. And thanks, man. It's a fucking pleasure to make your acquaintance."

The reporter's grin never wavered as he motioned the bartender to set them up. "Nothing like a cool one on a hot day, right?"

"Goddamn right," Ryan answered happily, rising a little unsteadily to his feet. "Keep an eye on those, will ya? I got to go take a leak."

"Sure thing," the reporter answered. Ryan staggered slowly back toward the rest rooms, hands on his fly, and Mike went back to washing glasses. The woman in the corner rose and edged over to the jukebox to feed it a dollar as the first of the lunchtime patrons came straggling in.

John Campion reached for the envelope, flipping through its contents with well-practiced speed. He found what he was looking for and slid a photo expertly up his sleeve. He rose, glanced toward the rest rooms, and dropped a twenty on the bar before heading out into the broiling noonday sun.

He made the three blocks to the *Star* building in record time, entering the lobby and punching the elevator button for the floor where Kate Loveless and the rest of the corporate heads resided. Her assistant was apparently on her lunch break, so he entered the inner office without ceremony just as his managing editor was hanging up the phone.

"Dammit, Campion," she snarled at him. "Where the hell have you been? There's been another murder. That girl who worked for Meredith."

Campion flashed a broad smile. "I know," he answered. "I checked my messages."

Kate's black eyes sparked with rage. "Correct me if I'm wrong, but aren't you supposed to be working on this? The TV cameras were on the scene at five o'clock this morning. Where the fuck have you been?"

"Oh," he answered smugly. "I've been having a very good day."

He eased himself, quick as a cat, around the back of her leather executive's chair and began to rub the tension from her shoulders until she swatted him away.

"Cut it out! What if somebody walked in here? You want to get both our asses fired?"

Campion maintained his position behind her chair. She tried to swing around to face him, but he blocked the movement with his knee. Loveless sputtered in irritation.

"Look, Campion," she went on. "I don't have time for games. Channel 12 scooped everybody on this one and we've got to catch up. I sent Jenkins and McGaffey down to headquarters, but the cops aren't divulging any details. We got shit."

For an answer, Campion plucked up a fistful of Kate's platinum hair and twisted so that she cried out in surprise. "Oh," he whispered softly in her ear. "We have much more than shit, Kate my dear. Thanks to me."

With a flourish, he reached into his sleeve and withdrew the police photo, laying it gently on the desk in front of her. He edged back around to face her, enjoying the look of shocked astonishment that played across her face.

Kate stared at the photo uncomprehendingly for a few moments. "What is that?" she breathed. "What is that? Where did you get this?"

Campion shook his head slowly. "Tut, tut, Kate darling. Can't divulge a source." He paused dramatically, looking at his fingernails. "Let's just say I was in the right place at the right time."

Kate's eyes narrowed. "This is for real?"

Campion laughed harshly. "Oh," he answered, "it's for real all right. Crime scene photo, fresh from the lab. I figured this one was right for the front page of the next edition. Leaves so much to the imagination, don't you think?"

Kate's eyes never drifted to the photo. "Fucking weird, you mean," she replied. "Is that supposed to be spray paint?"

Campion rose abruptly to his feet. "I knew you wouldn't let me run the photo of the body on the front page. She was nude and you know how the Bible Belters hate nudity. Looks like the killer outlined the body with the paint after he strung her up from the curtain rod."

Kate's head jerked up as she glared at him. "How do you know that?" she demanded. "Can we print it?"

"Print whatever you want," Campion replied. "I saw the rest of the pictures, and that's what happened."

Kate took the photo in trembling fingers and plucked up the telephone with the other hand. "We'll go color with the shot. It'll be more effective. What have you got for copy?"

Campion was already headed for the door. "Use Jenkins to write it up," he answered. "I've got to see that shrink today, and pull my commentary together. Now that there's been another murder, it's almost time."

Kate called after him as he was halfway out the door. "Campion! Wait a minute. You scored the picture. You telling me you don't want the byline?"

Campion only shrugged. "Anybody can walk through the ABCs of the story," he said. "I want to use the column. Put a little perspective on it instead."

Kate stared at him, frustrated and mystified at once. "Give me a caption at least."

John Campion paused on the threshold, a little smile playing around the corners of his mouth. He met Kate's eyes. They were so much alike, the two of them. More than she knew.

"Oh," he answered, "how about 'Angel of Death'?"

TWELVE

A little before two that afternoon, Campion signed in at the reception desk in Dr. McTeague's uptown office. He was about to turn and assume a seat in the comfortable waiting area when he paused, noting suddenly that the receptionist had fixed him with a curious, expectant look, a bemused little smile playing around the corners of her lipsticked mouth. It was a look he knew very well. He cast a surreptitious glance at the nameplate near her elbow.

"Is there something else, uhh, Lori?" he asked, giving her the benefit of his best boyish grin.

The young woman blushed furiously. "What? Oh no. That is—well—you turned in your insurance forms, right?"

"Yeah, sure I did," Campion answered easily. This Lori looked like so many young women, he thought. That same cookie-cutter blondness, those voracious, empty eyes. He saw that her teeth were slightly crooked, adding to the hesitant self-consciousness of her smile. He leaned an elbow on the countertop and propped his head against one hand.

Lori bloomed like a flower under the handsome new patient's

unexpected attention. "Then I guess there's nothing, Mr. Campion," she drawled softly. "You can just make yourself comfortable. The doctor's still in session, but it will only be a few more minutes."

Campion smiled. "What if I told you I was comfortable right where I am?" watching as the rabbity-looking receptionist's jaw all but dropped in surprise. He was enjoying the way she looked at him, the way her hands restlessly shuffled papers along the countertop as they spoke, as if he were making her nervous. He wondered briefly what Kate might think, seeing him chatting up the secretary. He wondered if her black eyes would narrow in the way he had come to know so well, if that painted mouth would compress itself into one of those grim lines that made poor Kate look so much older than she realized. People were always giving themselves away, he reckoned silently, still smiling down at Lori. They never even knew. All you had to do was keep your eyes open, your wits about you. Then a good reporter might find out any number of things.

"You worked here long?" he asked casually.

"Three years," Lori answered proudly.

"You must like it." Campion shifted himself a little, as if leaning toward her to better meet her eyes.

"It's okay," Lori answered shyly. "Just like anything, some days are better than others."

Campion inclined his head toward the consultation rooms in the back. "She a nice boss?"

Lori sat up a little straighter in her chair. "Oh yeah," she assured him. "She gets pretty disorganized sometimes. You know, all the paperwork. But she has me for that. I pretty much run that part of it."

Campion continued to stare at her, as if transfixed by the sheer import of what she had to say. "So I guess you find out a lot, huh? About the doctor's, uh, clients?"

Lori shook her head resolutely. "No way," she replied firmly. "Dr. McTeague's rules. Patient files are all completely confidential."

Liar, thought Campion. His smile brightened a little. The girl might be useful, if he played her just right. Through her, he might be able to find out just how well his game with McTeague was going. He allowed himself a little sigh. "Well," he went on softly, "all I know is, if I had a file on somebody like you, I'd read it. I don't know that I could help myself."

Lori's eyes widened. She looked like someone who'd just won the lottery, happy and thunderstruck and still a little unconvinced that so much money belonged to her.

The intercom chirped at her and Lori fumbled for the headset. "Mr. Campion is here," she murmured. "Uh-huh. I'll send him right in."

She replaced the equipment and looked up at him, still too confused to return his lingering smile. "You can go on back, Mr. Campion," she told him.

Campion straightened up just as a sniffling woman made her way from the hallway to the reception desk, dabbing her eyes with a crumpled tissue. "Call me John," he said and winked. He turned from the flabbergasted Lori and, still grinning, headed slowly down the hall to the room where McTeague was waiting. He'd been right about one thing, he thought wickedly as he knocked softly on the door to the consultation room. He was having a very good day.

Mentally, he ran through a quick rehearsal of his problems for the day, like some penitent on his way to confession. She'd want the family history for sure. They always wanted that. The door swung inward and he raised his sad, dark-gold eyes to the woman who stood behind it, his face arranged in an expression of suitable suffering.

"Hello, John," Portia said as she ushered him in and closed the door. For a long moment, she looked at him, trying to fathom from his expression whether he'd seen her at last night's crime scene. Yet nothing at all registered in his face. He hadn't known she'd been there, then. He was just another reporter covering a story. "I've just been going over your file," she continued with something like relief. "Let's get started, shall we?"

Campion glanced at her and managed a rueful smile. This time, he chose one of the more comfortable chairs, an overstuffed pastel near the window, and settled in. "Let the games begin," he said.

Portia settled herself in a nearby bentwood rocker and took up her pad of notes. Campion's clinical history had indicated a marked paranoid depressive tendency, and some problems with alcohol, but not much else of interest. Prescription tranquilizers seemed to have alleviated much of his previous job stress, but Campion's personal history was sketchy and incomplete. Which either meant that Campion had not chosen to discuss his family background with his previous doctor, which was likely, or that his doctor had found Campion as difficult and withholding as she had in their first session. Either way, it was something she would try to address.

"John," she began. "Like I said, I've been going over your file. And I wonder if you could tell me, how would you describe your relationship with your previous therapist, down in Florida, I mean?"

For a split second, the question appeared to take him off guard. Portia could see his knuckles whiten a bit as he gripped the arms of his chair. Just outside the open window, a bird began a high, mournful fragment of song. Campion shrugged. "He was okay, I guess. Dr. Masters. You know, he did his job. I don't think he was as easy to talk to as you are, though."

Portia glanced at her patient. If Campion found her easy to talk to, his sessions with Masters must have been like pulling teeth. "Well," she continued smoothly, "I'm glad you feel that way, John. It's a sign to me that you're really ready to work on some of the things that have been troubling you."

He nodded vigorously, his eyes bright, waiting for her to go on. Her face had assumed a mask of concern as she studied him. Portia McTeague truly cared about her patients, or pretended that she did. He wished fervently that he'd had a camera with him at that moment. The shot of her in the rocking chair, with her head slightly tilted and a pencil in her hand, would have been perfect for the front page.

"John, I know you're going through a bad time right now. You have a lot of issues connected with your job. But you also have to know that your writer's block isn't hurting anyone but you. It's something that is preventing you from doing a job you care about. And sometimes, when people are caught in behaviors like that, it's a sign that something else is bothering them. It's my opinion that this writer's block of yours has its roots in your past. Maybe in your family history."

Campion feigned a moment of confusion. Bingo, he thought. "Gee," he said aloud. "I don't know, maybe. But actually my family was pretty normal. Pretty boring, if you want to know the truth. Heck, I know everybody's supposed to be really into their childhoods and everything. But I never was. I don't even remember too much about growing up. Except that I was bored."

Portia continued to study him. "Tell me about being bored," she prompted him. "Maybe that will spark something."

Campion relaxed a little into the chair, clasping his hands behind his head. "I was born in Pennsylvania. Ever been there?"

"I was in Philadelphia a few times," Portia answered.

"Well, this was a long fucking way from Philadelphia, believe me," Campion answered. "A steel town. No, not a steel town. The steel was gone long before I got there. The jobs, too. My old man did a bunch of stuff to keep us going. He ran a gas station/convenience store for a while. Then a laundromat. Then he went broke and then he got something else—I don't know what it was. I don't remember. We didn't ever move or go for anything better because Armpit, PA, was the place we called home. Or at least that's what the old man told me. The real reason was that we couldn't fucking afford to get out."

"What about your mother?" Portia asked quietly.

Campion only shrugged. "She was burnt out, I guess. At least by the time I came along. I was the youngest of five kids. My next oldest brother was almost ten when I was born. So I don't think she was too thrilled about the stork showing up. You know what I mean?"

Portia nodded without looking up, taking notes on the legal pad in her lap. "Go on," she said.

Campion shifted position again. "What can I say? We all went to church on Sunday and we all went to school and we had to make do with what we had. And everybody we knew was exactly the same as we were, so you didn't really notice so much. It was the original American nightmare, Doctor—family values, roots, all that shit. You watched *Gilligan's Island* and *The Brady Bunch* and you tried not to notice that you lived in a place where everything was fucking dying."

"Dying?" Portia prompted him.

"You say that word like you don't know what I'm talking about," Campion retorted. "C'mon, Doctor. Never shit a shitter. I've just described thirty percent of the towns in North America. Steel towns, farm towns, tobacco towns—every place you look. And all I could think about when I was a kid was, God, get me the fuck out of here."

Portia eyed him carefully. "It doesn't sound as if you felt very connected."

"Connected?" Campion hooted with laughter. "What the fuck was there to connect to, Doctor? Church suppers? Stealing cars? Some girl who couldn't wait to have you knock her up so she could get married and drop out of high school?"

Campion leaned forward, his eyes alight with some gleeful inner fire. "You want to know what I remember best about my childhood?"

Portia gazed at him, fighting the sudden certainty that John Campion was about to make some awful confession—that he'd mangled some house pet or dumped gasoline on a vagrant. "What?" she managed after a moment.

"I remember the night my oldest brother was blown to pieces on the six o'clock news. In living fucking color—blam! Bob's a goner. Cut back to Cronkite in the studio."

Jesus. Portia could only stare at him for a moment, unsure if she'd heard him correctly. Campion leaned back in his chair, confident of the impact of his statement, waiting for her to say something.

Portia wet her lips. "Was it an accident?" she asked.

Campion laughed again. "There's a question," he replied. "Was Vietnam an accident? You tell me." Her patient's eyes held a glittering challenge. "No, Doctor," he went on acidly. "Bob was a Green Beret. Last year of the war. Back when all the best families sent their sons off to the rumble in the jungle. CBS pulled the best film coverage that year. But back in Armpit, PA, it was just an ordinary evening. The old man was drinking beer and dozing in front of the tube and Mom was in the kitchen making supper. I saw Bob go down right on camera. I knew it was him. He was turning around to wave at some buddy of his and stepped on a land mine. And the rest, as they say, is history."

Portia spoke softly into the silence of the room. "What did your parents do?"

Campion shrugged. He managed a small, painful chuckle. "They didn't do anything. When I told 'em I'd seen Bob go down on the news, they blew me off. Watching too much TV, they said. All that violence—it wasn't healthy. My mom actually told me I needed more fresh air." Campion paused, spreading his hands wide. "Here are two God-fearing adults, okay? They sent their fucking son half-way around the world to be fucking target practice for the Cong. But violence on TV just wasn't healthy." Campion snickered unpleasantly. "It sure wasn't healthy for Bob."

The only sound in the room was that of Portia's pencil as she hastily scratched her notes. "When did your parents understand what had happened?" she asked.

Campion smiled thinly. "I don't think they ever did," he answered. "Understand, I mean. But some army guy finally turned up with Bob's dog tags, about three months later. Three whole months. And all the time CBS had it on film."

Portia considered how to phrase her next question. Gruesome as it seemed, Campion believed he'd seen his brother die in Vietnam on the nightly news. Whether or not he actually had was beyond proving, but that hardly mattered. She herself had known enough of those soldiers, childhood friends and classmates and cousins, to know Campion's story was one like thousands of others. And that the emotions he'd experienced as a result of the incident and his family's connection to that war could be related to any number of his subsequent decisions, doubtless including the one to become a journalist. Still, she hesitated. Campion's demeanor had never changed in the telling of his terrible recollection. Despite all of the obvious emotional and psychological implications, he'd never lost his breezy cynicism, his way with words. It wasn't even that his affect had been flat or even inappropriate. It was only that he'd betrayed no real emotion on the subject, as though he were instead describing some movie he'd seen, the plot of some play. She gazed at her patient thoughtfully. It was as though he'd been telling her a story, she thought suddenly. And that his brother's death had become for him a tale told so often it had ceased to have any reality anymore. It was something only to be told and retold, some terrible invention beyond truth or feeling, save for the emotions it inspired in his audience. To Campion, it meant nothing. The truth, if in fact he was telling the truth, was nothing. Only the reaction mattered.

As if to corroborate her silent speculation, Campion leaned forward eagerly, anticipating her next question. "Aren't you going to ask me if dear old Bob was the reason I became a reporter?" The careless cynicism of his tone held a new, nasty little edge.

Portia smiled blandly. "I'm sure that it must have been part of your motivation," she answered. "But I'm more interested in what you felt at that time. It must have been very traumatic for you."

Campion stiffened slightly in his chair. His eyes again rested on some invisible spot on her forehead, just above where they should have been. He flashed his tense, movie star smile. "I'm not sure what you mean," he hedged.

"Bob was your brother," she prompted softly. "He died."

Campion glanced uncertainly at the ceiling. "Oh, I see what you're saying," he answered. "Well, he was a lot older than me. I told you that. It's not as if we were close. I barely even knew the guy." He glanced at her uncertainly. "I was sad, I guess."

"What about your relationship with your parents, John? How did you feel when they didn't believe you? That must have hurt."

Campion fixed his attention somewhere beyond the window, his nervousness gone, gazing dreamily out to the sun-blasted lawns. "Hurt?" he asked softly. "No, I don't think I was hurt. I don't remember that. I remember thinking how stupid they were. What hypocrites. But it was more like finding out something you'd always known. And once you knew it for sure, it didn't matter anymore. It just—set me free. You know what I mean?"

Portia nodded. "I think so."

"My brother was only the beginning. The whole world was on fire. And I got to see it," Campion continued. "The race riots and the war and Nixon. My parents . . . were just sleepwalkers. They didn't get it. They were just like the rest of them. But I always knew there was more. The real world was out there every night on TV. All of it. Just waiting for me."

The intercom chirped, signaling the end of their session. Portia rose, trying to absorb all that she had heard. She began to understand John Campion in a new light. The obsessive, almost dandified grooming, his choice of career, even his subsequent problems with it. She found she felt deeply for the child who had all but grown up in front of a television, isolated and alone. A child who saw the world of television as far more real than anything his world had to offer. Yet Campion was simply one of the first of generations of children to follow him, their perceptions of reality forged by the world of the media. Vidiots, her neighbor Aggie was fond of calling them. A part of Portia agreed, and a part of her debated. John Campion was a product of his culture, perhaps. But he clearly wasn't stupid. Just mildly sociopathic. She managed a small smile as Campion stepped to the door.

"Next week, same time, right?"

Portia nodded. "I'm looking forward to it. I think we can make real progress here, John."

Campion only smiled. "Me too."

After he had gone, Portia sat alone at her desk, reviewing their session, idly flipping through his case file. Despite his revelations, something about him still struck her as odd. Something that defied an easy label or psychological definition. In their first session he'd appeared almost borderline. Today, however, he'd been more at ease. He'd had his moments of hostility and projection, to be sure. But then he'd confided his tales of childhood so readily, so confidently, like an actor.

Portia stared unseeingly through her window, watching the broad, powerfully built man as he made his way out of her office and into the blistering sunlight. Something was wrong with that man. Something that went way beyond writer's block.

And that something, whatever it was, lay deep beneath the surface.

The question was, would Campion, with his bright, phony smile and carefully cultivated image, let anyone get to what lay buried?

THIRTEEN

Two calls on the cell phone failed to turn up any news on the investigation from Dave Goodman, and Portia, still ruminating over her newest patient, made her way almost thankfully to her afternoon's shift at the Help Line center. Despite her best efforts to come to some conclusion about the killings of Tamara Meredith and Angel Tirado, despite the furor over the double homicide, she still felt she'd been unable to offer Goodman much that was illuminating in the way of a psychological profile. And now, for perhaps the hundredth time, she mentally went through the personality inventory of a possible suspect.

He (and it was almost certainly a male) was probably white, aged twenty-five to thirty-five. More than likely lived alone or possibly with a parent. He was a loner, with highly developed compensatory fantasies of domination and control. The standard profiling criteria pointed to a blue-collar profession, but Portia had decided against that. Blue-collar workers didn't dabble much in New Age philosophy, and the rules of opportunity dictated Meredith's killer had to be either a client, or someone already in the building at the hour of her death. And since Dave Goodman had questioned all the building's security and maintenance personnel down to the executive bathroom attendants and come up absolutely empty, she was left with little choice but to suppose the killer had some kind of white-collar job. If, in fact, he had one. Something like the loss of gainful employment was sometimes enough to push a person over the edge. Maybe their killer was unemployed, downsized from some corporation. She puzzled over the possibility for another moment and then discarded it almost immediately. The strange, almost symbolic quality of both murder scenes indicated some kind of aesthetic education. Although Portia was at a loss to explain exactly what the killer's bizarre tableaux were supposed to represent, they were nevertheless quite creative.

Still, she considered the New Age connection significant, and suspected the killer's profile would correspond at least marginally with other subscribers to that particular school of thought. After all, he'd had to learn about Meredith and what she did and become obsessed with her. That meant something. In fact, it might mean everything.

She sighed heavily as she swung her Volvo into the dilapidated parking lot near the Help Line office. Beyond the standard psychological characteristics, the only links between the murders were the obvious ones. Whoever had killed Meredith had killed Angel, probably because Tirado might have been able to identify him. Nothing unusual about that, save for those bizarre signatures. Clearly the killer meant to taunt the authorities. And from the sound of Dave Goodman's strained voice over the phone, he was doing a remarkably good job. Yet, as far as anyone could tell, he'd made no attempt beyond that to insinuate himself into the police investigation. And serial killers always found a way to get inside the investigation. It was part and parcel of the control fantasy. If the killer was smarter than the cops, then he could hide among them without fear of discovery. If he was more powerful than the authorities, he could break all the rules.

After locating a parking space, she locked the car and made her way toward the building, mentally trying to switch gears. Help Line callers were usually in crisis; as a volunteer, she knew, she couldn't afford to give them less than her full attention. Whatever the mysteries surrounding the murders, they would have to wait a few hours.

The phone room was in its usual state of disarray. A woman named Miriam Daunt sat at the main desk, a phone propped up against one shoulder as she spoke animatedly to whoever was on the other end of the line. Portia knew Miriam from previous volunteer shifts, and she surreptitiously examined her profile as Miriam continued to talk. She was healing nicely; Portia could see that much from where she stood. Only a bright, thin line of scar tissue ran down one side of her face to a point just below the hollow of her jawbone. Portia couldn't help smiling at the sight of it.

Miriam had been a prime candidate for facial reconstructive surgery after years of domestic violence at the hands of her husband. A number of Charlotte's private plastic surgeons had been solicited to volunteer their talents to help severely battered women as they began the long process of winning back their lives and self-esteem after years of abuse. When they'd first met, Miriam's nose had been reduced to an all but unrecognizable pulp, both cheekbones had been smashed, and her jaw had been dislocated so often she couldn't so much as yawn without pain. Though she was only in her mid-thirties, Miriam had looked twice that before surgery. Now, with the help of a willing team of doctors, she looked like a million bucks.

Portia took an empty seat in front of a waiting phone console as Miriam finished up her call. She grinned as Miriam caught sight of her and, after another few moments, hung up.

"Hey, gorgeous," Portia said warmly. "I haven't seen you in a few weeks. You look wonderful."

Miriam smiled gratefully, reaching up to touch her face as if to reassure herself. "I still can't believe it. It's been almost three months and I still wake up every morning and run to the mirror. It's like a miracle."

"No miracle," Portia answered. "Just a little help from your friends."

Miriam nodded. "That was another one," she said, indicating the telephone. "A woman I met when I first entered the shelter. Tracy.

Her old man cut her face and neck. Destroyed a lot of nerve endings. She looks like a stroke victim now, and she's got keloid scarring to boot." Miriam sighed heavily. "I hope the plastic surgery program can help. The waiting list is a mile long."

Portia nodded. "They'll do what they can," she said comfortingly. Privately, though, she wasn't so sure. From what she knew of the program, there were far more victims than volunteer surgeons.

Miriam frowned down at the mess of notes and assorted papers scattered over her desk. "I almost forgot," she said, rifling through a sheaf of pink message slips. "Some guy keeps calling for you." She selected one of the slips and handed it to Portia. "He called just after two. Didn't leave a number, but I told him to try again this afternoon."

Portia took the slip. Something inside her turned cold and uneasy even before she could identify the name scrawled in Miriam's untidy script—Ivan.

Miriam eyed her curiously. "Everything okay? I hope it's all right. That I told him you'd be in today, I mean. I asked him if he wanted somebody else—you know—if he was in trouble or anything. But he said no. He just wanted to thank you for something. Personally."

Portia glanced up and managed a smile at Miriam's concerned expression.

Stupid, she chided herself inwardly. *A week into a murder investigation and already you're jumping at shadows.*

Mentally, she ran through a quick replay of her conversation with the caller who'd identified himself as Ivan. Rape fantasies, obsessive-compulsive rumination. Fantasies, and that was all. He was probably calling to thank her for having gotten him into therapy.

"You okay?" Miriam asked. "You look a little funny."

"Yeah," Portia answered, crumpling the pink slip of paper and tossing it into the wastebasket. "These murders—I guess they've got me a little spooked."

Miriam had withdrawn a small compact and lipstick from her purse and was applying a subtle coral shade to her newly shaped mouth with all the self-conscious pride of a teenager. "You and everybody else," she answered when she had finished. "I couldn't believe it when I saw the paper."

Portia stared at her, disturbed. "The paper?"

Miriam snatched the afternoon edition from the desk and tossed it in Portia's direction. The color photo of Angel Tirado's spray-painted window showed back from the page in sickening clarity. Portia's insides went cold when she read the headline—splayed across the page in sixty-point type.

"Jesus," she breathed, her mind reeling. She'd stood in front of that window only a few hours before. How could the photo have made it to the newspapers so quickly? And why would Goodman have allowed it?

Miriam glanced at the page and sighed. "To paraphrase Mae West," she answered, "Jesus had nothing to do with it. Whoever did that," she went on, pointing at the page, "is nuts."

Portia could only nod in mute agreement.

Miriam slung her purse over her shoulder. "You going to be okay? Roster had Dan Plumb on with you, but he had a final. So you're solo for another forty-five minutes or so. Then Dr. Bob comes on. It's not too bad, though. Lines have been slow." Miriam paused and glanced uneasily at her watch. "I've got to pick up my daughter from counseling," she said. "But I can give you twenty minutes, if you want."

Portia swung her chair around as a telephone jangled. "I'll be fine," she answered. "Go."

Miriam waved as Portia picked up the phone, her heart pounding inexplicably.

"Help Line. This is Portia."

A woman's voice came hesitantly over the wire and something inside Portia went nearly weak with relief. She spent the next minutes helping the caller find a suitable special education program for her son, while at the same time she struggled to identify her own feelings of trepidation. The sight of the photo in the newspaper had unnerved her in some way she found difficult to pin down.

The phone rang again, not a full minute after she'd hung up from the first call.

"This is Portia," she answered.

"It's me," a male voice answered, "Ivan. You remember?"

"Uh, sure, Ivan," she answered, glancing around the empty office. "Sure I remember. They told me you'd called. How are things going?"

Ivan chuckled, a low, sinister sound that made Portia flinch. "Weird," he answered. "Actually, things have gotten really weird."

Caution and concern played across the psychologist's features as she switched the phone to her other ear.

Easy now, she warned herself. "How do you mean, Ivan?"

The caller's voice went edgy with disdain. "I guess you could say my condition's deteriorated, Doctor." He placed an unpleasant little emphasis on the last word.

A half-formed thought skittered somewhere on the edges of her mind and was gone. "Talk to me," she went on, making an effort to keep her voice steady. "Tell me what's going on."

On the other end of the line, Ivan inhaled with a noisy hiss. "Oh, well now. If I told you, it wouldn't be the same, would it? It's better if you guess. Guessing is part of the game."

Fitfully, Portia rattled her pencil against the countertop. "Did you get to a therapist? Like we talked about last time?"

"Oh yeah—" he answered. "Yeah. But we—me and the shrink— we didn't hit it off so good. I don't think I'll be going back."

"How come?" Portia inquired. "Ivan, what happened?"

"Nothing happened. I talk, they don't get it. You people never fucking get it, all right?"

Portia bit at the eraser end of the pencil, trying to sort out what she was hearing. "But you said a therapist had helped you. Before, when your mother died."

Ivan snickered. "Well, here's a clue, lady. Mom's still dead and I'm still fucked up." There was a little pause. "What's that joke? You know—the light bulb one? That's who I am, okay? I am the light bulb that doesn't want to change. Hah, hah!"

Portia closed her eyes against a sudden drumroll of a headache. "So how come you're on the phone, Ivan? What made you call me today?"

There was a short, uneasy pause before he answered. "I don't want to talk about that. It isn't important now, anyway."

Somewhere on the other end of the line she could hear voices—a television or radio blaring in the background, the oddly identifiable voice of a local news anchor. "It is important, Ivan," she insisted. "Can you tell me who you saw? I gave you a list of names. Remember? Doctors you could call? Who did you see?"

Ivan's voice came distantly, almost drowsily over the wire. "They're so beautiful, aren't they?" he asked sleepily. "Are you beautiful, too? You sound beautiful."

"Ivan, listen to me," Portia insisted. "What are you talking about?"

"Oh," the caller answered as if it were somehow obvious. "The women, of course. The ones on TV. Haven't you seen them?"

Portia struggled to make sense of Ivan's increasingly disjointed conversation. "Which women, Ivan?"

More laughter. He was definitely high this time, but it was impossible to immediately identify Ivan's drug of choice. Maybe his sleepy and disjointed speech was the result of something as simple as a snootful of liquor. Or maybe it was something far stronger—sedatives or heroin—enough to kill. There was no way to know for sure.

"Ivan," she went on, her voice low and urgent, trying to keep him on the line. "Talk to me."

"They're soooo pretty," Ivan sighed. "So "

She wanted to scream at him. Her voice grew throaty with the struggle to keep calm. "So what, Ivan? Tell me about the women."

"Dead." Ivan snapped. "They're so beautiful. And sooo fucking dead. What's the matter, lady? Don't you watch the news?"

The news?

Suddenly, part of this bizarre conversation began to come clear. "Are you talking about the murders, Ivan? Tamara Meredith and Angel Tirado?"

There was a long pause before the caller answered. Portia silently cursed her status as the lone volunteer manning the phones. In ten more minutes, someone would be there to help—to trace the call. But for the moment there was nobody. Just her and Ivan, and the disembodied voice of a news anchor echoing eerily over the wires.

"Is that who you mean?" she repeated. "Ivan, are you talking about the victims?"

"One guy's victim is another guy's groove," replied the caller. "That's what's so cool about it."

"What do you mean, Ivan?"

"You don't understand, I don't want to talk to anybody but you. That's why I keep calling. You're easy to talk to, not like those others. All those others. You understand, don't you?"

"Yes," she answered slowly. "Sure I do, Ivan. Just—keep talking. Tell me what's going on."

"I was watching TV," Ivan slurred. "So fucking cool. It's like somebody got inside my head. Like they knew me. You ever have that happen?"

Portia silently debated, not at all sure of where he was going with this. Before she could form some answer, Ivan's voice suddenly thundered at her, cold and threatening.

"I SAID, BITCH, *DID YOU EVER HAVE THAT HAPPEN?*"

"Sure I have," Portia faltered. Ivan's rage level sent up a flurry of red flags in her mind. He was acting out his need for control. And if he could act it out over the phone, he could act it out . . .

Anywhere.

Her own voice sounded strange in the empty room. "Everybody's had that happen, Ivan."

"I thought so." Seemingly satisfied, his voice dropped to little more than a whisper. "I was going to do somebody," he confided, as though it were some delectable secret. "I was thinking about it all the time. And then—it happened. Right there on the TV. Don't you get it? My dreams are coming true."

Portia still held the pencil, now poised shakily over the blank notepad in front of her. The dark shape of her instinct rose up again, clamoring for her attention. There was something—something he'd said. But she pushed it down. Her feelings didn't matter. Ivan was in trouble. Whoever and wherever he was, he was sinking—fast.

She began again in a firm voice. "You understand you're talking crazy, right? Those women are dead—murdered. It's for real, Ivan. It's not a dream. You know that, right?"

"Everything is gonna change," rambled the caller, his voice rising again with some internal excitement. "I can feel it. You know what's gonna happen then?"

"What, Ivan? What's going to happen?"

"I won't need you anymore," Ivan whispered. "All you bitches. You promise to help me. Heal me. But you're lying. All of you. You're just setting me up. You can't fix anything, can you? *YOU DON'T HELP ANYBODY!*"

Portia stared, wide-eyed and trembling, around the empty room, her mouth suddenly dry. She would have given her eyeteeth to have Dave Goodman in the room at that moment, listening in. But Goodman wasn't there. Nobody was there. Nobody but her. And Ivan.

Get a grip. You can't know it's him.

"Ivan," she managed finally. "Try to think. Try to remember. Did you hurt . . . somebody? You can tell me. You know that, right? It'll be okay. I can help you."

"I can help you—" The caller mimicked her voice in a high, mocking falsetto. "Are you deaf, bitch? Haven't you been listening?"

"Ivan—"

"Tell you what, lady. You want to help me?"

"Yes, Ivan, yes."

Again, that evil giggling, a sound that broke off so abruptly it made Portia go cold inside.

"Well, now," the caller whispered, low and vicious. "You have to find me first."

And then, in the next instant, he was gone, leaving her alone. Portia sat paralyzed in the sudden silence, punctuated only by the drone of the dial tone still buzzing in her ear.

Ivan, she thought, the name repeating in her thoughts like some awful dirge. Ivan. She knew the killer's name. His name was Ivan. She sat there for a long moment, too stunned to make sense of anything. Part of her dimly realized she should call the phone company, the police. There would be a record of the call somewhere. And if they could find it, they could find him. Because they had to find him, wherever he was. And soon. And yet she made no move.

Some part of her still hoped she was wrong. That the call was simply about some terrible blending of Ivan's fantasies with the horrible images on the six o'clock news.

Make up your mind, Portia. You've got your killer, haven't you?

I can't be sure of that. Maybe I don't have anything.

What do you want, another body?

No! Portia thumped the desk in front of her with a frustrated fist.

How can you set yourself up as some sort of expert when you can't trust your own opinion?

She stared unseeingly ahead of her. She'd spent the whole of her professional life giving criminals the benefit of the doubt, trying to understand the hurt and the damage that led them to kill. Now, in an instant, all that was irrevocably changed. The caller had killed those women. And it was because she understood that she could stop him from killing again. Because Ivan would kill again. And from the sound of him, it would be soon.

She turned back to the phone and had just begun to punch in Dave Goodman's private number when Bob Shade came unnoticed through the door and up behind her. When he placed a hand on her shoulder she nearly jumped out of her skin. She leaped to her feet and turned to him, trembling.

"Hey! Take it easy," he said. "What's with you today? Run out of Xanax?"

Portia sat heavily down, legs all but buckling beneath her. "Christ," she managed after a moment, "you scared me to death."

Shade cocked an eyebrow. "From the looks of you when I walked in here, somebody got a head start. What's up?"

"I've got to call the police, get a trace out on that last call," Portia answered shakily. A sheen of cold perspiration had broken out on her face and she passed a hand over her forehead, astonished at herself.

Bob Shade slid into a nearby chair. "Suicide?"

She shook her head slowly and looked at him. "Worse," she answered. "Suspect. Call the phone company for me, will you? They might have a record. I've got to try and get in touch with Homicide."

She watched as Shade's expression changed from concern to

something like disapproval. "You'd better tell me what went down," he answered quietly.

"Bob! There's no time for that now!" Urgently, her fingers moved for the buttons on the telephone console.

"Make time," he answered, reaching out and sliding the console just out of her reach. "You know you can't put a trace on any call to this location. Not unless you suspect a suicide."

"What if I suspect homicide?" Portia snapped back. "What if I told you I think the guy I just got off the phone with might be Tamara Meredith's killer?"

Shade looked momentarily confounded by this piece of information. "How could you know that?" he asked. "Did he confess or something?"

"No . . . it's just that . . . well." Distractedly, Portia jumped to her feet and began to pace the length of the room, as if unable to control the energy boiling inside her. "This is between you and me, okay? I'm working with the task force on the murder investigation. Both Meredith and the other one—Tirado."

Shade nodded thoughtfully. "I saw the photo in the late edition," he offered.

"The cops think they might have a serial killer on their hands. And I'm helping to put together a psychological profile."

Shade's eyes narrowed, yet he remained outwardly unmoved. Slow and deliberate as some farm animal. It infuriated her.

"Okay," he responded. "So what's that got to do with your caller?"

Portia sputtered in her impatience. "Same personality traits. Rape fantasies. He was watching the news just now. He had it on in the background. I could hear it. He was high as a kite and talking about how beautiful the victims were. How all his dreams were coming true. He kept calling here because he wanted to talk to me. Apparently, he's made some fantasy connection that I'm the only one who understands. I think it's the same guy, Bob. He calls himself Ivan."

Shade shifted uncomfortably as he chewed on this information. "Maybe," he answered slowly. "But you can't trace the call—"

Portia wanted to slap him. "Why the hell not?"

Shade sat back in his chair and held out his large, knotty hands in a conciliatory gesture. Staring down at them, Portia thought it suddenly odd that a doctor should possess such hands. Doctors' hands should be scrubbed-looking, even delicate. Shade's were big and clumsily formed, with big knuckled fingers and spatulate nails, the hands of a laborer or a peasant. She forced herself to look at his face.

"I talked to him, Bob," she insisted quietly. "And I was wrong the first time. You were here. I thought he was just fantasizing. Obsessive-compulsive. But I was wrong. His rage level is over the top. He wants help, but I think he's convinced himself that anybody who tries to help him is setting him up for a fall. That's why he killed Meredith. He went there to be healed, right? And when it didn't happen, he went ballistic."

Shade's perpetually forlorn eyes filled with a quiet understanding. It made her want to scream. "You've been knocking yourself out with this investigation, haven't you?" he asked.

"What's that supposed to mean?" she snapped.

"All I'm saying is that maybe you're feeling the pressure. Or maybe you're feeling guilt because your first hit on the guy may have been off the mark. And now, all of a sudden, things fall into place. Thanks to the caller, you have a theory." He paused then and sighed, as if hating to be the bearer of bad news.

"But that's all you've got, Portia. A theory—no facts. So far, the only real connection between the caller and the murders is the one you've made in your head."

The last statement caught Portia up short. For a moment, she could only stare at him, openmouthed, as Shade continued.

"Look," he went on smoothly. "This is the only service of its kind around here. We're supposed to help people in trouble, not blow the whistle on 'em."

"But he is in trouble, dammit!" Portia exploded. "He's dangerous!"

Shade held up a hand. "If you say so. The point is, crisis calls are confidential. Period. And if you take it upon yourself to breach that confidentiality, especially on the strength of what you've just told me, the whole program goes down the toilet. Think a minute, if word gets out that the cops have traced calls from here, we lose all our credibility with the people who need us most. For a whole lot of people, this crisis line is all the help they can find."

"Bob," she protested. "For crying out loud, doesn't it mean anything to you that there might be a serial killer out there? This is a matter of life and death!"

"Even if your theory's correct, and the caller and the killer are one and the same, he's just one guy, Portia. And there are hundreds of other people out there who need this line. Battered women, kids, runaways, drug addicts. And just plain crazies. None of those are isolated incidents in a city like this. And they're all at risk. Every one of them is a matter of life and death. A whole lot of those folks would be dead by now if it wasn't for the work we do down here. You know that as well as I do."

Portia turned silently away, sinking reluctantly back into her chair, feeling like some reprimanded schoolgirl. Part of her wanted to fight with him, tell him to shut the fuck up, while another part couldn't help suspecting her own motives.

You really trying to save somebody? Or are you just desperate to be right?

"Do the math, woman," Shade went on urgently. "Compare the possible body counts, and then tell me keeping these lines alive isn't more important than catching one looney tune."

Portia stared down at the phone console, her mind moving dully through the options. Shade was only a volunteer, like herself. Technically, he had no authority over her decision to have a Help Line call traced to its point of origin through the authorities. For that, she would have to answer to the Line's board of directors. A board made up of people like Miriam Daunt. People who knew better than anybody what the Help Line meant to those who had nowhere else to turn.

She met Shade's basset hound eyes. "Okay, so I've got a conflict of interest. You're right, and I know that. But every instinct I've got tells me he did it."

Shade managed a small, empathetic nod. "I believe you. And for what it's worth, I hope they catch the guy. But you're a psychologist, Portia, not a cop."

Portia rolled her eyes to the ceiling. It was one thing to have said it herself. It was quite another to hear it from someone else. "I was wrong. When he called here the first time, just after Meredith. He was already over the line, and I didn't see it. He even described how a woman looked. Only I thought it was a fantasy. But Jesus, Bob, it wasn't."

Shade almost smiled. "So show me a shrink who hasn't made a bad call. Show me any doctor who knows everything. And that's all you are—a doctor. You're not a miracle worker, and you're not a policeman. Besides, even if you had suspected him the first time, you'd still be in the place you're in now."

Maybe Ivan's not so crazy after all, her inner voice reminded her. *Aren't you a case in point? You can't help him and set him up for a fall at the same time.*

She faced her colleague with miserable eyes. "What do I do?"

"I don't know," Shade answered. "But if the guy has really fixated on you, I can guarantee you one thing. He'll call back."

His words had barely time to register before Portia was on her feet, making her way to the filing cabinets. She all but threw open the top drawer, rifling through the tattered folders anxiously.

"What're you doing?" Shade asked.

"Holy shit," Portia muttered. "Holy SHIT!"

"What is it?"

She turned to him, her green eyes wide with an awful guilt. "Last time, when we were here together. You remember me telling you about him?"

Shade shrugged. "Yeah," he conceded. "But that was before you'd decided he was Jack the Ripper."

Hastily, she laid open the manila folder on the nearest desk. "I took notes. A few, anyway."

"So?"

"Did you file them with the evening report?"

Shade rose and came to stand beside her, peering over her shoulder. "Sure, just like I always do," he answered. "What's the problem?"

She turned to stare at him then, a mixture of impatience and something very close to terror written on her features. "The referral list," she told him, shoving a stack of papers into his hand. "Just find it."

Shade thumbed awkwardly through the two dozen or so pieces of paper in his hands. "Here," he answered, after another moment. "Here's the call sheet and your notes on this Ivan character."

Portia snatched it from him with greedy fingers. "Thank God," she breathed.

Shade looked at her, thoroughly bewildered. "What gives? What's so important about that stuff? It's all standard."

But she was already headed for the battered copying machine in the corner. She ran the two sheets through it without even bothering to close the lid. Her face, as she answered him, was bathed in an otherworldly light.

"I gave him a list of five names." She began plucking the first sheet from the tray and squinting against the glare. "Here, two psychologists, one clinical social worker, one psychiatrist, and a minister."

"So?" Shade demanded. "Like I said. Standard procedure."

The copy machine ground to a sudden halt as Portia gathered the papers to her chest. "Three of those names were female," she told him in a hushed voice. "If I'm right, and Ivan is killing people who try to help him . . ." She faltered, swallowing hard. "I'm the one who gave him his shopping list."

Then, in the next moment, that dark unformed thing that had been crying for her attention took shape in her mind, so startling it was as if the sun had fallen from the sky. She turned and snatched up her purse, not daring to say aloud the words that whispered in her mind like some terrible accusation—too afraid of what it would mean if she made them real by saying them aloud. She would take the list to Goodman and pray she wasn't too late. The whispers could wait and the single, awful thought taking shape in her heart could only be pushed aside.

He knows that I'm a doctor.

FOURTEEN

At five-thirty that same evening, over on the other side of town, Detective Dave Goodman sat forlornly in his minuscule precinct office, feeling as though he had something dark and tentacled sitting on his chest.

He'd spent the better part of the afternoon at the mayor's office, enumerating the nuts and bolts of a homicide investigation for an assortment of political animals who had neither listened to his report nor especially given a damn about anything he'd had to say. It was as if he'd been summoned to the press conference as a kind of court jester in the crime-solving drama the media had been summoned to witness. He felt as if his only role was to supply punch lines and sound bites to an ever greedy press. He flinched a little, imagining what he must have looked like on camera, blinking owlishly in the Klieg lights, as he'd struggled to respond to the reporters' barking queries, awkwardly fingering his gaudy tie.

"Can you tell us what was behind the decision to release the police photo, Detective? Do you think the killer is trying to send the authorities a message? Are you close to an arrest?"

Miserably, he thought of calling home. He imagined hearing his wife Cindy's lazy Alabama accent and the clamor of his children in the background as they fought for dibs over that evening's video selection. That thought brought him to another. In his mind, he saw his children's faces, rapt with attention, shining blue in the light of the TV screen, absorbed in the Disneyfied version of *The Hunchback of Notre Dame*.

The Festival of Fools, that was what this investigation felt like; and Detective Dave Goodman had just been crowned king. A poor hunchback gifted by his cruel keeper with the name of Quasimodo. Quasimodo—it meant half formed.

Just like his case.

He turned and picked up the telephone. But he didn't call home. Instead, he called Portia McTeague.

She answered on the fifth ring, a little out of breath from running in from the garage.

"This is Portia," she said, some part of her mind still unable to tear herself away from the Help Line.

"And this is Goodman," he answered. "Have you seen the news?"

Portia sank heavily into a nearby chair. "I saw the paper," she told him. "I can't imagine the news got any better than that."

Goodman sighed. "His honor decided to call a press conference to explain that little breach of security," he explained. "With yours truly as the whipping boy. You should have been there."

For a moment Portia could think of nothing to say. "I'm sorry," she managed.

"Don't be. It's not as though they came up with anything real original. I just hate like hell to give this thing any publicity at all. The thought that this guy is out there somewhere, sucking on all the publicity, makes me a little sick. But since the photo got out, we had to make it look like a deliberate leak. Otherwise we just look like a bunch of jerks."

The disembodied voices of the television news that had formed the background for Ivan's call echoed again in Portia's mind. She had so much to tell Goodman that she had to clench her teeth against the torrent of information bubbling to her lips.

"But hey," Goodman continued. "I didn't call you to tell you my troubles. I just wanted to know if you'd come up with anything new for me."

Portia hesitated for only an instant, frantically trying to reveal what she knew without giving away any clues to the source of her information. She took a deep breath. "He's still in the area," she began. "I know that much. And you're right, he probably is getting off on all the coverage. But I don't think that's to our disadvantage. Publicity, fame—it's part of what he wants. And I think he wants it enough to go on killing to get it. If you want me to make a prediction—"

"Please," Goodman interrupted weakly. "No predictions. Half the psychics in North Carolina are calling me with their predictions, offering to work on the case. And every last one of them has a different version."

"Oh, Lord," Portia said. "I hadn't thought of that. But, of course, with Meredith being who she was—"

"One guy swears he's the reincarnation of John the Baptist," Goodman went on wearily. "I took that call myself. He lives in some trailer park in Monroe. I ask you, does that make sense? I mean, if there is such a thing as reincarnation, why would a big shot like John the Baptist have to come back as trailer park trash?"

Portia grinned, grateful for this brief tangent in the conversation. She wasn't looking forward to revealing what she knew, and so she allowed the banter to go on. Besides, she suspected Goodman's quirky sense of humor had rescued him more than once when life on the police force got too bleak to bear. "What did he tell you?" she prompted, sinking into a nearby chair.

"Oh," Goodman answered. "He said the guy was possessed by demons and would require a full exorcism. He even volunteered to perform the ceremony once we catch him. I took a number."

"Good for you," Portia answered. "And here you thought you had no talent for public relations."

"Tell that to the mayor," Goodman responded. "So what have

you got, Doc? Believe me, something on the scientific side would be very welcome at this point."

Instantly, the conversation struck a more serious note. Portia scowled at nothing as she spoke into the phone, wondering with one part of her mind if what she had might indeed be referred to as science, or if it were, as Bob Shade had said, only another theory, barely distinguishable from the so-called "psychic" visions of all those other willing volunteers.

"His rage is building," she began. "Based on the Tirado scene, I think he's going to continue to drift in and out of reality. He knows that. And feeling like he's losing his grip is going to make him more and more insistent on control. And that means bodies, Dave. The only way this guy really feels in control is when he kills somebody." She took a deep shuddering breath and went on. "What if he really was a client, Dave? What if he went to Meredith for healing? And what if he killed her because he was disappointed somehow, enraged because she couldn't fix whatever is wrong with him?"

"Works," Goodman agreed cautiously. "Go on."

"If it's true, if the healing thing is tied to motive, then we have to assume he's going to select potential victims from the helping professions. He's going to keep looking for help, or safety, or security, or whatever it is that he needs. And when he doesn't get it, he's going to perceive those women as withholding something from him. That will spark his rage and need for dominance. His sense of powerlessness expresses itself in the compulsion to reassert control."

She heard the intake of breath on Goodman's end of the line. "I'm not sure I'm following this."

Portia hastened to elaborate. "My guess is our killer perceives needing or asking for help as a loss of power. A concession of some kind. And when he doesn't get his problem fixed, he's humiliated and enraged to the point of violence." She paused, already knowing she had said too much, yet unable to stop herself from going on. "He's looking for a miracle, Dave. And he's going to keep on killing till he finds one."

Goodman's admiration was evident. "How did you put this together?" he asked. "You sound like you've been talking to the guy."

The irony of his statement wasn't lost on Portia. She took another breath and steadied herself. In for a penny . . . she thought.
"I think I might have," she replied. "I can't tell you all of it, but I
recently spoke to a man who identified himself as someone called
Ivan . . ." Then, before she had the time to change her mind, she
went on to reiterate the gist of their conversations, taking care not
to specify the exact circumstances. "I can't even be sure it's the
same man," she said when she had finished. "But I can tell you
there are certain similarities in the psychological profile."

She heard Goodman give a long, low whistle through his teeth.
"Ivan," he breathed. "It isn't enough."

She felt a hysterical little giggle rise up in her throat. "When this
is over, I need you to come to my group therapy session. You'd have
them rolling in the aisles."

"When this is over, I may need to," he answered. Then, in a tone
so elaborately casual he might have been discussing the weather or
a mere change of clothes, he said, "You know I need to be able to
trace those calls."

"Yeah," Portia answered. "And you know I can't compromise
confidentiality by telling you where I got the information. I'd lose
my license, for one thing."

"Fuck your license," he went on in the same easy tone. "I could
subpoena you."

"And then you'd lose your expert," Portia rejoined in a tone that
sounded far calmer than she felt. "Either way, I can't tell you any
more. If I hear from Ivan again, I'll agree to provide you with my
assessment of his psychological state. But that's between us. No
cops, no DA, no traces."

"Is he a patient of yours?"

"I can't tell you that."

"So how come you talked to him?" Goodman speculated. "If
he's not a patient, how do you know so much about where he's
coming from?"

"I can't tell you that, either."

Goodman made a sort of grumbling sound by way of reply.

"I'm sorry, Dave," she went on. "It's the best I can do. And it may be only a theory. A coincidence."

Liar. Tell him already.

She spoke into the telephone, her mouth dry. "All I mean is, we've got to allow for the fact that I may be shadowboxing here, coming up with answers that aren't there just because I need answers. There may be no real connection at all."

"My eye," the detective answered. "So tell me, you got any other little bombshells you want to drop? Any other little missiles of information tucked up your sleeve?"

Portia shifted the phone to her other ear, her stomach churning. "Um. Just one," she said.

"Dear God," said Goodman. "I knew it."

"I referred him to some people for counseling," she began. "And based on what I know about his deterioration, I'm afraid one of those people will be his next victim. I think he may be stalking one of them, or at least looking for help. I think they ought to be watched. Or at least alerted to the possibility that they may be in danger from a client. Especially the females."

"How do you know that?" blurted Goodman.

Portia sighed. "Just . . . please. I think it's important."

"Christ on a bike," muttered Goodman. "Lemme get a pen. Who are they?"

She fumbled in her handbag for a copy of the Help Line report on Ivan's initial call. "Marcy Forest is a psychologist who works out of a clinic downtown. Doctor's Park." She rattled off the number and address. "Got it?"

"Yeah, who else?"

"Ann McCleod. She's a clinical social worker. Works the school system and has private clients. Two numbers." She dictated them and went to the last possibility. "Reverend Elizabeth Welch. Heads a congregation on Decatur Avenue. I guess she's a minister, but she's got a psychologist's license."

"Is that it?" Goodman asked.

"That's it for the females. They're the likeliest targets." She paused and sighed heavily, the sound of Ivan's mad giggling echoing in her mind. She had told Goodman so much, and yet she knew it was hardly enough. She stared out through the windows, over the preternatural green of the neighbors' twilight-tinted lawns. Ivan was out there. Somewhere.

"Look, Goodman," she went on, her voice low and intense. "I know that the man I spoke to is at least potentially dangerous. Whether or not it's the same man is anybody's guess."

"Yeah, well. Guessing's half the fun, ain't it?"

The odd echo of Ivan's statement made her feel as if her flesh would crawl off its bones. Setting her teeth, Portia fought a second little wave of hysteria.

"Has forensics come up with anything off the victims? Hair? Fibers? Anything?"

"I'm expecting the results of the DNA tests on Meredith in two more weeks," Goodman answered. "That should give us something. They got some flakes and they got some residue. But forensics says it's spermicide, not semen. Looks like our boy wore a raincoat."

Lubricated with spermicide, finished Portia silently. How considerate for the victim. She began to play with the possible reasons for such a tidy assault, her thoughts tumbling like balls in a lottery machine.

Goodman's voice jolted her back to the moment. "You still there?"

"What?" she answered. "Yeah, I was just thinking, the condom thing. He's protecting himself. From getting caught, sure, but also from any possibility of disease. It's very organized behavior. Almost . . . compulsive." All at once, she was struck by yet another possibility. "Hey, wait a minute. I just had another idea."

"Yeah? I'm not sure how much more I can handle."

"It's a shot in the dark."

"Better you shoot than somebody else," Goodman replied. "Dark or not."

"What if we continued to work the publicity leak? Release some detail about the murders, something totally inaccurate. And we make sure it gets into the media loop. TV, the papers, everything. Have the mayor call another press conference if you have to. I'm guessing, but I'm almost sure this guy's internal structure is such that it would smoke him out somehow. At least to the point where he might feel compelled to correct the information. He may even go so far as to insinuate himself into the police investigation. What do you think?"

"Give out a lie to make the guy crazy. It's not like it hasn't been done before," Goodman reflected. "I'm game. Let me run it by the DA and the mayor. See if anybody salutes."

"Right," said Portia.

From another corner of the house, Portia heard the front door bang as Alice returned from next door.

"Mom?" the little girl cried noisily as Portia detected the sound of Alice hurtling in the direction of the kitchen. "MOM!" Again, louder and more demanding.

"In here!" Portia called. "Listen, Dave," she said into the phone.

"I heard," Goodman answered. "The call of the wild. I'll call you when I know anything more."

"Thanks," Portia said. "We'll talk soon."

"Just one more thing—"

"Sure."

"What you said about his deterioration. How long do we have before he does it again?"

Portia exhaled softly, not quite a sigh. When she answered him, it was with more resignation than conviction.

"I don't know. We don't know enough about his cycle. Most serial killers have cycles, like phases of the moon or PMS. I'm willing to bet this guy does too, but I can't begin to tell you what it is."

"But if your Ivan and our killer are the same man?"

"I don't know, Dave," she insisted quietly. "Fact is, we just don't have enough bodies yet."

If Alan Simpson's smile got any wider, he was going to hurt himself. Portia sat ensconced at a sticky table near the vast bright maze of nets and slides and primary colors that comprised Charlotte's newest McDonald's monster play area. A place where, presumably, children were supposed to frolic while their defeated parents munched cholesterol sandwiches and pleaded for them to come and eat.

The excursion that evening had been Alan's idea, his latest attempt to woo Alice's affections. Now he stood with his muscled arms akimbo, that bright fake smile still plastered across his features, begging the recalcitrant little girl to come out from the farthest reaches of a red plastic tunnel.

"C'mon out, honey," he coaxed. "Your McNuggets are getting cold."

"I'm not hungry," Alice said belligerently. "And stop bothering me!"

Portia ducked her head to hide a smile at Alan's crestfallen expression. There was a time when she had believed there could be no woman on earth impervious to his considerable charm. She had been wrong. For it appeared that Alice was made of sterner stuff. Ever since their first meeting, her daughter had harassed poor Alan with the implacable, single-minded resentment that was the special province of the very young, knowing in some part of her childish bones that this man, whoever he was, was trying to win himself a permanent place in her beloved mother's heart.

Now Alan turned to Portia with a helpless gesture, his hands spread wide, confusion on his face. Poor Alan, she thought. He was so unused to rejection.

"Leave her alone and come and eat something," she instructed him, not unkindly. "She'll come out when she's ready."

He slid into the booth beside her. "I just thought it would be nice," he said, his blue eyes straying to a whisper of movement inside the tunnel. "I thought she'd enjoy herself."

"She is enjoying herself, Alan. In her own way."

He turned to her, startled. "But her Happy Meal is getting all cold."

This time, Portia couldn't hide her grin. She draped an arm around his neck and offered a brief massage to the knotted muscles there. "She loves cold food," she said. "Believe me, to her, cold french fries taste just as good as hot ones."

Alan sighed and began to tear the box away from a double cheeseburger. "She hates me," he said miserably.

"No, she doesn't, she's just yanking your chain. Testing your limits. They do that with all new adults who enter their territory. Once she finds out you can handle it, she'll settle down."

Alan chewed thoughtfully. "I'm not sure I *can* handle it," he said around a mouthful. "That kid of yours is one tough customer."

Portia glanced at Alice, now bouncing along a section of trampoline on her skinny butt. "Tell me about it," she replied. "But she needed to be tough. Think about where she came from. Considering her background, she could be a lot worse."

He nodded, perhaps remembering Alice's hard beginnings. The poverty, the drug-addicted mother. She'd been a prison client who'd begged Portia to adopt the little girl. The day after she'd signed the papers, the mother had killed herself in the prison laundry.

"Don't take it so seriously—" Portia was saying. "Alice is going to adjust to our relationship. You just have to give it some time. Look at the way she's taken to Dec Dylan. They're thicker than thieves." Of course, she added silently, her old friend, attorney Declan Dylan, had known Alice since just after her first birthday. Dec was the closest thing to a father Alice had.

Alan paused with his cheeseburger halfway to his mouth. "What's that supposed to mean?"

She bristled at his tone without quite knowing why. "Nothing—" she insisted. Privately, however, she was less sure than she sounded. The situation between Alice and Alan seemed to have worsened over the last weeks, and Portia was at a loss to explain it. The harder Alan tried to make friends with her daughter, the greater seemed the child's contempt for him. And the more Alan was rejected, the needier he became. Now, watching him watching the defiant Alice, he looked like a kid who hadn't been invited to a birthday party. She struggled to reassure him. "Alice gets along fine with other friends of mine and she'll eventually get along with you."

"Is that what I am to you?" Alan's voice was harsh. "A friend?"

Portia dropped her burger back to the tray. "Oh, for crying out loud, Alan. Lighten up."

His blue eyes turned icy. "You're the one who brought up Dylan, not me," he told her quietly. "I just don't appreciate the comparison."

"You're paranoid!"

"Am I?" he said coldly. "Why did you bring him up?"

Good question.

Portia made a futile little gesture, blushing in spite of herself. "I don't know—he's been in London for months. Maybe I just miss him."

And part of her, at least, knew that it was true. She plucked up a french fry. Somehow, without her quite being aware of it, Alan had turned his campaign for Alice's affection into a sort of popularity contest, something the more confident Dec would never have done. She looked at Alan for a long moment, trying to think how she might undo the damage her innocent comment had caused.

Innocent, right. Tell me another.

Portia scowled. Maybe she was trying to keep her distance from Alan, and maybe without her quite knowing why, she'd used the mention of Dec to do it. Men, in her experience, were not especially anxious to take on the rigors of domestic life, especially men like Alan, who'd spent so much of his life doing exactly as he pleased. But his nascent career crisis seemed to have spawned a number of other issues. And she couldn't help wondering if this sudden interest in her family had more to do with wanting to secure his own place in an uncertain universe than with any genuine affection for her or for Alice.

Awfully suspicious, aren't you? How can you expect Alice to trust a man you can't even trust yourself? The voice inside her head chortled with satisfaction.

"What?" Alan was looking at her as if she'd spoken aloud. There were lines of fatigue and worry etched around his eyes, lines that had not been there a few months before. His easy confidence was slipping away by degrees.

She managed a small smile. "Nothing," she answered a little too brightly. "I was only thinking." They ought to talk about it, she knew. But not tonight.

Chicken.

Alice wandered over at that point, and slid silently into the booth. She snatched disconsolately at a chicken nugget and chewed, her black eyes fixed on Alan, silently challenging him to say something stupid.

Portia tried to diffuse the tension. "What did you think of the play equipment?" she inquired conversationally.

Alice tore her steady, unnerving gaze from Alan's face long enough to look at Portia. An unspoken warning passed from mother to daughter, and Alice ducked her head. "It was okay, I guess," she answered, not quite able to keep the sullenness from her tone.

Unable to stop himself, Alan blundered in, his smile bright and strained. "So, Alice, what's going on at school? You learn anything new today?"

"Nope."

"Alice—" Portia cautioned.

The little girl sipped orange soda, pursing her lips around the straw and facing her mother with an expression of the purest innocence. "We're going to have career day soon," she said by way of a peace offering. "People are going to talk about their jobs."

"Oh yeah?" Alan said enthusiastically. "That'll be fun. Do you know who's coming to speak to you? Maybe a nurse? Or a fireman? People like that?"

Again, Alice fixed him with her merciless eyes. "I'm going to be a journalist," she announced gravely.

"I see—" Alan bobbed his head, clearly flummoxed by this new piece of information.

Portia glanced heavenward. Forgive him, Lord, he knows not what he does. She lowered her eyes, shooting a glance at Alan's sculptured profile. He really didn't realize he was talking down to the kid; he thought he was being friendly.

On the other side of the table, though, Alice, seeing a moment of weakness in her adversary, moved in for the kill. "Did you get a job yet?" she asked.

"Alice," Portia intervened, "for heaven's sake!"

"What?" the child demanded. "I was just asking a question."

"I've explained to you that Alan works, well, off and on." She could feel his eyes boring into the side of her face, caught the flush of his rising color out of the corner of her eye. "What I mean is, Alan works on cases. Just like I do. And sometimes he has a case to work on, and sometimes he doesn't. Just now he doesn't. That's how come he was free to have dinner with us tonight."

"That's right, honey, and I—"

Alice silenced Alan with a withering glance. If the information about the ups and downs of self-employment registered at all, it had fallen well below her standards of acceptability.

"But you got a new case, Mom. You told me."

Dread and french fry grease made for a nauseating mix in the pit of Portia's stomach. She had told Alice about working with the police on a case. There seemed to be little point in keeping it a secret from her daughter, especially since most of the news had come by way of Aggie and Reg next door. The problem was, she'd not yet mentioned it to Alan, the man with whom she was supposedly conducting an intimate relationship.

He met her eyes, clearly confounded. "What case?"

Portia smiled uneasily. "Alice, sweetie. Go back and play for a minute, will you? Alan and I need to talk. Grown-up stuff."

Satisfied with her evening's work, Alice was transformed into a model of sudden obedience, skipping off toward the circular slide with a wide grin.

As soon as she was out of earshot, Alan turned to Portia. "What was that all about?" he demanded. "You're on a court case?"

Portia shook her head. "Not exactly—"

"Not exactly? Portia, either you are or you aren't. I thought we talked about this. I thought you were going to devote yourself to private practice and get out of the forensics work. We both know the toll it takes on you. You get in over your head and the whole rest of your life suffers. That's why you decided to quit!"

"No!" The force of her response shocked them both, but Portia did nothing to repress the sudden tide of anger that threatened to overwhelm her. "You decided I should quit, Alan. YOU." She let the word hang between them, her eyes blazing. "But just in case you're interested, it isn't a court case. I'm working with the task force on the Meredith murders. Profiling the killer, okay?"

Taken aback by her outburst, Alan couldn't seem to find a place to put his eyes. "It's the same thing, though, isn't it? God, I wish you could see yourself sometimes. I can feel it happening already."

Portia wanted to pound on the table, her fingers already curling into a fist. "Feel what happening?"

He looked at her then, his blue eyes dispassionate and oddly resigned, so clear she could see her own face reflected in them, twin images of jutting jaw and defiant eyes. He offered a ghost of his old smile. "You," he answered simply. "Drawing away. It's like an obsession or something. You let those vampires suck your energy and your thoughts and all your attention until there's nothing left, Portia."

"I do not," she insisted. "And my so-called obsessions are none of your damn business!"

"Oh? Then tell me this: Why is it that every time you get involved with a murder case, you become completely unavailable to anyone else in your life? Emotionally and every other way." He paused and took a ragged breath, staring down at the plastic tabletop as though he could find some answer there. "I don't know what it is with you," he finished almost sadly.

That sadness, more than anything, set her blood to boiling. She wanted to hurt him for trying to make her feel guilty, for trying to patronize her. "Oh, come now, Alan. Are you sure you're not just a little jealous that I've found a way to stay involved in a job I love? Are you sure you're not just pissed at me for being willing to evolve in my career while you're stuck in the same old rut?"

Clearly, the remark hit home, but Alan, ever the gentleman, proved enough of one not to take the bait. "Maybe that's true," he acknowledged. "Or maybe it's true that you've got a blind spot. You can't see how you isolate yourself, how you shut everyone but Alice out of your life."

"Leave Alice out of this!" she hissed at him. "Or do you mean to sit there and tell me you're actually jealous of a little girl?"

"No, I don't. But think about it, Portia. We made love the other night. Then you get some phone call, presumably to do with this murder, and suddenly I'm no more to you than a stick of furniture. How do you think that makes me feel?"

"Look." Portia felt the razor's edge of her rage begin to dull. "It wasn't anything personal. I just had to go, that's all. You're a little depressed, and it's made you hypersensitive."

Alan held up a hand. "Please," he said. "Spare me the sidewalk therapy, okay? It was personal. Very personal. And you just don't get it."

Portia sat there, struggling to absorb it all, unsure of how exactly their conversation had gone so suddenly, wildly beyond her control. The last thing she wanted was to fight with Alan, but at the same time, every part of her rebelled against his accusations. She was doing fine with the profiling work, and it represented a chance for her to excel at something she was truly good at. No matter what he said.

Alan passed a weary hand over his eyes. "Maybe I've got some things to sort out in my own life, fine. But what makes you so immune? You can't go on shoving people into little compartments while you go off and crawl around inside the heads of killers."

"I don't do that!"

Alan smiled wanly, a look in his eyes that came very close to breaking her heart. "Whatever," he replied. "But that's the thing with me these days, you know. I don't want to be stuck in some convenient little compartment. And I don't want to have to wait for my chance to make a different kind of life. I don't want it to hinge on whether you happen to be on some case or not."

"Then don't let it," Portia answered flatly. She shifted uncomfortably, suddenly desperate to be away from this place with its bright colors and falsely cheery atmosphere. "Alice!" she called, so sharply that Alice, on the far side of the play space, snapped to instant attention. "C'mon, we're ready to leave."

She glanced irritably at Alan. "You want me to drop you someplace?" she asked, her eyes gone cold and defensive.

"Don't bother," he answered. "I can find my own way home."

He rose and stood aside, allowing her to slide out of the booth.

Ronald McDonald grinned hideously from a far corner of the room, as if enjoying their discomfiture.

"Suit yourself," she told him, not quite able to keep the tremor from her voice. "But I still think you're being unreasonable."

He smiled then, his eyes kind and filled with a quiet understanding. It made her uneasy.

"Watch that blind spot, hon," he said, bending to graze her cheek with his lips. "That's how the bad guys know where to get you."

Alice sidled up and slid underneath Portia's elbow as they watched Alan's broad shoulders disappear through the doors and into the street.

"Mom?" she inquired.

"What?"

"Did you guys have a fight?"

Portia glanced down at her, surprised at the unerringness of the child's intuition. "Not a fight, really," she answered. "A discussion."

Alice skipped ahead and held the door open as Portia passed through. "It was a fight," she said confidently as they came upon the Volvo in the simmering parking lot. She swung open the passenger door and scrambled into the back. "I can tell."

Portia hooked her seat belt and placed the key in the ignition. She caught sight of her own eyes in the rearview mirror, helpless and bewildered, and then directly behind that, Alice's impish reflection, her face a portrait of quiet mischief and gleeful, "I told you so" triumph.

"Oh, Alice," Portia sighed, feeling as if she were in pain someplace. "Do Mommy a favor, will you? Just—please—shut up."

FIFTEEN

Elizabeth Welch sat alone in her office, working the Internet for signs of God. It had become something of a habit with her in the past months. Her computer had a siren's call she couldn't quite shake, beckoning her as it did with all those worlds of promise and information.

The screen came alive in shimmering colors and bits of animation as she surfed the Web sites of a hundred souls' voices or more, each of them shouting out their prayers and their beliefs and their cries and their frustrations. Dogma dickered with doctrine on these pages, enlightenment with the most primitive fears. But for all of the advertising and grandstanding and plain buffoonery documented with a few simple strokes on a keyboard, she'd found cyberspace a lively enough place, teeming as it was with discussion groups and theorists, online worship services; prophets and plain lunatics from all walks of the world.

Shadows gathered in the long corners of the Reverend Welch's study, yet her face was illuminated by an eerie, almost supernatural light as she sat squarely in front of the monitor. Surely the simple shepherds of the biblical world might have mistaken her for some angel sitting there, long white hair flowing loose across her shoulders, broad, aristocratic bones that had saved her beauty from many of the ravages of time, bright blue eyes rendered fiery in that electric, otherworldly glow.

Long, knotted fingers moved lightly, rhythmically over her keyboard, searching for some truth among the dross, carefully researching, through endless lists and texts and chat rooms. Looking for the meaning of God in this brave new universe, looking for his light in the dawn of a new era.

She did not hear the footsteps as they entered the vestibule to her left. She was deep in conversation in the Armageddon chat room, talking with a Dutch cleric as he debated the fine points of the Book of Revelation. Privately, Elizabeth considered the good man quite out of his mind, but even via modem and lines of type, she was too polite to say so. She had been a psychologist before coming to her truer vocation as a woman of God, and she had always held a special tolerance in her heart for fanatics, a special fascination. For their views were so utterly defined, their lines between good and evil, black and white, so clearly delineated here in the confusion of the world.

The figure entered the office and paused to watch her for a few moments, hidden in the shadows. She will be different, he reckoned silently. He had seen it in her from that first moment. This time, he was sure, he would not be disappointed.

He made a soft noise to get her attention. Not at all surprised, Elizabeth turned to him and smiled.

"Is it time already? Goodness, have a seat. Just give me a moment to sign off." She turned and did so quickly, cutting the poor Dutchman off in mid-tirade. "There," she said, swiveling back to her guest, who had seated himself, fixing her with an oddly innocent stare, a self-conscious smile frozen across his features.

Elizabeth returned the smile with a more genuine one of her own. "I'm glad you came back," she told him. "After our last conversation, I wasn't sure that you would."

The man nodded, clasping his hands together in an attitude of prayer. "I thought about it . . . what you said."

Elizabeth studied him, a concerned expression in her eyes. "And did you come to any conclusions?"

A sigh escaped him and he seemed to settle himself more deeply in the chair, stretching his legs out in front of him.

"Go on," Elizabeth coaxed. "It can't be so much more difficult to speak with me in person than via computer, can it?" For that was how the two had made their first acquaintance less than a month before. The young man in front of her had been a regular contributor to one of the larger religious forums, and his comments had first tripped her psychologist's, rather than her minister's sensors. Though his rapid-fire comments had shown her he was well educated and surprisingly versed in some of the more esoteric doctrines, he was also quite depressed, searching, as so many were, for a spiritual context in his life. Her client was one of those who'd lost his footing on the road, a quality that never failed to awaken the good reverend's more nurturing side.

After a number of private chat sessions, she'd managed to discover that he lived close by. And, with some further persuasion, he'd agreed to come to the small suburban Episcopal church for spiritual counseling. Their first meeting had been awkward, but not overly so, and they had engaged one another in a conversation about the nature of sin and forgiveness. As an exercise, the reverend had challenged him to write down his sins and to decide for himself if he might be forgiven. Apparently she had touched some unknown nerve, for the young man had turned sullen and angry at the suggestion, and left shortly thereafter. Inwardly, Elizabeth was pleased that he'd chosen to keep this appointment, offered via e-mail from her office three days before. It reaffirmed her notion that God indeed worked in mysterious ways—even on the Internet.

"So," she said. "Where were we?"

She caught his eye then, and was struck by the pain she saw there. "I want to confess my sins," he answered simply. "I want you to forgive me."

Elizabeth's heart sank a little. It always came to this—the need for absolution, for a fresh start. Sometimes she believed that the rite of confession, for both the devout and unbelievers alike, was a sort of last hope for the spiritually bankrupt. A magical means whereby guilt and debt and trespasses were wiped away and it became possible to start again.

"That isn't what I do," she explained, as kindly as she could. "I'm happy to sit here with you and discuss the things that are troubling you, but that's all. I'll help you if I can. But only Catholics hear confession."

"I don't want to see some priest, I want to talk to you. I want to confess."

Elizabeth Welch looked hard at the young man slouched in the chair, seeing the quiet misery etched around his mouth, the shadows beneath his eyes. What had he done? she wondered. What was the thing that so tortured his soul? There was so much pain in him. So much need.

But much as she wanted to help him, she could not bring herself to lie, even to save a soul.

Her penitent sat in stony silence, almost visibly drawing inward, perhaps the better to converse with his personal demons. She struggled to bring him back.

"Confession isn't a cure. It's a ritual. And the simple performance of a ritual is not an answer. The act of confessing one's sins is essentially a valuable psychological process. It's a means of taking your own inventory. A means of self-examination. The urge to confess is very much a part of human nature. I believe the church understood that from the beginning. That's why the ritual exists. But the ritual itself is not essential. Self-examination is the real key."

The man looked at her, bathed in the soft glow of the desk lamp. "What about forgiveness?" he asked.

Elizabeth opened her hands to him, as if offering him something. "Forgiveness means nothing if you don't first forgive yourself."

"I thought God forgave everything," he countered, eyes narrowing.

Elizabeth looked at him. He was challenging her, testing her own faith to see if it was strong enough to pit against his great, unspoken guilt. It was. She was sure that it was.

"I believe that is true," she went on quietly. "But I also believe that the Lord helps those who help themselves. If you can talk about your past, if you can share the burden with another person, your burden will be lightened. Whatever you have to talk about, I promise you that together we will be able to work it through."

"That's a pretty secular interpretation, isn't it, Reverend Welch?" His voice rose sharply in the quiet study.

Elizabeth shrugged lightly, fingering the golden chain that hung from her neck. "I don't think the life of the mind and the life of what we call the soul are so easily separated. The point is self-awareness. Knowledge, especially self-knowledge, is power. Self-knowledge is the key that enables us to face the mystery of God without fear, it is the element that enables us to accept his love and forgiveness. If you're aware of something about yourself that is troubling to you, you have it within your power to change. And if you need help making those changes, know that God is there for you. You are his child."

The man smiled ruefully, his eyes distant. "Oh, Reverend," he said as though it were something quite obvious. "God can't save me."

"You must have faith," Elizabeth answered earnestly. "Whatever you have done, God can and does forgive. Think of the soul as that portion of yourself that will always belong to God. The idea of salvation becomes then not a question of being 'saved' but simply of finding a means to return to our truest natures, our higher selves. Each of us is part of God's creation."

She saw that his eyes were harder now in the dim light of the desk lamp. And when he spoke, his voice held the fine edge of self-loathing. "Every act of creation has its by-products, Reverend. Even God makes garbage, don't you think?"

Elizabeth leaned back in her chair, frowning a little. So tutored in the good was she that her generous heart still believed she could reach him. She voiced a silent prayer to her own beneficent deity. "I promise you, there is no soul beyond redemption," she assured him.

The young man rose and looked at her, and it was as if some mask had fallen from his face. He smiled again, and for him it was genuine this time, an icy leering look that chilled her to her bones. For the first time, the Reverend Elizabeth Welch looked into those fathomless eyes and recognized what she saw there. Not some troubled spirit, not the defense and anger of the frightened lamb, but evil—real as the day.

He leaned across her desk, so close she could feel the sudden unwelcome heat of his breath on her skin. Those terrible eyes held her like a trap and she saw darkness and cold and a menace so pure even her great, strong faith had no choice but to desert her, its light shriveling in fear and pain as his hands closed around her wrists, pinning her arms to the desk with an audible snap. When he spoke, his voice seemed to come from a long distance, echoing up from the echelons of hell.

"What if you don't have a soul?"

The Reverend Elizabeth Welch at last heard the young man's confession, her body lashed to a plain wooden cross that rose above a plainer altar. He knelt down before her and prayed like a child, all the long hours of the night—watching her suffocate by slow degrees.

SIXTEEN

CRUCIFIED!!!

CHARLOTTE, N.C. The body of 68-year-old minister Elizabeth Welch was found this morning by a custodian in the small Church of Our Fathers on Gatling Road. She had been crucified.

Police sources disclosed that the Reverend Welch's wounds corresponded to the wounds of Christ according to biblical descriptions, nails through the hands and feet and a puncture wound on the left side, just below the heart. Authorities refused to speculate, but there can be little doubt the horrifying crime was committed by a deranged religious fanatic, possibly someone who objected to a female taking over as head of the congregation.

A former psychologist, the Reverend Welch took up the ministry ten years ago and came to the Church of Our Fathers in January of last year.

This death is the third in the Charlotte

area in recent weeks. Tamara Meredith, well-known television psychic, and her assistant, graduate student Angel Tirado, believed to be the only person able to identify Meredith's killer, both died in torture murders. When pressed for a comment regarding a possible connection between Welch's death and the two previous crimes, sources at the mayor's special task force declined to comment.

Still, there is a ritualistic aspect to the murders that is difficult to ignore. If Charlotte has spawned a serial killer, it will be the second such series of crimes in less than three years in this city known as "The Queen City of the South."

Kate Loveless smiled benignly down at the morning edition, feeling as if all was right with the world. Sunlight flooded the pale mauves and greens of the managing editor's office. Her desktop was dominated by a huge floral arrangement of yellow orchids and birds-of-paradise, courtesy of corporate headquarters. Subscriptions were up; newsstand sales were over the top. Kate smiled at nothing in particular as she glanced once more at the glaring headline in front of her. A cub downstairs had been working the scanners and picked up the 911 call from the custodian. It was nothing more than the dumbest luck that the *Star* had managed to scoop the story. The kid had worked up the copy before Welch's body was even cold. Less than an hour later, another reporter's police source had given up the details, and the presses were rolling for the morning edition.

It was just too good, Kate thought. Another spectacular murder, Campion's column due to debut in a couple of days. She smelled a Pulitzer in it somewhere, another promotion in the wind. The syndicate was currently eyeing a respectable sort of rag in DC, whose management's refusal to change with changing times had left it all but bankrupt. If the acquisition went through, they were planning to revamp the format and go to a political-style tabloid. And they would need a managing editor.

Kate stretched contentedly, dreaming her dreams. She would like Washington, she knew. She would fit in so beautifully among the power mongers and diplomats. It was nice living, if you had the money. Nice parties, if you had the connections. And if you had the brains, you could dig up dirt on anybody, a notion that filled her with a delicious, heady sense of power. No one was safe in the new world of journalism, politicians least of all.

Besides, even Kate had to admit it was time to move on. The "Queen" City of the South was beginning to get on her nerves. And then there was the matter of Campion.

She glanced uneasily at the telephone. Campion. Without quite being able to pinpoint the reason why, John Campion, too, had begun to make her edgy. He was increasingly cocky, taking care not to cross forbidden lines but at the same time broadcasting the unspoken message that he considered her authority over him nothing more than an accident—an inconvenience he was prepared, at least in his own mind, to overcome. Without ever saying so, he managed to imply that he considered himself her equal, even her better, because of their relationship outside the office. And it disappointed her a little, for she considered John Campion to be one of the smarter talents she'd ever managed to lead astray. But something had gone wrong—something for which there was no cure or explanation. It was time to move on. For even as her mind skirted the issues, Kate knew, with a deep, feral instinct, that there was simply no telling how a man like Campion would react when he realized he would never be her equal, despite his grand aspirations. He was, and would remain, her toy.

Yes, thought Kate, thoroughly satisfied with herself. It was time to move on. First, though, she would have to make sure his debut column came in on time and that his exposé was all he'd promised it would be. Heads were sure to roll down at City Hall when the *Star* was the first to offer a solid theory to support a serial killer roaming the streets; she smiled to think of it. With a little influence in the right places, a story like that could get Campion's career off the ground.

But even if it didn't, it was enough to use as a springboard with corporate. Enough of a sensation to ride the wave of sales all the way to a new managing editorship up in Washington. Long, manicured fingers plucked up the telephone receiver and she punched in the numbers for Campion's extension, listening to it ring, a faint frown creasing her carefully made-up brow. No answer.

She hung up the phone and smiled again at her flowers. He was out somewhere, she reckoned silently. Doing his research, seeing that shrink. This new murder made all the difference, she knew—he could use it as a linchpin to tie together the rest of his cases. The headline caught her eye once more, and she broke into a grin. Crucified. God, it was too good—too bizarre. And the *Star* had scooped them all.

Then, another part of her mind stirred with an uneasy thought. What if it were, well—too bizarre? What if this weren't a serial killer at all, just some nutcase with a grudge against his minister?

The telephone jangled at her elbow, shattering her reverie, making her jump. She picked up the receiver, eyes shining when she learned who it was. A producer from *Hard Copy*, looking for details.

In the end, it hardly mattered if it was a serial killer, she decided. Establishing that connection was Campion's problem.

For herself, it was definitely time to move on.

On the other side of town, Campion sat in his underwear at a small kitchen table, a bottle of Finnish vodka fresh from the freezer within easy reach. He heard the phone ringing and decided to ignore it, already knowing who it was. He'd had his office calls forwarded home and he closed his eyes against the plaintive bleating on the speakerphone as she left a message on his voice mail.

"Hi. This is Kate Loveless. I can only hope you've seen the paper. Give me a call. I'll need a progress report on that column of yours for the afternoon meeting."

Blah, blah, blah, thought Campion. Who did that ball-busting bitch think she was, anyway? He allowed himself a longing glance at the cobalt blue bottle perched next to his laptop. Not yet, he thought. But soon. A little something to get the wheels turning, change his perspective. The story had been going so well—so right. Everything had been right. Until this morning. Until—this.

He lowered his head into his hands, fingertips feeling the expensive plugs that were no longer tender to the touch, but still somehow foreign. He had to get it together—the story, the quotes from

McTeague. He had to weave those infinite scraps and pictures and bits of evidence into something bigger—he had to form some shroud-like fabric of fact and reason to wrap those corpses in. The morning edition screamed at him from the table, demanding answers.

John Campion raised his head, snapped open his laptop, and paused to power up. He poured himself three fingers of vodka. He stared at the blinking light of the cursor until he could close his eyes and still see it there, patient and silent and relentless as it waited on the empty screen.

And he fervently wished his managing editor into the pitiless reaches of hell.

It was just after nine in the morning when McTeague pulled into the parking lot of the small, blond-brick church on Gatling Road. Law enforcement officials, ordinary cops, and ambulance personnel stood in little clumps on the wide green lawn, stomping through the good minister's riotous beds of pansies and marigolds as they went about the painstaking business of securing a murder scene. On the opposite side of the walk, she saw cameras and reporters in a desperate throng behind the lines of yellow police tape, waving hands and notebooks, holding cameras high as they angled for a shot of the covered gurney rolling down the walk. Slipping on a pair of sunglasses, Portia avoided notice and headed for a side entrance.

It took her tired eyes a moment to adjust to the dimness inside. It was funny how churches all smelled the same, she thought as she made her way through the vestibule. Modern or gothic, plain or fancy, they shared that common, weirdly identifiable scent, something like wax and something like flowers, something like old books and, in this instance at least, something like death.

She paused just outside a set of pale bleached oak doors that led to the sanctuary as the low murmur of voices inside suddenly rose. Her eye was caught by a bulletin board with announcements of single parent socials, teen talks, and after-school Bible classes. There was a small photograph tacked up in one corner identified as the Reverend Welch. It showed a beautiful woman with long, snow-white hair, smiling easily into the lens.

Portia stared at the photo for some moments, captivated by the face. It was beautiful, true, but there was strength in it too. The reverend's wide-set eyes shone from the picture with the kind of confidence that came only with time and living; the lines around her mouth revealed an easy, compassionate humor that neither judged nor allowed itself to be judged, except perhaps by those Elizabeth Welch had considered her real employers. Portia studied her in detail, as if the face itself might reveal some quality in its owner that had resulted in her terrible end, as if it might suddenly begin to come alive and talk to her.

She was startled when Detective Goodman burst through the doors at breakneck speed, all but knocking her down as he passed.

"Good God," he exclaimed. "What're you doing here?"

"She's a victim," Portia answered quietly. "And it's my fault. I gave Ivan her name. It was on the referral list."

"It's not your fault," Goodman replied. "Shit happens, that's all."

Portia turned to face him. "Right," she answered bitterly. "Is that why you forgot to call me to come down here?"

Goodman averted his eyes and for a moment Portia knew that she'd embarrassed him. "No," he replied uneasily. "I knew you'd be taking this hard but it wasn't the whole reason I didn't tell you right away."

"What's that supposed to mean?"

Goodman exhaled in a rush. "Look, I went ahead and did what you said. I had some rookie leak it to the press that she was nailed up. But she wasn't. She was tied up there, hanging maybe all night. Coroner says it's something about the angle. They die from slow suffocation." The homicide detective couldn't seem to find anything to look at. His eyes moved uneasily from her face to the floor to the doors and back again. "Anyway," he went on, "they ran it this morning."

Portia nodded grimly. "It's something," she said. "That kind of detail is important. Our guy is going to find the inaccuracy very disturbing. But Dave, I heard it on the radio. Why didn't you call?"

Goodman looked oddly ashamed of himself. "I did," he answered. "That is—I was just going to. But—I had to straighten something out first."

Portia frowned, her senses suddenly on the alert. "I heard the shouting," she said, jerking her thumb in the direction of the altar. "What's up? You have a suspect? Am I fired?" she asked, half in jest. From the look of him, this had not been one of Goodman's better mornings.

The detective's head wagged in the negative, but he still refused to meet her eyes. "It's the mayor. He pulled some strings. Apparently when this broke, the shit really hit down at City Hall. The DA and the mayor are crawling up each other's butts. Everybody yammering for action—you know the routine." He glanced at her curiously as if noticing her for the first time. "You look awful," he said matter-of-factly.

Portia nodded. "I know—" she answered flatly. "No sleep."

Goodman rubbed his chin and took a deep breath, trying to decide what to say next. The psychologist's face made it clear she wasn't interested in any further questions about her personal life, which left him little choice but to break the worst of the morning's news.

"Bottom line is, they're sending a guy down from Quantico, day after tomorrow."

Portia's bloodshot eyes went wide. "You mean special services?" she asked. "A profiler?"

Goodman met her look squarely, nodding.

"So I *am* fired?" It hung there, halfway between a question and a statement, followed by her short harsh laugh.

"You're good," she said acidly. "You're really good. Here you just stand there, letting me fill in the blanks. How many suspects have you pulled that little trick on, Dave? How many families of victims?" She stamped her foot in rage and frustration. "If you want me off the case why can't you just tell me, dammit? Why make me do all the work?"

The detective shoved his hands into his pockets, inhaling the church smell deeply. "Because I don't want you off the case," he answered quietly. "Not yet."

Portia eyed him angrily. "Coyness isn't my style, Dave," she said. "And up until now, it wasn't yours, either."

"McTeague," he interjected, "calm down, will you?"

"What the hell for?" she hissed, a tumult of emotions taking shape inside her as the news began to sink in. She was fired. Off the case. Dismissed by the same old good-old-boy establishment she'd been fighting for the whole of her career.

And maybe you deserve it. Welch might be alive if it wasn't for you and your precious rules of confidentiality.

"All I wanted to do was to be able to finish what I started!" She spoke aloud. To Goodman—to herself. To that awful taskmaster she carried around in her head. A hot flush of rage bloomed in her cheeks as she confronted the detective, green eyes blazing.

"How the hell could you let this happen?" she demanded. "We were almost there!"

Goodman's eyes widened suddenly, as if he'd been struck by some truly surprising piece of information. Then impossibly, he grinned, a lopsided sort of look that caught Portia completely off guard.

"Geez," breathed the detective, grasping her firmly by the elbow and steering her down a nearby hallway. "It's real. I never would have believed it."

"What's real? Get your hands off me!" Portia fumed. "Listen, just because you're a cop doesn't mean—"

In the hallway off the main entrance, Goodman turned her around to face him and leaned her gently against the wall. He shushed her, placing a pudgy finger to his own lips. When she had subsided into icy silence, he spoke again.

"The red hair," he answered. "I swear to God. I thought it was a dye job. But with a temper like that, I figure it's got to be real." He pulled distractedly at his earlobe, still grinning at her outraged expression. "You got one short fuse, you know that, Doc?"

Portia set her mouth in a thin line. She'd overreacted, it was true.

But being dumped off the case like a bad date, together with the huge irrational guilt over Welch's death, had hit her with unexpected force.

But she was not about to admit that to a cop. Especially a cop like Dave Goodman.

"I'm fine," she assured him icily.

"Yeah," he said. "Sure you are. And I'm twenty-five. Look, it's like I told you, they've called in Quantico. And unless we catch our boy Ivan in the next forty-eight hours, there's nothing we can do about it."

Portia clenched her teeth, fuming. He was right, of course. The system was the system. But that didn't mean she had to like it. "Well," she said sourly. "At least you know his name."

Goodman silenced her with a wave of his hand. "We can still pull this out, okay? Calling in the Feds is just more bells and whistles— window dressing. They've set up the agent for a fucking press conference the minute he sets foot off the plane."

Portia crossed her arms over her chest. "So?"

"So I cut you a deal."

The psychologist's eyes narrowed to slits as she looked at him. "What deal?"

"You show up at the press conference," he answered simply. "I want you on the podium. Make it look like you're making nice and handing over the reins of the investigation. Local talent bowing to the greater authority. All that crap.

"Then he spills the agency's goods. If I know my Feds, he'll start feeding the media sharks the standard profiler party line. Then you begin to take him apart, all very polite, very civilized. Point for point, you go through and show him how the profile doesn't work. The mayor's happy, the press is happier. And we get our investigation back." His eyes crinkled wickedly. "How does that sound?"

Portia could only stare at him for a long moment, attempting to fathom what it was that made a man like Goodman able to come up with that kind of plan in the space of what? Less than an hour? Two hours, tops? "Sounds pretty Machiavellian for a guy who wears cartoon ties," she said. She fixed her attention on his current choice, which depicted a slobbering Sylvester chasing the hapless Tweety over an endless polyester field.

"Aww—don't be like that—"

"Like what?" she demanded furiously. "You're using me to look good with the commissioner!"

Unexpectedly Goodman blushed. "Yeah, but—"

"You want me to be grateful? Sorry, Dave. You'll forgive me if I forget to thank you for offering to make me the human sacrifice." She started to move past him, but he stepped in front of her, blocking her passage through the narrow hall.

"I thought you wanted to see this through," he told her quietly.

"We agreed to keep my association with the case out of the media," she reminded him. "You promised me—no press. It's the only thing I asked for."

But Goodman only shrugged, as some part of her had already known he would. "That was then," he answered. "This is now. Things have changed. And, like it or not, you're a celebrity around here. I'm willing to throw them that, if it's what it takes to save somebody else. I don't have time to dance with the Feds."

"But you're willing to let me do it," she interjected.

"Because you can, Doctor. Experts are the way the game is played—in the courts, and in the press. You know that as well as I do. Look," he went on, beseeching her with his eyes. "I hate this crap. But I have to deal with it. And the reason I have to is because I want to catch this guy. That's the priority." He paused, searching her face. "Don't you see? If I get up there, I'm nobody, I'm just a cop. And cops have zero credibility until they have a suspect. In the meantime, you're all I've got."

There was a moment of stony silence. "What if it doesn't work? What if my getting up there only succeeds in pissing everyone off?"

He sighed. "I'm willing to take that chance; are you?" Warily, Goodman went a little further. "You *are* an expert," he went on. "You can't be willing to be that in private if you're not willing to face them in public."

Bastard, she thought, more in resignation than anger. Calmer now, Portia leaned farther into the wall, eyeing the detective doubtfully. "It may not work, Goodman," she said again. "I think you've really overestimated my popularity here."

He shook his head. "Doesn't matter," he replied. "They don't have to like you to know who you are."

Portia drew herself up then, turned, and made her way back to the place where their conversation had begun, in the vestibule where Elizabeth Welch's kind eyes looked out at all who passed beneath them. Goodman ambled after her, coming to a stop as Portia gazed at the photograph in grim silence.

"What time is the press conference?" she asked after a moment.

"Four, on Thursday," he said. "City Hall."

There was another long, uneasy silence as they faced the smiling victim.

"Is she still in there?" Portia asked.

Goodman spread his hands wide. "Yeah, but—"

Portia whirled on him fiercely and Goodman felt his protests die in his throat. Her eyes were hard as emeralds and just about as warm.

"I need to see her," Portia said, and pushed past him through the doors.

SEVENTEEN

Twenty minutes later, she was back behind the wheel, heading north into town, and feeling as though she were about to be roasted on a slow-burning fire. Blood throbbed in her temples as she raced a yellow light through a crowded intersection, and all the old issues rose up, vying for her attention. She had no right to take it personally, she knew. Goodman was only doing what had to be done. They both knew the rules of the game. And those rules frequently dictated that justice came down to a war of expert opinion, and that being right, in the end, was a question of surviving the system long enough to be vindicated.

The Volvo sped along a wide boulevard, hemmed in by semis on either side. The press, she thought bitterly. The fucking press. They lived in a world where a princess had died in a deadly race with the paparazzi, where speculation turned to fact and fact to fiction at the touch of the TV remote. She thought of the upcoming press conference and cringed in anticipation. Not because the prospect of going head to head with a Federal agent was so frightening to her, but because the things that would transpire the day after tomorrow in the glare of flashbulbs and shouted questions were already far too familiar.

For, in the end, she knew that Goodman's reasoning was utterly sound. It was, after all, that same reasoning that had made her urge him to leak erroneous details to the papers. The same that had caused the mayor and the DA to form a task force to catch a small-time madman. They were all playing by rules where information, right or wrong, good or bad, was the only currency that mattered. Where media was the only real power left—absolute and absolutely corrupted.

They would not be after the facts, she knew, but after the story. And she was the story. The local expert, the former psychologist for the defense, now working for the cops, now come over to what the public would doubtless perceive as the "right" side of the fence. It would not matter that she was trying to put her talents and knowledge to their best use; it would not matter that her basic convictions about personality damage and its effect on criminal behavior were largely unchanged. The press would see her appearance as a kind of defection from her liberal ways. Even if she did succeed in calling off the Feds, the local media would play her like a violin. And she wondered if she would be able to withstand the scrutiny, even if it meant the killer, whoever he was, might finally be caught.

She began to make out a familiar landmark or two, and slowed the car past a school zone. Three blocks over was a rambling Victorian mansion. Portia made a quick decision, jerking the wheel and sliding into the turning lane at the next intersection. It was only a little before eleven. For a moment, she eyed the cell phone on the seat beside her. Portia knew it wasn't entirely correct of her to just barge in on her therapist without calling first. But she was so close, so in need of Sophie's quiet wisdom at that moment. She was verging on a crisis, and she desperately needed someone to talk to, someone who would try to help her make sense of it all. Perhaps Sophie would see that. Two short blocks later, the Volvo rolled to a stop in front of the house, the gingerbread trim and lacy woodwork beckoning Portia like a beacon in the sun. Just a few minutes, she promised herself, already forming an apology for the intrusion as she made her way up the flower-lined walk. Just a few moments, she promised herself.

Sophie would understand.

She felt almost foolish, standing there on the wide porch straining to peek through the lacy curtains of the front windows. Then, without warning, the front door slid open a few inches and Sophie herself stood behind it, peering uncertainly at her.

"Oh," Portia said. "You are home, after all. I was just about to leave."

"Yes," Sophie replied. "I'm here."

There was an awkward moment. "Look, Sophie, I know I don't usually do this, and I certainly don't want to mess up your day, but could we talk for a minute? I'm—just—well, I feel like I'm going off in a million directions. I need to sort it out."

Sophie's black eyes shone out from a network of fine lines as she seemed to look Portia up and down. "Of course," she answered, not smiling. "Come in."

She reached up with knotty fingers to undo the lock and swung the door inward.

Portia hesitated on the threshold. "Are you sure it's all right?" she asked.

In answer, Sophie reached out and took Portia's hand, leading her into the dimness of the hallway. Her skin felt dry as paper, the bones fragile and birdlike against the dampness of Portia's own.

"We can sit in here," Sophie instructed, leading her to a sort of parlor off to the left. "I was just having some tea. And thinking."

The old woman indicated a dusky velvet chair that looked as if it belonged in another century, and settled herself into a platform rocker. A small china tea service graced a table between them, and Portia noted a spill near the teapot, where old hands had trembled over the cup. She looked away.

"What's on your mind, my dear?"

The musty, cluttered comfort of Sophie's parlor had a sudden, almost draining effect. Portia wanted nothing more than to curl up on one of the ancient sofas, tuck an afghan around her knees, and fall asleep.

"I'm not even sure where to begin," she said quietly, "so much has been happening."

"Take your time," Sophie offered evenly. "I have nothing to do."

Yet there was something in the older woman's tone that struck Portia wrong. A resignation, a fatigue she had never heard there before. But, caught up as she was in her own dilemma, she chose, for the moment, to let it pass.

"It's the investigation, partly," Portia hurried on, striving to put her thoughts in some kind of order, "the profiling work I told you about."

Sophie nodded mutely. Had Portia been watching, she might have seen a shadow cross her face, like the sun obscured behind a cloud, before the brightness returned to her eyes.

"And I broke up with Alan," Portia confessed, suddenly aware of the disjointedness of her own statements. "Or, at least we're cooling it for a while. I don't know, Sophie—he was making me feel so crowded all of a sudden. I needed some space." Portia paused, throwing up her hands in exasperation. "Or maybe you were right all along. Maybe I was just acting out some adolescent fantasy with him. All I know is, it was making me crazy."

"What specifically was making you crazy, Portia? The sex? The companionship?"

"No, of course not. It was just . . . the whole thing."

"So, what caused this turnaround in your feelings?"

"I don't know!" Portia shot back. "He was crowding me, that's all. Me and Alice both. He wanted some big commitment all of a sudden. And we argued about it. I thought it was because he's at loose ends himself. With his career so up in the air, I figured he just wanted security, that's all. So we argued. And then he accused me of being unavailable to him. Because of my work on the investigation." She met Sophie's eyes. "He told me I was obsessed."

Feathery white brows rose, delicate as fairy wings. "I see," answered Sophie. "Are you?"

"No—at least, I was pretty sure of that until this morning. I thought it was going fine. We're really very close to catching this killer—I can feel it."

Sophie observed her without expression. "What happened this morning?"

Portia inhaled with a hiss. "Goodman—the detective. He wants me to go public. They've called in the FBI, Sophie. And we both know this killer doesn't fit the standard profiles. So he wants me to go head to head with special services. He figures he can keep control of the investigation if he puts me out front."

"So," interjected Sophie. "He's making you a sort of scapegoat, is that what you're telling me?"

"No, not at all. I don't think he wants this any more than I do. He's just playing by the rules. Media's rules. If I can be the bigger story, I get to stay the principal profiler on the case because I satisfy the media. You know, the local celebrity thing." She stopped short, shaking her head. "The press," she continued ruefully. "You can't escape it. Good Lord, Sophie, I even have a reporter as a patient. He came to me with writer's block, for crying out loud."

"So?" Sophie interjected mildly. "It's not unheard of."

Portia stared at nothing, momentarily distracted by thoughts of Campion. "He's so, I don't know, weird. Nice diagnostic, huh? Okay, no—the point is, he supposedly came to me for help with this block of his, but there's always this subtext going on. I observe him, but he's observing me at the same time. It's like I'm under a microscope. Like I'm being interviewed or something." Portia threw up her hands, unable to explain further. "Or maybe it's because I know he's from the press and that pushes my buttons. Like I can't trust him. Help him." Portia chuckled softly, running a distracted hand through her hair.

"God," she finished. "Listen to me. Maybe I should just unblock him and give him an exclusive. That way, I wouldn't have to face those cameras day after tomorrow."

But Sophie failed to pick up on her lame attempt at humor, steering her back to the subject at hand. "I thought you'd expressed a desire to stay out of the public eye, to concentrate on your personal life," she reminded Portia quietly. "It doesn't seem to be the case, does it?"

"It's still true," Portia insisted. "I do want that. But I have to finish what I start, don't I? My God, Sophie. There's a killer out there."

"Why must you be the one to catch the bad guy?" Sophie countered. "Why must you solve the mystery? You're a psychologist, Portia—not a policeman."

Portia stared at her hands, lying still and strangely white in her lap. "Alan said that too," she murmured. "Something like it, anyway. But I can't quit, Sophie. We're too close. I know who the killer is. I've . . . spoken to him."

A rare look of surprise crossed Sophie's face. "And how is that?"

Portia went on to explain her Help Line caller. And how Ivan—whoever he was—was drawn to certain victims because of his own needs. "Serial killers," she finished, "and I believe that's what he is, always want simultaneously to be caught and not to be caught. I didn't think so at first, but to me, Ivan's impulse to get help is also his way of trying to be stopped."

There was a long silence after she was done. Sophie rocked pensively in her chair, her chin propped up on gnarled fingers. A clock ticked loudly somewhere in the hall, marking the minutes' passage.

"I want you to know something before I say anything else," Sophie began, shattering the quiet. "Elizabeth Welch was my friend. We belonged to the same gardening group. We shared a number of interests. I respected her deeply, and I will miss her very much."

Portia rose halfway from her chair, then fell back again as the same awful guilt took hold of her insides.

You gave him those names . . .

"Oh God, Sophie, I'm so sorry. I didn't know—"

Sophie silenced her by holding a crooked finger in the air. "Please," she said. "It isn't your fault."

Oh yes it is—

"I wanted you to know that simply because I wanted you to be aware that my opinion here may not be entirely objective. A mutual acquaintance phoned me with the news this morning. And the loss of my friend is still quite fresh in my mind."

Portia sank back onto velvet, stunned into silence, even as she struggled for some word of comfort. But there was nothing. Nothing she knew of the death of Elizabeth Welch could comfort Sophie now. There was no peace to offer her in the things Portia had seen that morning.

"But you are my friend too, Portia McTeague," Sophie went on. "We've known one another for a long time. And I think we understand one another a little."

"Sophie, please," Portia protested. "I'm so sorry. This isn't the time."

Sophie managed a wan smile. "There is no good time for tragedy," she replied. "More importantly, you are alive. But I have an obligation to you—both as my friend and as my client. And that is to tell you that you're chasing ghosts. And for that reason, I am afraid for you."

"Ghosts?" Portia looked at her without comprehension.

"Yes," Sophie replied. "The ghosts of your own past." Sophie's voice sounded low and urgent in the stillness of the room. "The ghosts are that of the abuser and that of the victim. Think about it, my dear. Whenever your life seems to be going well, you feel compelled to resurrect some very old patterns. You try, over and over, to fight this same contest. You sacrifice everything to win, to be right. You separate yourself from all that should have meaning in your life so that you can fight this same war. Why else would it be that you feel such an obligation to do the kind of work you do? To face these horrors again and again?"

"It's not an obligation," Portia shot back, surprised at the edge in her voice. "I'm trying to do some good here!"

Sophie fixed her with an unwavering gaze. "Are you?" she challenged. "Or are you putting yourself at risk? I want you to ask yourself something, Portia. What is to keep this caller of yours from attaching his obsession to you, if he hasn't already? What makes you think that because you call yourself a scientist, you cannot be killed?"

"You're overreacting, Sophie. I've talked to this man. I think I can—"

"You think you can what? Help him? Understand him? Catch him? You're playing by your own rules, Portia, no one else's. You think if you can somehow master the abuser you will not have to be a victim anymore. You are trying to decide within yourself who will win the battle for your soul—Portia the victim, or Portia the abuser."

Portia gawked at her, openmouthed. In all the years they'd known each other, Sophie had never spoken to her like this. There was frustration in the old woman's eyes as she looked at her, even anger. And there was something else, something like fear.

"Sophie . . ." she protested weakly. And the name died in the air between them.

"Your war is with yourself, Portia. These ghosts you battle are the ghosts of your past, your own fears."

As if her outburst had cost her a great deal of energy, Sophie leaned heavily against the rocker, closing her eyes. "I know what it is to live with ghosts," she murmured. "At my age, every death brings them back to me." When the old eyes fluttered open again, she seemed to be looking at Portia from some great distance, wise as the ages, full of sad history.

Portia sat perched in the velvet chair, feeling somehow foolish as she struggled to absorb it all. She had come here expecting her therapist's understanding, a willing shoulder to share her burdens. But Sophie herself seemed to have changed into someone Portia hardly knew. All this faintly Jungian discourse on ghosts and shadows and battles for the soul left her cold in that moment, a little impatient with the old woman's rhetoric. Yet, even as those thoughts arose they were replaced with guilt at her own disloyalty.

"We will talk about this again," Sophie said, sounding exhausted, her voice little more than a sigh. "Perhaps you are right. Perhaps this is not the time."

Portia stood a little unsteadily, groping for her purse and looking down at the elderly woman with concern. "I'm sorry—" she offered lamely. "For this. For Elizabeth, too."

"I am sorry, too," Sophie replied. "But please, try to think about it a little. You cannot perceive the real dangers of your position if you are busy fighting shadows."

Portia paused uncertainly. "Sophie," she began. "Please don't be concerned. I'm not in any danger. I promise you that. I'm working with the police this time, remember? And we'll find Ivan. I know we will."

The old woman held Portia's eyes for a long moment. And in the dimness of the parlor, Portia thought for the barest instant that she saw tears there.

"I was talking to Elizabeth not long ago." Sophie looked away and resumed rocking, gazing out the window. "She mentioned a young man she'd met on one of those computer networks. A troubled man, apparently. She'd begun to counsel him, I know."

"Oh God—" Portia breathed, feeling a tightening in her stomach. "Ivan—"

"Maybe, we cannot be sure." Sophie shrugged, as if the killer's identity were something unimportant. "But I recall discussing it with her. I remember cautioning her. You see," Sophie said, twisting back enough to meet Portia's eyes full on. "Elizabeth wasn't afraid, either."

Holding her breath, Portia leaned over to graze the old woman's cheek. "Soon," she promised, and left her there, rocking in the half-light of the crowded, musty room.

Portia slung her bag over one shoulder as she headed hastily down the walk, anxious to be back in her office, a place where the world, at least temporarily, might make some sense, where she might exercise the notion of being in control.

She slid behind the wheel and slammed the door harder than she'd intended, glancing in the rearview mirror as if to reassure herself that she was still there. She sped away from the curb with a tug of conscience, haunted for an instant by the mental image of a white-haired woman, rocking away the afternoon in the silence of her parlor.

They would make it right, Portia promised herself. She and Sophie. They would find a way. In another session—some other day.

At the moment, however, she was grateful to be gone, away from the smells of dust and age and Sophie's talk of ghosts.

For Portia knew one thing as she slowed through an intersection and headed toward the clean, modern, uncomplicated skyline of Charlotte's business district. Knew it as surely as she knew the all too familiar loneliness that rose up with the knowledge.

Sophie did not understand.

EIGHTEEN

She knows the aching first, the emptiness and loss. She wanders the streets uptown, uncomfortable as she tugs fretfully at her suit, strangely conscious of her height in high-heeled shoes. A sudden desire to weep overcomes her as the familiar streets are transformed to a landscape of dreams. The cold, loveless outlines of the skyscrapers shine against a dull pinkish sky. She hears the deserted echo of her footsteps on the walk.

Everyone is gone, she thinks. Everyone is hiding. And she feels a thousand pairs of eyes watching her from the darkened windows of the uptown skyscrapers. The buildings stand like sentinels guarding their secrets.

She comes to the foot of a granite staircase, pauses, looking uneasily around. Her chest tightens with grief and fear. She glances up toward darkened doors. And suddenly she sees that place light up, burning in the glow of the camera lights. They are waiting.

Don't go, a voice hisses inside her mind. Not yet. You know what they'll do to you.

And then, without thinking, she flees, seeking the cover of the shadows—away from the lights and all those unseen eyes. She feels as if she is made of shadows, there on the empty streets. She knows the loneliness, the awful hurt she has buried like bones. She cannot—should not—be alone. She cannot face them alone.

But maybe there is time, she thinks. Still time to find him.

Running now, hearing the steady *thock, thock* of her shoes on the pavement, she zigzags across the empty city, running for the comfort of the one she has lost. She can find him, she knows it. Feels his presence, almost catches the scent of his skin. She was wrong. He hasn't gone at all. Her lover is waiting. She has only to find him—help him understand. There is still time.

A tall man is selling red balloons from a cart. He smiles as she passes him, tries to stop her, calls her name.

Pokey-Pokey, come back!

No! she shouts and runs on. The balloons are some trick, a trap to keep her there.

Now the running slows a little. She comes to another part of town, passes a park where the lawns glow strangely bright, preternaturally green. A small pond glistens in the eerie light, and an old woman, all in black, nods in her wheelchair.

And in the dream, she is sure that she knows her, even before the woman lifts her head and beckons her with a crooked finger, the smile wide and toothless. But she cannot go. Her lover is waiting. So she shakes her head and turns away. And the old woman begins to cry.

Leg muscles grow sluggish, her feet heavy in the awful high-heeled shoes. She shivers in her own sweat as the air grows bitter cold and the pond turns to ice and the old woman is a black dot in the distance.

It's better this way, she tells herself. Better to run. The old lady doesn't know the truth; she is too crippled—too old to know the truth. She might have killed her with a touch.

The landscape alters again and she is closer now. The wide streets narrow. The sidewalks are pitted, glittering with shards of broken glass. Pages of a newspaper dance like ghosts on the pavement. She is panting from the exertion; her lungs turn to fire with every breath. But nothing will stop her as she runs through the city, nothing can make her give up.

Then there is a church that she has never seen, its stained-glass windows vandalized, their jagged edges sharp enough to draw blood. Lines and shapes are painted over the bricks of the old facade, rising impossibly high, the pattern glowing in the light. She strains to see it all at once, backing away to get a better look.

The tree of life. The map of death.

And then she is inside the church. And there are telephones everywhere, blinking from the toppled pews. The broken altar has become a ragged office, lined with tables and still more telephones, all bleeping and ringing and filling the place with a deafening chorus of sound.

She walks, takes her place on the altar. She picks a phone, her voice strained and hesitant.

"Alan?" she asks.

But there is nothing, only air, the ghost of a ringing in her ear.

She feels his hand then, hot upon the cooling skin of her neck. And she knows her lover has come to her at last. Fingers stroke her skin lightly, seductively, sending floods of warmth and gratitude through her veins. It isn't too late, she thinks. There is still time.

The hands travel over her shoulders and neck, light as whispers, urgent as fire.

Alan.

There is a voice close to her ear as the hands come around to cup her breasts and she feels the tug of her body's reply. "Don't turn around," it whispers.

Lips on her neck. She moans, hair falling forward over her face as she strains against the hands. He pinches her nipples erect, gently at first, then harder. Reaches to hike up her skirt and stroke her thighs. She strains against him, tries to turn. But the hands hold her firmly to her chair.

She can feel his breath as he tells her his secrets, low murmurs that fall like kisses on her skin.

Please—she tells him. Let me see you. I've missed you . . .

She rises, turns, but there is no one. And she cries out in the emptiness as the phones begin to ring.

No!

And then she does see him, a black silhouette far above her, half hidden in the deep shadows of the choir loft. He has not left her, then. She has not lost him. He is only waiting, waiting for her to come to him. To be his beloved at last.

Ivan.

Portia sat patiently as an accountant described his homosexual fantasies. Mr. (call me Chip) Greggs seemed unaware that the latest in what had proved to be a series of sexually charged racquetball dreams pointed to precisely that possibility, but his therapist was far too preoccupied with her own dreams that morning to feel ready to break the news. Instead she found herself doodling on the yellow legal pad in front of her, drawing again and again the strange outline that glimmered from the corners of her memory. The lines and shapes from the front of the church. They struck her as familiar somehow as she murmured a polite encouragement to Chip's description of scoring the final point, puzzling over what the pattern might mean.

At length Chip rose, smiling, and thanked her for what he called a "dynamite" hour, no less ignorant of the working of his psyche as when he'd walked in. Portia ushered him to the door, trying to feel guilty over having been so absent from their session, and wondering with another part of her mind why Chip hadn't noticed the difference.

She made her way out to the lobby, feeling sluggish and strangely depressed. Her nightmare stayed with her like a hangover. She felt weary, yes, but it was more than that too. Details had floated in and out of her consciousness since breakfast, like parts of a song she couldn't quite remember. And at the same time, she shied from any clear recollection, assuring herself it was simply the stress of the past few days, the uncertainty of the ones to come.

She laid the yellow pad carelessly on Lori's counter and headed for the coffeepot, sipping gratefully and closing her eyes. Lori was on the phone juggling appointments to clear a space for the doctor's press conference the following afternoon. When she'd hung up her eyes traveled curiously to the strange design etched again and again in place of what was supposed to have been McTeague's clinical notes on Chip Greggs. She frowned, glanced at Portia, then back again.

"Interesting session?" she asked.

An exhausted little sigh escaped Portia's lips and she flipped through the waiting files, arranged according to the day's appointments. "The usual, I guess," she answered absently. "Who's up next?"

A guilty flicker crossed Lori's blond features, an expression that Portia failed to see. "Mr. Campion," she answered quickly. "He's not here yet."

Portia swallowed more coffee and yawned hugely. "I'll be waiting," she mumbled.

She started to head back to her consultation room as Lori called after her. "You want this? Or should I file it?" She held up the legal pad, the top page covered with its strange designs.

Portia saw it, blushed, and came to retrieve it from Lori's efficient fingers. "I guess I was a little preoccupied," she admitted.

"I guess," Lori agreed. "This case has you into some weird stuff."

Portia glanced up, frowning. "Weird?"

"It's none of my business," Lori assured her. "I just work here."

Portia stared at her. "But what did you mean just now? When you said it was weird?"

Lori's eyes held a measure of surprise. "Why, the drawing, of course—the design or whatever you call it."

"You mean this?" Portia glanced down at the page, frowning at it as though she had never seen it before. "Do you know what it is?"

Lori nodded self-importantly. "We reviewed it as part of my acupressure class. The one I take at the community college. You know I'm working to get my license."

Actually Portia hadn't known that, but she was far more interested in the design at that moment. "But you've seen this before, right? This—symbol. Or whatever it is."

"Sure," Lori said nonchalantly, unable to resist adding, "but I thought you weren't into New Age stuff."

"Lori," Portia had to fight an impulse to reach across the counter and slap her, "it could be important. What does it mean?"

Lori, sensing her employer's mood, scooted her chair over a few inches toward the file cabinets. "It's a diagram of the energy centers of the human body. Most people call them chakras, but they can be called a lot of different names. In my class we call them chi points." She paused, spelling it out.

"So anyway, chi is basically just energy, right? Life force. And chakras are connected by energy channels. You know?"

Portia didn't but nodded curtly. "Explain."

Lori's eyes shone enthusiastically at the chance to prove her knowledge. "Well, the ancients believed that there are invisible energy channels in the body that connect the seven major chakra centers where energy and life essence or chi are concentrated. And that people get sick and stuff where the energy gets blocked. Alternative healing tries to unblock the channels and establish a flow between all the centers. That," she finished, pointing to the page, "is a diagram of the connections between the centers. My teacher said we should think of it as sort of a spiritual X ray."

Portia could only stare for a moment, unsure how to respond. Somehow, Lori's explanation of the strange and yet familiar design she had sketched left her more confused as to its meaning than before.

"So," Lori continued, eyeing her oddly, "I didn't think you were into this stuff. Where did you see it?"

Portia shook her head in confusion. "I—don't know. That's what I was trying to figure out. A dream maybe. Or something—I don't know." Suddenly, the realization of just where she'd seen that design hit her like a thunderbolt. She sank down heavily into the nearest chair. "Jesus Christ," she breathed. "Jesus fucking Christ!"

Lori's eyebrows shot up quizzically. "What?"

Portia looked up at her assistant, still too flabbergasted to make sense of it all. "Meredith," she answered softly. "The design—it was cut into her body."

Lori only shrugged. "It's not for me to say—but that's probably why you dreamed it. Like, that image is part of the collective, you know? I think your intuition is telling you you know more about this guy than you think you do."

Portia gazed for a moment beyond Lori's bright blond curls to the window. In the parking lot, she saw a car pull up and her next patient emerge. John Campion looked oddly disheveled from this distance, and the psychologist was brought instantly back to the moment. Intuition notwithstanding, she felt she owed her patients better than she'd given so far that morning.

"He's here," she said, gathering up the yellow legal pad and Campion's patient file. "Send him back."

Lori's bright anticipatory smile faded almost immediately as Campion strode unsteadily through the outer doors and toward the reception desk. His handsome face looked oddly bloated, covered with a few days' growth of beard, and the irises of his eyes showed almost yellow against the bloodshot whites. His smile never wavered, though, as he crossed to the front desk and took care to reach up and self-consciously straighten the knot of his tie.

"How're you this morning, darlin'?" He grinned lasciviously at Lori over the counter, and she caught a waft of stale booze coming off him, so sharp it took her breath away. It was as if he'd showered in Smirnoff, rinsed in melted ice.

Disappointment showed like tears in her eyes as she shot him a glance that seemed to swallow him whole. She'd already broken the rules for him. In secret, she'd skimmed his patient file, looking for clues to his personality. She'd refused to believe McTeague's preliminary diagnosis of borderline traits and overdependency. Not to mention the possibility of substance abuse. Instead, Lori had privately cherished the belief that the handsome Mr. Campion might benefit from some alternative healing. Something to realign his energy and unblock the wealth of creative force that Lori was convinced lurked beneath that carefully maintained facade. The truth was, she'd even been planning to ask him to attend one of her classes at the community college.

Now, in an instant, her fantasy turned to dust. She met his eyes and could see that her presence barely registered there. He saw her only as a reflection of himself—her attraction as a mirror in which to preen. His yellow eyes read her secrets, knew her guilt. And he baited her with the knowledge.

"I'm fine," she managed with a cold efficiency. "You can go on back, Mr. Campion, the doctor's waiting."

But he chose to linger another moment, leaning heavily on the counter that stretched between them. "I'm a little under the weather," he confided in a mock confidential tone, still smiling. "Sick. You wouldn't hold that against a fellow, would you, Lori? The pressure, you know."

Lori glanced up again uncertainly, some part of her still unwilling to believe the loss of her short-lived dream. And she saw that he read that uncertainty in her eyes, and was daring her to believe that her own heart had not so deceived her. She felt naked under that look, imperfect and alone. And she could see that he knew his power over her and reveled in it.

"Tell me," he said. "You get a peek at my file?"

He saw her blush with guilt and disappointment. Their eyes locked. And she knew that he knew what she had done.

And he began to laugh.

She was jolted by the office intercom buzzer at her elbow and snatched at the telephone headset like a lifeline, feeling a coldness settle in the pit of her stomach. "Mr. Campion is here," she announced.

"I'm ready," answered Portia. "Send him back."

Hearing the voice, Campion bowed elaborately from the waist, still mocking Lori with his eyes. "See you later, love," he whispered. "Got to go get cured." And lightly blew her a kiss.

Shaken, Lori watched him disappear down the hall. His steps were steady and his shoulders square, despite his breath and bloodshot eyes. Uneasy guilt and anger fought for a place in her thoughts as she turned back to her duties, along with the inarticulate certainty that Campion's flirting had only been testing her, setting her up as sport. That a man as handsome as that could take advantage of his looks came as no real surprise to a woman like Lori. That he had read her attraction for him and then laughed at her did.

She stared for a long moment down the hall, wondering how it was that her intuition could have so betrayed her, and thinking that perhaps Portia had been right. John Campion was better left to the professionals. Maybe a shrink could get to the bottom of it. The sound of his laughter echoed in her thoughts and she was stung once more by his derision.

"Sick is right," she said to no one.

And was pulled back to the moment as the phone rang once more.

"So," Portia began back in the consultation room. "How are you doing?" Privately, she was taken aback at his appearance. She, too, had caught the odor of old liquor emanating from his pores and noted the fatigue etched in the lines of his face. Suddenly it struck her as truly ironic that the two of them had been thrown together in this place and at this moment in time. She, dreading the on-slaught of media that would come with her appearance at the press conference the following day; he, a member of that enemy camp, blocked and apparently deteriorating under the pressure. And nei-ther of them doing very well.

But Campion smiled blissfully, his bloodshot eyes half closed. "Tired," he admitted. "But I think it's going to be all right. For the first time—I don't know. You've really helped me get back the sense of being in control of my shit. You know?"

Portia raised an eyebrow. The comment seemed oddly out of character. "How so?" she prompted him.

"The writing, you know. It's really flowing now. The whole thing's finally coming together for me. I've just got a couple of details, a few things left to research, and then . . ." He paused, making an expansive gesture. His flashy smile widened to a grin. "Man oh man, is this town going to sit up and take notice. Once it hits—"

"When does your column debut?" Portia interjected. Campion was different today, something about him subtly altered. The smell of booze and the beard stubble, the bloodshot eyes, all indicated the reporter had gone on a bender. Yet his attitude belied deterioration. He was almost relaxed, confident without the brave phoniness he'd shown her in their previous sessions. She frowned a little, trying to intuit the meaning of the change. He might, in fact, be deteriorating. Or he might have passed his crisis. Professionally at least. She had to allow for the fact that whatever his psychological problems, he had come to her with writer's block. If he had overcome it, she might be witnessing nothing more than the aftermath of a hard night of celebration.

Now, he fixed her with his startling eyes. "Sunday morning," he answered. "Just a few more days. God, it's weird to feel so close, isn't it?"

Portia stirred restlessly. Tell me about it, she thought. Aloud she said, "Close to what?"

This time, the smile turned mysterious. "The dream, of course. My dream."

Portia fought with the uneasy sensation that there was a subtext to this conversation, as though Campion were reading from some script whose contents she could only guess at. She caught the image of the strange diagram impressed on the fresh sheet of yellow paper in front of her. The dream.

She glanced at her patient quickly. "I don't mean to be negative here, John. But this is your first column at this newspaper. Just the first. And as glad as I am that you're writing again, I don't want you to lose perspective."

Or succumb to delusions, she added silently.

Campion stretched like a cat in his chair, fixing her again with those peculiar eyes. For a long moment, he said nothing.

"What're you thinking?" Portia prompted him.

His teeth showed white. "Nothing. Or something. Maybe I shouldn't say it."

"Say it, John. That's why you come here, isn't it? To tell me what's on your mind?"

He examined his fingers for a long moment. Portia followed his gaze. Powerful hands, covered with a network of dark hairs.

"I was thinking how interesting it would be if we had met under different circumstances, Doctor." He glanced up suddenly as if surprised at his own words. "Am I allowed to say that?"

Despite herself, Portia managed a small smile. "Of course you can," she said kindly. Here we go, she thought. Borderline overdependency spiced up with some serious transference. In Campion's case it was almost a good sign. At least he was connecting with something.

"Of course, I meant in the professional sense," he added quickly, searching her eyes. "You see, I've been doing all this research. For the column. I caught up on a lot of your court work. Your forensics cases. And I have to tell you, I was blown away. You're really good—you know that? As a criminologist, I mean."

Portia studied her patient. She'd been prepared for a crush, even some overtly sexual remark. It wouldn't have been the first time a troubled male patient had found a female therapist populating his fantasy life. Campion, however, showed no sign of that. Instead he admired her criminal work. Now there was a twist she could never have anticipated.

"Thanks," she offered, for want of anything better to say.

Campion leaned forward encouragingly. "I bet you have an idea who's doing all those women, don't you?" he asked, hardly able to keep the excitement from his voice. "I mean, with your knowledge of psychology."

Portia shook her head, both flattered and strangely embarrassed. "John," she said as gently as she could, "I know you're really excited by your writing right now. And it's natural for you to be interested in the news, but—"

He leaned back in his chair. "But what? An expert like you? Are you telling me you have no opinion? This guy is probably a serial killer, right?"

Portia hesitated. "Well, yes, but I can't really speculate on that."

She caught the edge of anger that crept into Campion's next, more demanding question.

"Why not?" he asked. "Didn't you just tell me I could talk about whatever I wanted?"

"Yes, but . . ."

He looked at her then, his eyes wide and innocent as the rage faded from his voice. "I was trying to pay you a compliment, Doctor. To tell you I respected your work."

Portia blushed, suddenly clear on why in the world Campion had chosen to be a newspaper reporter. He was just like all the rest of them, pushy and angry and manipulative. Another pit bull in a sports coat.

She took a deep breath. "And I appreciate that. But . . ."

"So you've gotta have an opinion on the murders," Campion insisted. "I mean, why not you? Everybody else does."

"Look," Portia interrupted. "We're here to talk about you, not me. And not about the murders." So shut up, goddammit, she added silently.

But Campion was not about to give up. "What if I was a killer?" he asked suddenly. "I mean, that could happen, right? You could have a patient you knew was dangerous?"

Portia shook her head, and suddenly some part of her relented. Stop overreacting, she chided herself. He's just a reporter, hyped up on his job. How many times had she done the same thing, asked the same question over and over, trying to get to the bottom of a criminal case?

It's more than that—you know it is. You almost want to tell him, don't you? It would almost be a relief.

Portia looked at nothing for a long moment. She couldn't lay blame at Campion's door. He didn't know she was working on the case; he couldn't know that was what lay at the bottom of her internal struggle. That was her job; his was something different. She was spooked, that was all. Spooked by the prospect of that stupid press conference.

She willed herself to relax as she faced him, forcing a small, tense smile. "That could happen," she agreed. "But you have to remember that if a patient comes to me for therapy, he's probably not a serial killer. Even though there are certain sets of symptoms that relate to a predisposition for violence, the killer is usually the one who doesn't seek help. Those who do usually get it."

Campion's eyes glittered. "Do they?"

"Absolutely," Portia answered. *Coward. Why don't you tell him the truth? That you don't even know how to help yourself?*

"So, if somebody like you, an expert in psychology, I mean, were after this killer, you could find him, right?"

"No," Portia admitted, again conscious of the terrible irony of their situation, even as thoughts of Ivan beckoned from another, darker corner of her mind. "Based on what I knew about his psychology, maybe I could help. But that's as far as it goes, I'm afraid. Your research has to tell you that serial killers are extraordinarily difficult to apprehend. Even for a psychologist," she admitted. "With sociopaths," she finished lamely, "it's pretty much a question of degree. How far does a person have to deteriorate before he kills? And why does that vary from one individual to another? The answers are as individual as people are."

Campion laced his fingers together and nodded understandingly. "I guess," he replied. "It must be hard, though—like a guessing game almost."

Again Portia's attention was momentarily drawn to the impression of the strange design on the page. "Sometimes it is," she answered quietly.

"So what makes it work?" Campion continued. "I mean, I know you've helped me so much. Getting over my block and all. It's like you really understand. But on the other hand, it must be frustrating for you. I mean, when you get right down to it, psychology's awfully inexact, isn't it. Imprecise?"

"The patients make it work," Portia answered. "By working together with me. At least that's part of it."

"Part of it?" Campion's eyebrows rose. He smiled again. "What's the other part?"

Portia could only shrug.

"Intuition," she answered.

And then, when he had gone, Portia thought for a long time about the things they had discussed, trying to identify the moment when John Campion had found it within himself to use their few sessions as a springboard for once again being able to work at a job he clearly was good at, one he clearly loved. She closed her eyes wearily, her thoughts rolling back and forth between Campion and her murder case, between the help she provided her patients and all the troubled ones she could not find, much less reach.

Perhaps she should not have discussed things so freely with the reporter. But on the other hand, by the same time tomorrow, her

position as a psychological consultant on the case would be all over
the news, so it hardly mattered. She even paused to wonder if Campion might attend the press conference. He certainly knew how to
ask the questions.

She gathered up the yellow pad after a few moments, intending
to take it out front and place the few notes she'd made in Campion's case file. She paused at her desk, her finger idly tracing that
strange embedded design, the same one that had haunted her
dream. What did it mean to the mind of a killer? Why had he
chosen to carve it upon Tamara Meredith's flesh?

Then it came to her in a single flash—the answer to a puzzle
looked at so often she had feared, with all of her scientific training,
that its meaning would be lost forever. The lines and the symbols
came together in a shock of sudden recognition as she found her
answer. She knew Ivan's need, his motivation, knew it as surely as
she knew her own name.

Intuition, she thought, smiling down triumphantly at the page. It
counted for something after all.

NINETEEN

The following afternoon, Agent Bob Carstairs took his place on the far side of the long, Formica-topped table where the mayor, the district attorney, the police commissioner, and an assortment of mid-level police brass, all looking grim and blinking in the camera lights, bobbing their heads or murmuring among themselves, sat lined up like human targets for members of the press.

Portia sat rigid in her chair, wearing a peacock-blue suit, her long neck framed by a white silk crescent of collar. Dave Goodman sat next to her, having been assigned the last place at the table, so close to the edge of the platform he was in danger of falling off. Doubtless planned as yet another professional courtesy by the mayor and his boys. They wanted the homicide detective there, but well out of camera range. Portia doubted his microphone even worked.

"As you know," the mayor was saying, "this special task force was formed to provide special assistance to the members of the police force in the aftermath of the shocking murders that have plagued this fair city. Ladies and gentlemen of the press, Charlotte has known murderers before. It, like any modern city, has known its share of crime. But I have pledged to the people of this community, this state, and this country that we will not tolerate mayhem in our midst. That's why this special task force was formed. That's why I have used my considerable influence in our capital to . . ."

Portia tuned the mayor out, and busied herself for a moment trying to read Goodman's mind. His broad face betrayed nothing at all. Instead, he sat as relaxed and comfortable as he might have been in his own living room. Portia, by contrast, had continually to restrain the impulse to fidget as the mayor introduced the police commissioner and the first speech dovetailed into a second.

She leaned back, unable to get a clear look at Special Agent Carstairs, who was sandwiched between the mayor and the district attorney.

The better to photograph you, my dear, she thought disgustedly. One more Federal photo op.

She did manage to glean a dim impression of a dark suit and a strong profile, and she allowed herself to wonder if the Feds ever hired anybody without a strong profile, someone with a receding chin perhaps. Or a wart on his nose.

Struck by the absurdity of it all, she had to fight a sudden impulse to giggle at the thought. A small snicker escaped her lips and she quickly covered it with a cough, catching Goodman's eye as he shot her a curious glance. She sipped water, meeting his eyes over the glass.

Take it easy, Doc, his brown eyes told her. You can do this.

Yeah, her green eyes answered. But frankly, I'd rather have boils.

A sudden smattering of applause brought her attention back to the podium, as she realized her name had just been spoken. Tentatively, she reached for the microphone in front of her as her innards dissolved into a thousand butterflies.

"Thank you, Commissioner," she said. "Like any citizen, it has been my pleasure to assist the authorities in this matter. And I want Agent Carstairs to know that I will do anything I can to—"

"Thank you, Dr. McTeague." The commissioner interrupted so abruptly even Goodman raised an eyebrow in surprise. "And now, before the questions begin, let's hear from Agent Carstairs himself.

I'm sure he can throw considerable light onto this baffling and truly distressing situation."

Bob Carstairs rose and strode to the center of the platform, opening a manila file folder and pretending to read it with theatrical concentration. He looked out over his audience, as if surprised to find them there, and began.

"Well," he said. "Based on my preliminary findings, I think we are looking at a male between eighteen and twenty-four years old—"

Wrong, dipshit, thought Portia. He's older.

"The suspect we are seeking in these cases probably is a drifter or manual laborer of some kind. An itinerant with no real abode. Thus, we can infer that if he is not apprehended relatively soon, he will move on."

Now that's really brilliant. He's telling them if nobody catches him, it won't matter because the killer will leave town.

Carstairs rattled paper. "Further, I believe that the most significant aspect of these murders is the perpetrator's obvious religious mania, probably augmented with regular drug abuse. I believe we are seeking a person who is compelled to desecrate what he believes are sacred or holy people and places. Thus it is the Bureau's sense that we may be seeking a Satanist or someone belonging to a similar cult."

This was too much.

"Excuse me—" Portia interjected.

Carstairs glanced at her, irritated. "Yes?"

Portia flashed a wide, slightly unpleasant smile. "How are you getting Satanist here? There is no consistent ritual aspect to these murders at all, nor do they correspond in any way to significant dates on any known religious calendar."

Agent Carstairs looked momentarily confused. "Well, there's the crucifixion, of course. And the outline of the angel. We at the Bureau feel those are clear indications of the perpetrator's compulsion to desecrate accepted religious objects and values." Carstairs smiled as if he had just said something highly profound.

Oh, for crying out loud, Portia thought. And felt Goodman's knee gently nudge her own beneath the table. She glanced at him and saw he had a subtle finger entwined in a lock of his own hair. Hair. Her mind jumped back to his comment on her own auburn curls a few days before. He was warning her to keep her temper in check.

She spoke once more into her microphone. "Interesting," she said. "Please go on."

"The way the victims were attacked points to a blitz-style attack, where the victim is incapacitated very quickly, then overpowered by the killer. This is consistent with a disorganized type of killer. In a disorganized personality, the killer uses readily available weapons and implements such as the kitchen knife discovered at the Meredith scene, the spray paint used in the instance of Ms. Tirado, or even the nails used to crucify the Reverend Welch."

Portia's head snapped to attention as she heard those last words. Though she herself had given Goodman instructions to leak the wrong information to the press, she could not quite believe he'd kept the real details of the crucifixion from the rest of the task force. She glanced at him, wondering. Had this been his piece of insurance? A means of keeping her on the investigation? If the Feds and the press had been deliberately given wrong information, they might very well come to the wrong conclusions. Had Goodman made sure of that in order to retain control of his case?

Once more, his bland, slightly bored expression showed nothing as he gazed out on the blur of faces and cameras in front of him. Portia went positively weak with admiration. It was starting to become very clear that Dave Goodman knew exactly what he was doing.

"For this reason," Agent Carstairs' voice had risen against the wave of murmurs that swept the assembly, "we believe that the profile indicates an individual who works with his hands, possibly someone who works as a custodian or janitor, or a construction worker. Someone who is, for want of a better term, handy with such things as ordinary tools."

Mother of God, thought Portia. "I'm sorry for interrupting again, Mr. Carstairs," she said. "But you are aware, aren't you, that the homicide division has interviewed all custodial personnel at these scenes and come up with nothing to support that theory?"

She heard a low rumbling from the crowd. The press smelled blood.

"Well, yes," he admitted in a patronizing tone. "But for the moment, I believe we may have to backtrack a bit."

"Why?" she demanded. "When you're obviously looking for the wrong man?"

The rumbling rose to a roar and Special Agent Bob Carstairs looked very much taken aback as he glanced uneasily out over the crowd of waving hands, a hundred voices vying suddenly for his attention. Clearly, the members of the press had decided the floor was now open for questions.

"Hey, Carstairs," one voice jeered, "is it true the Feds catch fewer than fifty percent of suspected killers using their current profiling techniques?"

Carstairs coughed into the microphone. "We are dealing with a serial killer here. And serial killers are notoriously difficult to—"

Without waiting for him to finish his sentence, someone else shouted a question from the floor. "Dr. McTeague! How do you know? Why did you say they're after the wrong man?"

She reached for the microphone, hands slippery. "As a volunteer on this task force, I've studied the crime scenes carefully," she answered calmly. "We're looking at a highly organized, almost compulsive individual. He arranged his victims very carefully and left the bodies displayed in a distinct fashion. Each of the murders showed greater complexity—escalation—in terms of the way the corpses were displayed. The killer used very common objects as weapons not on impulse, but because they can't be readily traced. This is a highly intelligent individual, ladies and gentlemen, and he keeps learning with each new crime."

"What about the attack style?" someone shouted from the corner.

Portia drew a deep breath. "Each of the victims was overpowered almost instantly. But only one of them, Tirado, died instantly. The killer took his time with the other two. And according to the coroner's reports they took a very long time to die. That means the killer planned carefully. He knew he had hours before he would be in any danger of being discovered. It's more than likely that he stalked his victims, or at least staked them out."

Another clamor of questions, which Portia silenced with her hand. "I also think it serves to explain the discrepancy in the MO in the Tirado killing versus the other cases. With Tirado, he had to work very quickly because he was at greater risk for discovery. Either that or . . ." Here she hesitated for only a moment. "Tirado was a convenience killing. Not actually part of the killer's larger plan."

"Agent Carstairs!" Another voice rose from the general clamor. "Why do you think he's a janitor?"

Carstairs' Adam's apple slid up and down. "I didn't say that. I . . . meant he worked with his hands."

"I don't know that the sophistication of these murders points to that at all," Portia interjected. "Clearly, it's impossible to know what the killer does for a living. But we do know that he kills a certain kind of victim. Reverend Welch was a minister, but she was also a licensed therapist. Meredith was a healer and spiritual adviser. Blue collar just doesn't mesh with the choice of victim. Whoever he is, he's looking for help of some kind."

Someone shouted from the back. "What about the angel? The crucifix?"

"The symbols are significant," Portia went on. "But only as symbols. I think they're part of the killer's signature, his way of making sure his crimes will be noticed." She leaned forward, clutching the mike with both hands now. "He wants to be outrageous, and he knows how to shock—to push our buttons. He's using well-known symbols to do it. He wants to get all the recognition he can. Everything he does feeds into that need."

From the corner of her eye, she caught Carstairs gaping at her, his mouth hanging open in surprise.

"Besides," she went on, "there's a very technical aspect to his choices. Meredith bled to death, a little at a time. A design was carved into her flesh—lines and circles. She died very slowly, bleeding from those wounds. Elizabeth Welch died slowly too. Over many hours. Suffocation. The manner of death is critical in our search for the one who did it."

"Torture?" asked Carstairs, sinking back into his chair.

"No," Portia answered. "I don't believe it's that so much as he's trying somehow to absorb his victims as they die. He wants what they know. He needs their . . ." She paused and made a helpless little gesture. "Essence, for want of a better term."

She glanced around anxiously as a ghastly little silence came over the crowd. A hundred flashbulbs strobed in her face. Part of her panicked, even as she sat calmly in front of the microphone. She might have said too much, gone too far. Her job that day was to reestablish control over the case, to assure the media jackals that she was on top of things in a way the FBI could not be. She might have overdone it with her talk of symbols and essences. It sounded crazy. But then, their killer was turning out to be a very crazy man.

She sat there, feeling hot and cold at once, seeing the reporters at the front of the house frantically scribbling in their notebooks and mumbling into handheld tape recorders. The TV anchors braced for the kill, talking in hushed tones while the minicams rolled. Her sense of dread was confirmed when Madeline Mathews elbowed her way to the front waving her arms and refusing to be ignored.

Portia stiffened in her chair. Madeline Mathews worked the courthouse beat. For what seemed like years on end, Portia had been harassed by the ferret-faced reporter, deluged with the same six questions each time she emerged onto the courthouse steps. In Mathews' universe, Portia McTeague had been an advocate of nothing less than chaos in the streets—trying to turn Charlotte into a psychotic's playhouse, where the inmates ran the asylums and the criminals preyed on Christians by virtue of their unfortunate childhoods.

Now Portia's heart sank as she faced her old nemesis. Madeline Mathews was edging closer to the dais. And she was smiling.

"Dr. McTeague? Dr. McTeague!"

Portia glanced down, as if she had only just seen her. "Yes? You. In front."

Madeline's thin soprano grated on Portia's nerves like a knife on a whetstone. "Given your reputation, ma'am, as an expert witness and all, well, I can't help wondering why you're working with the police now, instead of defending criminals. Does this mean you're finally acknowledging the scope of Charlotte's growing crime problem?"

Portia squinted a little, conscious of a headache taking shape behind her eyes. That was the other thing about Madeline. She had a way of phrasing a question so it couldn't be adequately answered. "I volunteered my services to the task force because of my background in criminal and forensic psychology," she answered carefully.

But Madeline was not so easily deterred. "So, regardless of your involvement with this case, you're still as soft on crime as you ever were?"

And the horse you rode in on, Madeline, Portia thought. Resigned, she spoke again into the microphone. "I want to say for the record that it has never been my position that criminal behavior is justified by personality damage. I have only tried to illustrate the fact that the two are frequently, and sometimes tragically, related."

Madeline was opening her mouth when suddenly another voice came out of the crowd from somewhere to the left, high and controlled and hideously familiar to her.

"Dr. McTeague—isn't it true that nails were not used in the killing of Elizabeth Welch at all? That she was tied to her cross and that's how she suffocated. Won't you set the record straight?"

The blood froze in Portia's veins as she strained to make out the source through the glare of the lights and the new roar of questions being shouted from the floor. A hundred reporters demanded to know— Was it true? Why was wrong information deliberately being released to the media? Didn't they think the people had a right to know?

But Portia was blinded, squinting into the lights. The voice— that voice. Gone in the split second it took for the words to register in her brain—vanished as a hundred other voices took its place. She needed to tell Goodman, to make sure he knew Ivan was there—in that room. Correcting the details, just as she'd predicted—unable to stay away. She wanted to stand up, to shout, He's here, you idiots! The killer is here!

She twisted in her chair, turning to Goodman.

But Goodman was already gone.

TWENTY

Five minutes later, the county courthouse disgorged the remnants of that afternoon's press conference. The sidewalk was littered with TV anchors and remote equipment, worried reporters on cell phones chattering like madmen. And, as the newly christened woman of the hour, Portia McTeague marched headlong into the fray, frantically searching the throng for Dave Goodman even as she was waylaid by a young blond woman from Channel 3.

"Marcia Ray, Doctor," the woman said brightly, thrusting a microphone in her direction. "Channel 3 news. Tell our viewers—what's it like to be back in the spotlight?"

Portia shot her a murderous glance. "Excuse me," she said as politely as she was able. "My comments on this case are confined to the statements I made inside."

"Were you instrumental in managing the false information leaked to the media, Doctor? Are you hoping to set a psychological trap for the killer?" Portia met the woman's eyes, slanted and yellowish, almost like a salamander's.

And, from a rival station, another reporter edged closer. "Do you think the killing of Reverend Welch means the murderer had a mother complex?"

Portia made a sharp left as two different cameramen fell over their feet trying to get to her. "Back off!" she yelled over her shoulder.

But even as they retreated, others pursued her. She could not allow herself to think about the media now. All that counted at the moment was to find Goodman, to see if he had found Ivan in the crowd. She heard her name called again and again as she dashed for the parking garage across the street.

She paused in the shadows of the first level, panting a little, aware of the sound of her own breathing as it bounced and echoed in the concrete caverns that surrounded her. Then, from out of nowhere another voice came, calling a name—her name, but one that no reporter would ever know.

"Pokey? Pokey, for crying out loud. Where did you go?"

She edged around a concrete pillar toward the sound, unable to believe what she was hearing.

"Dec?" Her voice was no louder than a whisper. "Is that you?"

"Of course it's me," he answered in an irritated drawl. "My God, you're the only woman I ever saw who'd allow herself to be chased by a man in a wheelchair. It's undignified."

She emerged from behind the pillar to find Declan Dylan rolling up a nearby ramp, the whine of his electric chair echoing all around.

"How did you find me?" she asked, so happy to see him that her eyes filled with unexpected tears. "I thought you were in England. On a case."

"I was," he intoned sternly. "Got back the day before yesterday. And as for how I found you—how could I miss you, is more like it." He paused, searching her face for some explanation. "What in hell have you gotten yourself into, Pokey?" he asked, again using her daughter's nickname for her. "Half the reporters in the state are back there, all chasing each other's tails."

Portia made a helpless gesture, at a loss how to explain. "God, Dec, it's a long story."

He raised an eyebrow, taking her in with a glance that seemed to swallow her whole. "So start talking."

She looked restlessly around the deserted garage, feeling suddenly vulnerable and exposed. Though whether it was by the environment or by her old friend's all-encompassing look, it was difficult to say.

"Let's get out of here," she offered. "I need a drink or something. Where's your van?"

"Other side of the ramp," he told her, smiling. "Street level. They actually let me park in the handicapped space, for once."

She shook her head, smiling back at him almost gratefully. She thought she had never been so happy to see anyone in her life. "My hero," she said.

"Beans," he answered. "Your slave's more like it. I was yelling my head off for you back there. I almost threw a wheel getting across the street."

She drew a deep breath. Falling into the familiar rhythm of their banter was like slipping into a favorite old robe. "Thank God you didn't," she replied with the first real amusement she'd felt in what seemed like weeks. "Another media scandal avoided."

They came to his van, and Portia watched with renewed respect as Dec maneuvered the various electronic lifts and gadgets that allowed him to drive his own vehicle. Independently wealthy, Dec Dylan could have hired an army of chauffeurs, yet he had chosen another path, one that allowed him the most independence possible.

She climbed in beside him as he started the engine.

"What about your car?" he asked.

Portia leaned heavily against the rich upholstery and closed her eyes. "Stupid," she murmured wearily. "I parked on the street. So the press probably has it staked out by now. I'll get it later," she replied. "Right now, I just can't face another microphone."

Dec eyed her doubtfully as he drove. "Pewter Rose okay with you?" he asked.

"Sure," she answered. "Anywhere."

□   □   □   □

They drove in silence the few miles to the restaurant that graced the edge of one of Charlotte's finer neighborhoods. With characteristic restraint, to say nothing of his finely tuned attorney's instincts, Dec refrained from pressing her for too much information until they were settled at a comfortable table in the bar area, where the last of the day's light filtered through tall, leaded glass windows, and the whisper of a Vivaldi concerto formed a pleasing civilized background for the low conversations of the cocktail hour crowd.

Portia curled her long fingers around the stem of her wineglass, suddenly uncomfortable under her old friend's scrutiny. She knew him well enough to realize that his sudden appearance at the courthouse had not been an accident.

"So what were you doing there, Dec?" she asked a little defensively. "Checking up on your former star witness?"

Unsmiling, he lifted a rocks glass to his lips. "In a manner of speaking," he admitted. "I have to say, I was a little surprised when I found out you'd gone into profiling."

She shot him a warning look. "I haven't gone into it, Dec. For crying out loud. It's one case. Do I live in a fishbowl or something? I'm a forensic psychologist. Figuring out criminals is what I do."

He observed her annoyance with maddening calm. "I thought it's what you used to do," he replied.

Portia refused to meet his eyes. "Yeah, well. I changed my mind. Is that all right with you?"

"Changing your mind is fine with me," he answered. "It's when you try to change the world that you get in trouble."

She glanced at him sharply. "What's that supposed to mean?"

Dec flashed a grin, which only succeeded in irritating her further. "It means, my hypervigilant friend, that you've gone way out on a limb with your work on this case. Last time I talked to you, before I left for England, you made it pretty clear that you'd rather be strung up by your heels than do what you did today. You can yammer about the press all you want, Portia, but you're the one who took over that press conference. And you didn't stop until you'd wiped the floor with that agent, either."

"You don't know anything about it!" she snapped.

Dec clinked his ice cubes as he drained his bourbon and signaled for another. "As a matter of fact," he answered, "I know quite a bit about it. First because I was there, and second because your boy-friend came to see me yesterday."

Portia's eyes widened in surprise. "Alan," she breathed, more a statement than a question.

"Yes, Alan," Dec answered with an edge to his voice. "And drunk on his ass, I might add. He wanted to talk to me. About you."

Some part of her rose up indignantly at the thought of Alan and Dec discussing her behind her back. "How dare he—" she began.

Dec shook his head slowly. "You can shelve the outraged debu-tante stuff, all right? Drunk or not, he came because he's worried about you. And he came to me because he knows I've seen how you get when you're on a case."

Portia's cheeks flushed red. "How I get? Christ, Dec, you know this work—the level of dedication, the concentration it demands. How can you sit there and accuse me—"

Dec met her eyes. "I wasn't aware that I'd accused you of any-thing," he answered quietly. "But since you asked, yes, we talked about the work. The paranoia—the obsession, even. The growing conviction that winning a case, or in this instance, catching a crimi-nal, is all that matters. And we agreed that you have a worse case of that particular disease than most."

Portia stared at him, eyes blazing, jaw clenched. "Fuck you, Dec," she said contemptuously. "And fuck Alan too." Words tum-bled from her lips in furious succession. "I don't suppose he hap-pened to mention that he and I broke up? Or that he's jealous because he can't find a job while I'm working my ass off on this case? Or that his delicate male ego can't withstand even a whiff of professional competition?"

"Lower your voice, Portia," Dec interjected. "People are star-ing."

"You go to hell," she said menacingly. "This is none of your damn business. I never even discussed this case with Alan!"

Dec clasped his hands closer around his glass, as if it might afford him some protection. When he looked at her again, his blue eyes were sad, filled with a wordless understanding. Unable to face that, she turned away.

"Whatever my opinion of Simpson," Dec went on quietly, "he cares enough about you to want to know what's really going on. He cared enough to find out. For heaven's sake, Pokey. He's a private investigator! He's got sources at the police department. What makes you think your secrets are so damn sacred? And more importantly, what makes you think you've got to do this all alone?"

But Portia could not answer; she could only stare stubbornly down at the polished tabletop.

Dec let loose an exasperated sigh. "Fine," he said shortly. "But he left something with me. He wanted you to have it."

Portia glanced up as Dec handed her a padded Jiffy bag that he extracted from the slim leather briefcase he carried at his side. The unexpected weight of the package made her flinch as she took it from him. She met Dec's eyes and saw the flinty blue edge of anger in them as he looked at her.

"It's a pistol. A .22. Simpson wanted you to have it. For protection."

She stared at the package, completely bewildered. "I can't take this!" she protested.

"Take it," Dec urged. "If Simpson is right, and I'm not saying he is, mind you, you may be at risk. From this serial killer."

"That's insane!" Portia replied with more conviction than she felt. "I'm not in any danger!" She stared at her old friend through a fog of confused emotion. "Dec, for Christ's sake, I'm just trying to help here! I'm trying to save some lives. And I'm finally getting a handle on this case. You saw that press conference, you heard that idiot agent. They need me. I can help catch this guy, Dec. Because—"

He held up a hand to silence her, rolling his chair back from the table and snagging a passing waitress with a wave of a fifty-dollar bill. When he looked at her again, his blue eyes were filled with pity.

"I know," he answered. "Because you understand."

"Dec—"

"Keep the gun," he said flatly. "You may need it."

"I won't. I can't."

"Keep it," he snapped. "Even if you don't need to use it, you'll see Simpson before I do." He managed a thin smile. "After you catch the killer, of course," he added.

She stared at the package sitting like an unspoken challenge on the table between them, all but impervious to Dec's sarcasm. Then another thought took shape in her mind. Alan, depressed, drinking. So lost he was investigating her rather than dealing with his own life. Maybe Dec was right. Maybe she ought to keep it. At least until the smoke cleared. At least until things got better for all of them.

The change arrived on a small leather tray and Dec counted out a generous tip.

"Here," he said, handing her a twenty.

"What?" she asked, bewildered.

Dec's smile was cold, distant. "You work alone? Fine. You don't need advice. Swell, call yourself a cab."

And with that, he swung his chair around without another word, leaving her alone in the dimness of the small bar, the strains of Vivaldi swelling to a heartbreaking conclusion, and the wine she'd drunk turning slowly to acid, burning a hole in her stomach.

Once she was home again, Portia made herself and Alice a quick supper of macaroni and cheese from a box, augmented with broccoli and a tall glass of milk for each of them. She moved around the kitchen like a sleepwalker, still stung from her conversation with Dec, grateful for the few precious moments of normalcy her daughter provided—the chance to switch off her mind and take refuge in simple tasks like boiling water, running a bath, and tucking a child safely into bed.

Her weariness was evident as she made her way once more downstairs. She envied Alice her sleep, but for Portia the long day was far from done. First, she plucked up the telephone and dialed Lori's number at home.

"Hey!" her assistant cried joyfully. "I saw you on TV. You looked fabulous!"

Portia smiled ruefully at the wall. She was about to remind Lori of the importance of content over packaging, but decided against it. At the moment she was simply too exhausted. "Thanks, I guess. Listen, can you do me a favor on your way in tomorrow?"

"Sure," Lori said. "What's up?"

"I need you to pick up my car. I parked just across from the municipal building. You still have spare keys, right?"

"Well sure," Lori answered. "But how come you didn't drive it yourself?"

"Too many reporters," Portia half lied. "I just wanted to get out of there when the conference was over, so I flagged a cab."

"Okay." If her explanation was flimsy, Lori didn't appear to notice. "I'll take my usual bus uptown and pick it up from there."

"Thanks, Lori," Portia replied. "I'll catch a cab or something and meet you at the office."

They hung up. Kicking off her shoes, Portia padded over to an armchair and grabbed her pocketbook. Walking slowly back to her desk, she withdrew the package containing Alan's pistol, struck again by its awful weight. She laid it to one side and punched the button that would play back her messages, half hoping to have heard from him. Or Dec. But neither had called.

"Goodman," his voice barked into the phone. She could hear the hiss of traffic in the background as he recorded the rest. "We lost him—whoever he was. Sonofabitch disappeared with the rest of the press jackals. We figure he had a phony pass. I don't know. But hey, you done good up there today, Doc. Looks like you still have a job."

Portia smiled miserably and reached to switch on a small desk lamp. Warm yellow light pooled over the desk, but it failed to comfort her as the rest of the tape unwound. Ivan had disappeared into the crowd. She should call Goodman, tell him not to worry about it. That was the thing about killers—especially serial killers. They knew how to make themselves invisible.

"This is Ivan," someone whispered then. And Portia froze to the spot as a creeping terror swam through her veins.

"You were wonderful today," he whispered out of the machine. "So good, so very smart. I taped you. On the news. So I could watch you. It's like you know me, isn't it?" The voice uttered a small delighted laugh. "You know me. And I know you, too."

The message tape bleeped, startling her out of her paralysis. It was an unlisted number. How, then, had Ivan known it? She shivered in the warm lamplight, wondering if she should call someone, tell Goodman maybe. Call the Help Line to see if someone there had given out her home phone number. Call Alan, even. Ask him to come and stay the night. To hold her against him until the terrible coldness that had settled around her heart was gone.

But Portia didn't do any of those things. Instead she lifted the small padded bag that contained the gun and pulled the tape that would open it, spilling the shredded paper packing over her desk and the floor. She slid out the pistol, reassured this time rather than threatened by its weight in her hand. A simple .22 automatic. What one of her self-defense instructors had once referred to as a "girl gun." But she'd learned how to use one, nonetheless. She could kill with it if she had to.

She snapped open her pocketbook, dropped it inside, and closed the purse.

Then, not knowing what else to do, she slung the strap over her shoulder, turned out the lights, and locked the doors and windows before creeping upstairs to her bedroom, silent as a burglar. And still fully clothed, she lay down on her bed to watch the shadows dance on the ceiling until sometime just before dawn.

TWENTY-ONE

She had no regular patients until eleven the next morning. But a check of her appointment book revealed that she had a therapy session scheduled with Sophie Stransky at ten. She stood alone in her bright kitchen, lost for a long moment after Alice had bounded out of the house to the school bus parked at the curb, and debated whether or not to call and cancel. It wasn't as though she didn't have a good excuse—she was without transportation until Lori brought her car to the office.

Do you want to cancel, she asked herself, because you're afraid that Sophie is going to see the same thing Dec saw? And Alan—and everybody else.

She stared unseeingly out the window above her kitchen sink. Other people had an inner child, she thought without humor. She was stuck with an inner bitch. Feeling as though she lacked the strength to even argue with herself, she plucked up the Yellow Pages from a nearby drawer and searched out the number for a cab.

At ten to ten, she got out of the cab in a wash of mid-morning light, curiously conscious of the pistol tucked in her handbag. Though the worst of last night's terrors had faded with the morning, she brought it anyway, convincing herself that it was better to keep it with her than to risk hiding it in the house, where Alice might discover it.

She rang the bell with a faint, false smile arranged on her face, while inside a tumult of emotions raged. Her last conversation with Sophie seemed like a distant and distinctly unpleasant dream— some error of judgment that was better glossed over and left unaddressed. Yet she knew, even as Sophie herself answered the buzzer, swinging the heavy door inward and fixing her with those bright, birdlike eyes, that whatever the fault in their last communication, Sophie was not about to let it go without further discussion.

They settled into their usual places in Sophie's high-windowed consultation room.

"You look very tired," the older woman began. "Aren't you sleeping well?"

Portia eyed her with sudden, unexpected resentment. Was Sophie somehow unaware of what her last days had been like? Hadn't she seen the news? The endless loops of "film at eleven"? Portia forced herself to take a deep breath and tried to relax. For all she knew, Sophie didn't even own a television.

"Rough day yesterday, that's all," she replied. "I had trouble getting unwound." Portia began to pluck fretfully at the strap of her purse. She wanted to say something—to unburden herself of the terrible pressure that was building inside her. But, still unable to find someplace to begin, she began with Sophie instead.

"Are you all right?"

Sophie nodded, as if sensing the unspoken portion of the question. "Elizabeth's congregation held a memorial service yesterday afternoon," she replied. "It was—very uplifting."

"I'm glad," Portia replied, quite sincerely. Then, "Sophie, look, I feel really bad about what happened the other day. Between us. I don't know—with all that's been happening, I guess I felt like Alan and you . . ."

And now Dec, she added silently.

"I felt like you were ganging up on me."

Sophie raised an eyebrow. "You must know that wasn't my intention," she answered gently. "Or Alan's either, I suspect."

Portia recrossed her legs in her wing chair. "Oh, Alan," she said dismissively. She was temporarily distracted by a sudden and rather vivid vision of the two of them—Alan and Dec—sitting around Dec's plush well-appointed offices, discussing her life. The thought made her almost ill.

"The truth is, Sophie, he's at such a low point himself, I think he'd do almost anything to insinuate himself back into my life. Honestly, I think he's jealous or something." She glanced at her therapist, her green eyes gone hard.

"It's interesting that you would focus on his hidden motives, don't you think?" Sophie asked mildly. "That you would decide you know his mind better than he does?"

Portia sat sullenly in her chair. "If you say so," she acknowledged.

As if you knew the half of it.

"Isn't it possible that Alan truly cares for you?" Sophie prodded gently. "That he's concerned for your well-being? Even that he wants to protect you? It would seem probable, wouldn't it? Given your relationship, I mean."

Given what she was carrying in her purse, the irony was hard for Portia to bear. "I don't want to talk about him," she announced abruptly. Her fingers began to worry the purse strap once more.

"The truth is, it's you," she blurted suddenly. "Last time. You were so . . . judgmental! I never felt that way before coming here. Never!"

Sophie seemed to absorb the accusation with extraordinary calm. Portia watched as she made a small notation on the tablet in front of her. "I wasn't judging you, my dear," she said simply.

Portia sat up straighter, fixed Sophie with a wary look. "Okay, look. Maybe I am a little obsessed with this case, all right? I admit that—is that what you want me to say? So what? Maybe it is some sort of compulsion to feel that I have to get the job done. Why can't anybody understand that? Why can't anybody cut me some slack?"

She fell back in the chair, exasperated. "How can I explain this?"

she went on. "They need a psychologist. A good one. And I know what I'm doing."

"Who is they?" Sophie inquired calmly.

Portia stared at her, taken aback by the question. "The task force, of course," she snapped. "Dave Goodman—the detective who's supposed to be in charge. He seems confident. But, Sophie, he's up against the wall. He's just pretending he can handle it."

"I'm not entirely sure he's the only one pretending," Sophie added.

"Fine. What about that Federal profiler they brought down from Washington? Christ, he wouldn't know how to find this guy if he were sitting under his nose!"

"So how come you know?" Sophie insisted. "How come you are risking your relationships—even your safety? Think about it, Portia. Why is it that you, out of anyone in the world, doesn't need protection? Every time anyone even suggests to you that you might be vulnerable, or that you are just as human as anyone else, you are filled with rage."

"Rage?" Portia snapped back. "Of course I am. I'm filled with rage that those women had to die. And some part of me is angry that the killer went so crazy before anybody could help him. I'm angry and sad that it's going to go right on happening unless somebody does something about it. More people are going to die. You're right, okay? That makes me angry."

And let's not forget guilty, her inner voice reminded her. *Don't forget you gave Ivan that list because you were too dumb to know he was dangerous. Haven't told Sophie that one, have you? What are you hiding?*

"Portia . . ." Sophie's tone was pleading now. "Stop trying to fix everything."

"I'm not, damn you!" she spat back. "I'm angry enough to do something! To try and help. And for that I'm accused of being compulsive. Obsessed. Why the hell can't anybody allow me to have the good sense to be able to take care of myself?" She paused, breathless from her tirade, and so filled with emotion she felt she might explode. "Aren't you always telling me to follow my heart? To trust my instincts? That's what I'm trying to do. So let me do it! Leave me alone!"

She fought back tears of rage and frustration, turning away, rather than allowing Sophie to see those tears fall.

Many moments passed as Portia struggled to compose herself. When Sophie spoke again, her voice was low and distant, gentle and soothing as a cool rain.

"Sometimes the hardest thing to do is to do nothing," the older woman reflected. "I care for you, Portia—as a friend and as a colleague. I want so much to be able to protect you, to keep you safe, if I can. And yet all I can really do is to sit here and watch you and worry about you. Your decisions are your own. I know that.

"But all I am really asking you to do is nothing. To wait for the real nature of this compulsion—this obsession—to reveal itself to you. It may not be as clear as you think it is. And until your real motivations are clearer to you, I am afraid for you. You are a brilliant woman, Portia. A fine psychologist. But you don't know how to protect yourself. You don't know how to respect your own vulnerability. Respect it, Portia, listen to it. Allow yourself to be wrong for once."

But Portia McTeague had ceased to listen to anyone, least of all herself. She stood up abruptly, slinging her handbag over her shoulder, and felt the weight of the gun bang against her hip. "Listen," she said, averting her eyes. "I've—uhh—got some things to do. At the office."

Sophie's old eyes were pleading. "Think about this, Portia. Allow things to unfold."

Portia snatched at the doorknob. "Yeah," she answered almost casually. "I'll call you or something."

And with that, she left the old woman alone.

She kept thinking she ought to feel something as she bounced along on the interminable bus ride that would take her downtown. She'd run for the nearest stop upon emerging from Sophie's house and paid her fare after establishing from the bored driver that this line would in fact take her within blocks of her own office.

Now she sat wedged between an elderly gentleman who smelled of hair tonic and a middle-aged woman carrying a houseplant, both of whom ignored her presence with studied indifference.

But Portia McTeague felt nothing at all as she gazed out the window on the opposite side, no tug of regret or flash of realization. And part of her was almost proud of that detachment. After all, it wasn't the first time a therapist and patient had parted ways. People outgrew one another, that was all. She would call Sophie perhaps, sometime in the coming weeks. To settle her account and assure the old woman she was doing fine. She would even promise to call again, suggest they get together for tea. But it wouldn't happen. Portia herself had parted ways with too many patients, even those with whom she had formed a kind of friendship, to think that it would.

Sophie had helped her over the years; that was certainly true. But perhaps even more important, Portia had done the work. In the end she was the one who had helped herself. She felt good, strong, as she gazed out the window. The last thing she wanted was to keep covering the same old ground, opening all the same old wounds. She wanted to give herself permission to grow up—to move on at long last.

And now, finally, she could do that—without Sophie's help.

And so she was only mildly annoyed when she reached her office less than twenty minutes later and realized that Lori was nowhere in sight.

Portia glanced at her watch, perturbed. It was nearly eleven. Since Lori worked by the hour, it seemed impossible that she would not already be perched behind her desk in a too short skirt, rifling the day's files from the drawers with elaborately manicured nails while the waiting room filled with patients and the smell of freshly brewed coffee.

Portia fumbled her key in the lock and turned off the alarm system after only a few false tries as she resurrected the code from her jumbled memory. She flipped on the lights, her annoyance growing by the moment as she found her way through a thoroughly unfamiliar morning routine, flipping through the session schedule and searching the cabinets for coffee as the phone rang repeatedly, answered by an automatic voice mail system. Portia scanned the return telephone numbers from the caller ID—there were none that she recognized. She left the system turned on. After yesterday, she figured it wise. The relentless press would be ringing her phone off the hook.

Where is she? a part of Portia's mind demanded as the minutes ticked inexorably by. This wasn't like Lori at all. Had there been a problem with the Volvo? It didn't seem likely. She'd had it serviced less than two hundred miles ago. Besides, if that had been the case, the relentlessly efficient Lori would have been sure to call, if only to say "I told you so," or "I warned you about that funny noise in your transmission."

As Portia watched the coffee drip, the door burst open behind her and she turned, smiling broadly, ready to welcome her prodigal assistant home.

Instead she was confronted by Sandra Mahoney staring at her in disbelief, her naturally discontented mouth set in a disapproving line.

"I'm here for my eleven," the woman whined. "Nobody called to reschedule."

Portia's smile shifted until it was a sort of lopsided agreement. "Of course you aren't canceled, Sandra," she said. "I'm just a little behind this morning. I seem to have lost my assistant."

Sandra nodded, as if that were all the explanation she required. "Nobody has any sense of responsibility anymore, Doctor," she intoned. "Nobody. Just wait till you hear what my ex did this week. Just wait."

"Go on back and get comfortable, Sandra," she replied, bracing herself. "I'll just be a minute."

She grabbed Lori's favorite mug from the tree and poured, as if hoping her use of it would somehow cause her assistant to magically materialize. But even as she sipped the scalding liquid, nothing happened. The phone rang again, startling her from her thoughts. Portia glanced at the number blinking on the caller ID and ignored it. She glanced once more around the abandoned reception area, wondering what could have gone wrong. Perhaps it was only something silly. Something like Lori being unable to find the spare car keys after all.

The clock on the wall uttered a forlorn little click as it passed the hour, the result of a disabled chime mechanism. And, almost reluctantly, Portia edged down the hall toward the unhappy Sandra.

When she emerged forty-five minutes later, with the weeping Sandra padding noisily behind, she was shocked to see Dave Goodman ensconced in one of the chairs in her waiting room, wearing a tie commemorating Jean Harlow and thumbing through a worn-out copy of *Redbook*.

Portia said nothing at all, but waited until she'd patted Sandra comfortingly on her chubby shoulder and assured her she was making progress. Sandra only looked at her, sniffing doubtfully.

"What about my payment?" she whined.

"Lori's out today," Portia offered cautiously, suddenly struck by a new sickening certainty, forged by Goodman's silent presence, that this was not the case at all. "We'll do it next week," Portia assured her. She was not at all sure she even knew where the account books were kept.

"But I always pay as I go. Every time," Sandra insisted.

Portia walked resolutely to the outer door and opened it. "Next week, Sandra. I'll remember. I promise."

Portia closed the door behind her and turned to find that Dave Goodman had risen to his feet and was looking at her with an odd expression, made up half of sympathy and half of something rock-like and unmovable.

"You want to tell me what you're doing all the way down here?" Portia asked half jokingly, not quite able to keep the tremor from her voice. "No offense, Dave," she said, avoiding his eyes and circling to a safer point behind the reception counter. "But I'm swamped just now. My assistant didn't show up this morning."

"I know," he answered softly. She looked at him and saw that once again Dave Goodman hung back, watching her with those sad doggy eyes. He said nothing. He was letting her come around to it, letting her draw the conclusions. And still she resisted, fighting off the cry of protest that rose unbidden in her throat.

"I thought I'd better come over here myself," he offered. And the statement maddened her.

"What for?" she demanded sharply. A sort of shaking had over-come her, and she sat down hard in Lori's chair for fear her knees had begun to knock out loud. "Am I fired again?" she asked, her eyes filling with tears.

He only shook his head sadly, as if somehow confirming the unspoken awful words that had yet to pass between them.

"Jesus, Dave . . . stop it!" Her fingers curled into fists as she pounded them impotently on her knees. "Is it Lori? Where is she?"

"Dead," he answered simply. "In your car. Near the municipal building."

For a long moment, Portia could only look at him, struck mute by this new awfulness as the implications hit her like waves on some desolate shore. "How?" she croaked softly.

Goodman ducked his head and mumbled the answer into his tie. "Strangled," he answered. "Far as we can tell." He stopped sud-denly. He didn't want to tell her that it had taken Lori Stone a very long time to die. "I came here first," he went on. "I thought you might know next of kin. Somebody to come and ID her."

"I'll go," Portia said, her voice sounding small and unfamiliar. Then, "There was a sister—no, sister-in-law—she talked about." Portia ran both hands through her hair. Trying to think, to remem-ber. "It's in the file," she finished lamely. "Jesus, Lori. I can't be-lieve this!"

She began to cry weakly and Goodman sank down next to her, awkwardly squatting on his haunches. He gently took up the limp, icy fingers of one of her hands. "Believe it," he said softly. "And yeah, you're fired. From now on, you're under police protection. Twenty-four hours."

He reached inside the breast pocket of a rumpled jacket and withdrew a folded piece of paper, placing it between her fingers like some glass figurine.

She stared at it, then him, trying to find some meaning in it all.

Goodman sucked a quantity of air. "It's him," he told her, enun-ciating the words as though it cost him a great effort. "Ivan. For you. He left it in the car. Open it. Don't worry, it's been dusted for prints."

Her hands shook violently as she did so. And then it took a long time for her eyes to focus on the letters scrawled upon the page—longer still for the letters to form words or the thought they conveyed to register in her agonized mind.

"I know you," it said. "And you know me."

TWENTY-TWO

MY WORLD

By John Campion

The sickening slaughter that has plagued Charlotte's streets is now part of a larger terror. This reporter has discovered through meticulous research of law enforcement sites on the World Wide Web and other sources that the death of Lori Stone is merely the latest in a series of murders by an unknown killer stalking the unsuspecting women of the Southeast.

Through my research I have discovered that there have been other killings, unsolved murders like the ones we have seen here. Murders where the similarity in style of attack, and even the women's choice of profession, point to the same individual.

His victims are women. Good women, all of them. Women who had elected the helping professions. They cared for the sick, listened to the troubled. There is first a doctor in Virginia; struck down even as she carried her unborn child. Authorities there believe she had been stalked by a former mental patient at the hospital where she worked. Yet they never identified a suspect.

Then a nun in Georgia—overpowered, then raped, then horribly mutilated as the killer cut out the good sister's tongue. Then there was the nurse in Orlando, struck down in a parking lot after her shift. Her ears had been removed. These are crimes no one has solved—crimes that the police have not taken the trouble to link with the current river of blood running through our streets. And still the body count is rising.

By tying these crimes together, we discover a clear pattern of escalating violence following a classic blitz-style attack. The killer removes trophies of his kill; the tongue of she who spoke, the ears of one who listened, and now the hands of one who used them to heal. Angel Tirado was hanged from a curtain rod in a bizarre mockery of her name; the subsequent crucifixion of Elizabeth Welch was the most bizarre murder of all. The murders are serial in nature. All the evidence points to nothing else. And our killer is turning up the volume on his crimes to gain the attention and fame he so desperately needs. *Why will no one notice?*

Yes, Charlotte has another serial killer.

How do I know? Because I did my homework, because I researched and thought and interviewed. Because I put the clues together in a way the authorities, whether through carelessness, incompetence, or simple disinterest, have not cared to do. This menace grows smarter and more complex with every kill—and moves further and further from the reach of ordinary minds.

How do I know? In short, I did my job—thoroughly investigating a series of crimes I knew would be of interest to the people that matter most—my readers. I read the clues—I found the pattern.

And why can't the authorities do the same? Because the so-called experts have failed us again. Just as they failed Charlotte two years ago in the Henry Lee Wallace case. Fourteen murders in twenty months, and Henry Lee Wallace was right under their noses. Just as the experts failed this madman when he came to them for help, it's happening again.

The authorities have failed us. Our protectors have failed to protect us. Just as they will fail in some other city, some other town. Cops, lawyers, even psychologists—all those who purport to know the dark workings of the killer's impulse and the secrets of the human mind—all of them are competing for our attention, drawing our thoughts away from the real danger and onto themselves.

But the fact remains that less than fifty percent of all serial killers are ever caught, and those who are, are likely to be freed or to receive reduced sentences as the experts continue their war of words in court.

They are pretenders, all.

The bumbling bozos who make up the mayor's so-called task force, supposedly investigating the recent deaths of Tamara Meredith, Angel Tirado, Elizabeth Welch, and now Lori Stone, make the Keystone Kops look like a SWAT team. Agent Bob Carstairs, of the Federal Bureau of Investigation, appeared at a task force press conference last week with a profile that any TV scriptwriter could have put together, while his fascinating foil, Charlotte forensic psychologist Portia McTeague, filled in the blanks with a theory of her own. What was supposed to have been a meeting to inform the public turned into yet another war of words. And a killer roams at large.

I have had occasion to speak with Dr. McTeague in the past weeks. During our conversations, she admitted to me that if a serial killer walked into her office looking for help or intervention, she would not be able to identify him. She calls herself an expert, yet by her own admission her work is "imprecise" and forged by "intuition." She said in effect that her patients "do most of the work" of recovery.

Apparently if this killer is to be caught, he must be the light bulb that wants to change.

The best hope for solving this case is, then, an expert who would not know a killer if he were under her nose, working with a task force that cares more about publicity than punishment.

And now, Dr. McTeague's own employee is dead, a victim of the guessing game we have come to call criminal investigation. Is the killer trying to send Dr. McTeague a message? Or was Stone simply the latest instance of one man's obvious ability to outwit the experts? Another taunt as a madman cries—catch me if you can?

Is he sending a message not to one woman, but to the world?

Portia read the column slowly, her morning coffee cooling in her cup. Her eyes, still red with last night's weeping, moved beneath swollen, sandy lids. From the open window, she heard the delighted cries of children as Alice and Jessica ran races in the yard next door. The phone on the wall began to ring and she rose like a sleepwalker to turn off the signal. People would be calling after this, she knew. Friends, colleagues, more reporters for sure. The damning implications of Campion's column would follow her for weeks, maybe months to come. Bewildered, she stared down at the page and saw her patient's face grinning back at her, pleased with himself and utterly confident before the camera as he posed for the beckoning world. And she recalled the strange sense of subtext during their few sessions, her suspicions that he'd had some reason other than the one he stated for coming there. It all made sense now. It made all the sense in the world.

Her mind was dulled by lethargy and pain as she crossed to the front window and peered through the curtain, looking out at the familiar street as though she had never seen it before.

A uniformed officer sat in an unmarked car a few houses down, his knees up on the steering wheel, drinking coffee straight from a thermos and paging through the *Star*. She wondered what the officer would think when he read the column. She wondered how well she herself would protect someone who had bungled and betrayed a homicide investigation. So what if it was nothing more than a fabric of half-truths and suppositions? Enough was true, enough to feed the fires of her guilt over Lori's death into a roaring blaze.

Reg, her next-door neighbor, came out to his yard, and she saw him glance toward her house, scowling as he walked to his car. How did Reg feel, she wondered. What must he think of the woman who'd blundered so badly—the expert who'd been so blind she had been duped by a reporter, who then had made fools of them all?

Portia moved the small length of lace back over the windowpane, trying to shake the strange paralysis that threatened to overtake her. She clutched her bathrobe close around her and tried to think, to find some starting point. But her brain refused to cooperate. Every thought she began she left unfinished. Every plan she found some reason to leave undone.

She should call Dec, have him make the paper print a retraction; but then, there was nothing, really, to retract. She'd been quoted out of context, that was all. The words were her own. Besides, a retraction would be given a half inch at best, buried somewhere on the comics page, lost in the advertising section. And Dec would not help her now—not after their last conversation. No one could help her now. The damage was done.

Another sluggish, unwholesome thought took shape out of the swamp of her depression as she went back to the kitchen and dumped her cold coffee in the sink. Lori's funeral was tomorrow. The idea of going to some church and having to face Lori's family and friends made Portia sick and cold with apprehension. And a huge unnameable guilt overwhelmed her. They would accuse her, she knew. They would tell her with their eyes that it was all her fault. And they would be right. Lori was dead, and she was to blame.

Portia's eyes burned with sudden tears. She brushed them away and sat down heavily in a nearby chair, forcing herself to think of nothing at all, until finally that thought too receded from her consciousness. She wanted to be emptied of tears. She yearned for emptiness and quiet and sleep.

She sat there for some minutes, not knowing what to do, how to focus. Powerless to fight against the depression that overtook her. The long day stretched out before her in a wilderness of hours. Outside, the clouds rolled in thickly, blocking the morning sun as the day turned oppressive and dark. She was dimly aware that the girls' voices had faded and she knew that they had gone indoors to Aggie's house. Aggie's house—always bright and welcoming, away from the black vibrations and misery of her own.

It was almost like dying. She felt dead—was dead—save for the dull monotony of her still-beating heart. She felt nothing, saw nothing, even as the great inventory of her life's failures rose up in her mind. The damaged and abused girl grown into a damaged woman. Full of weary rage, trapped in an endless cycle of victim and abuser, changing as the circumstances required.

It was clear to her then what all those who had tried to love her had been saying. She had ruined her life, fooled herself into thinking that she was trying to save others, and she had never succeeded even at that. And the thought of all those who had died and those still waiting to die regardless of her work in the courts filled her with a crushing sense of hopelessness. She had believed this time would be different—she had believed and she had been terribly mistaken.

But Alan had been right and Sophie had been right and even Dec, and she had pushed them all away as she chased her shadows and fought her useless battles with her ghosts.

Now even Campion was right. He had won. All the years had taught her nothing, all her education and experience vanished in a terrible hurricane of betrayal and loss, as she sat alone at her kitchen table. She would not know a killer under her own nose. She had simply guessed and theorized and counted herself an expert in the eyes of the world. When in fact she had only been vain and stupid and stubborn to the end.

She was nothing more than a pretender; and the killer had known it all along. And the predator in him had smelled her lies like blood on the wind, daring her to be right. All those poor attempts at therapy, the clumsy tools of science—were just a disguise. The paper was still spread out on the table, and his words mocked her from the page. She had done nothing—helped no one.

Dr. Portia McTeague was nothing but a fake, a joke, a phony so damaged, so schooled in violence, it was the only thing left that made her feel alive. Lori was gone. And her work was over. She was used up and alone—a laughingstock in a profession she had loved more than her own life. There was nothing left to guess at anymore. A killer had won.

The game, it seemed, was over.

TWENTY-THREE

After the wonder boy shuddered to a noisy climax, Kate Loveless rolled away and spat delicately into a corner of a Battenburg pillowcase.

"Hmm—" murmured Campion. "Was it good for you?"

Kate sat up, brushing the straight platinum-white hair away from her face. "Not especially," she answered. "But I figure you deserved it. That column of yours sent sales through the roof."

"Didn't I tell you it would?" he answered, smiling dreamily at himself in the mirrors above her bed.

Kate knew better than to reply, but she found she couldn't resist. "I still don't get it, Campion. Okay, so you got people riled up. You drew attention to the murders. But what was the big deal? Why all the secrecy? The extra time?"

He turned to her and his eyes held an unpleasant little glimmer of contempt. "I had to wait until they were ready to believe," he said quietly. "I put off the column release until there were enough bodies." He glanced down at Kate's wrists. Angry red welts still showed where he'd tied her up a few hours before. He felt a renewed rush of triumph. Poor Kate, he thought. She had so much to learn.

Aloud he said, "At first I was going to do more with it—really play up the connections. But that part will keep for another week. Better to keep 'em a little hungry, don't you think? Hankering for just a little more."

He reached over with a single finger and began to run it up the length of her thigh.

Kate moved away at his touch, hugging herself around the knees. The sight of the dark hair that curled over the back of Campion's fingers made her suddenly ill. And the memory of last night's sport made her recoil with humiliation. She had been a fool, she knew it. She had let him go too far.

She got up abruptly. She wanted a shower, to brush her teeth. She wanted him gone. He'd left his readers wanting more. Well, that was fine with her. They could have him.

"I suppose you know corporate is pleased." She began rummaging through her closet for a short silk robe. She put it on and tried to smile, wanting to butter him up enough to soften her own bit of news. The job in Washington had materialized; she was flying out in the morning for the first of the takeover meetings. This was the last time she and Campion would share the sheets, wonder boy or not.

He turned to her then, apparently satisfied for the moment with his own reflection. "Yeah," he said, "Beekman called me himself. Said I could really go places in the syndicate." Campion chuckled. "He said I really had a feel for the human heart."

Kate fought back an impulse to scream at him, to tell him Beekman was a fool. "Really?" she answered. "What did you say to that?"

Campion rolled over on his back again, smiling up at the image of the single person in the world he truly loved. "I played him, you know. Told him I'd done my best, sir. All the usual crap. But the column's just the first step."

Suspicion coiled like a snake in her solar plexus. "The first step? What do you mean? You're not still after that book deal, are you?"

He glanced at her as though he'd suddenly just realized she was there. "Fuck the book," he answered. "I work this right and I go to TV land, don't you get it? Money, recognition." His eyes shone brightly. "All I need is a few more bodies. A couple of weeks. Then my phone's going to be ringing off the hook."

Kate could no longer contain herself. "Campion" she said, more sharply than she'd intended, "you're leaving. That is—I'm leaving. For Washington. They bought up the *Bugle* and I'm going up there to turn it around. They handed me the publisher's slot."

She could see the statement brought him up short. He stared at her, his odd eyes narrowing with a flicker of surprise. A vein began to throb in his temple and some survival instinct made her edge farther down the hall toward the bathroom, out of his reach. "I'm going," she said again. "And you're not going with me. So get dressed."

She stood there watching him, waiting for some sign, some shout—anything to signal that he had heard her. But he only continued to look at her, his face frozen in the same bright, awful smile now leering out from every copy of the Sunday *Star*. She shivered. And then he began to laugh.

"You fucking cunt," he said, chuckling. "For real?"

"For real, Campion. Now get the hell out."

She found his pants and tossed them to him. He sat up, swung his legs over the side of the bed. She kept her distance, watching for a breathless moment as he tugged on his pants, then the remainder of his clothes. His thick-muscled shoulders moved under the fabric of his shirt. And suddenly he reached out and tore at her robe, the thin fabric giving way in his hands.

Kate snatched at the remnants of the ruined garment. "Get the fuck out, do you hear me!" she screamed. "Get out or I'll call the fucking cops!"

He rose and edged nearer, laughing a little at the terror in her eyes. "Cops?" he snorted derisively. "Oh, that's good, Kate. Calling the cops." He bent and kissed her lightly on the lips. Her stomach flipped and shuddered at the stale smell of his breath—the coldness of his touch.

He snatched his jacket from the foot of the bed and slung it casually over his shoulder. He glanced upward, as if to bid goodbye to his own reflection, and smiled at himself in the smoky mirrors.

Kate stood shaking, trying with every part of herself to will him gone.

He looked at her.

"You bitch," he said. "I really ought to kill you. But it would ruin my career."

TWENTY-FOUR

Monday morning dawned sullen and strange. The first of the season's big hurricanes was moving up the eastern seaboard, and even at this distance, Charlotte's air was charged with electricity, stirred up by fitful winds.

Portia rose from a thick sleep and padded to the bathroom, aware of the silence in her house. Alice was at Jessica's, she realized with a dull pang of familiar guilt. Aggie had offered to take her when Portia had at last resorted to the prescription that finally helped her to sleep, the first rest she'd had in what seemed like days.

The funeral was today. Lori's funeral. She stared at herself for a long moment in the mirror above the sink, aware of how much she seemed to have aged over the weekend. Her hair was tangled, hanging limply near the grayish shadows under her cheekbones, and her eyes were those of some much older woman, crepey and immensely tired. The eyes of one who has seen too much, and cannot face the world anymore.

She rinsed her face in cold water, trying to dispel the grogginess and grief that had clouded her thoughts since that moment when Goodman had come to her office to tell her that Lori was dead. Dead. The enormity of it threatened her even now as she slipped from her stale-smelling nightclothes, trying to work her grief-dulled mind toward more ordinary thoughts—people to be called, her patients. She smiled grimly as she stepped into a scalding shower, remembering all over again the insult of Campion's column.

Patients indeed. She would be lucky if she had any patients left.

She soaped herself all over and washed her hair, feeling some stubborn part of her come to life under the steam and spray. Thoughts and images tugged at her and she pushed them resolutely away. She would not allow herself to think just yet, with the pain so fresh. When she knew she would need all her strength to get through the next few hours. Thinking led to feeling and to questions that had no answers. And still her depression gnawed hungrily at the edges of her consciousness, while the demons of guilt and responsibility cried to be fed.

Some part of her was dimly aware that she was in trouble. But she could not find a way to loose the stranglehold she kept on her emotions. She could not face her losses just yet, could find no way to absorb the notion of a future beyond the moment. Better just to move through this day detached and dissociated. She was still a psychologist—she knew how useful it could be, to push aside those things that could not be faced, to move like some robot through the next days and hours. A few short days before, she had still believed she had power—the power to know the workings of the mind, to read without fear the darkest impulses of the heart. But her power had deserted her. The weapons of knowledge had turned to dust in her hands.

Dragging a brush through her wet curls, Portia paused and gazed at herself once more in the mirror before heading downstairs to the coffeepot. She studied her reflection, a little disturbed by the emotionless mask that served to disguise the hollowness inside. She wondered for a moment if she had gone crazy. And she found she did not care very much if she had.

□ □ □ □

Later, after she had moved like a sleepwalker through most of the morning, choosing a dark dress and stockings, applying makeup in a careful disguise over her exhausted face, she glanced uneasily through the lace-framed window of the front door. Across the street, a new uniform sat behind the wheel of a standard Charlotte police vehicle, chewing gum and eyeing her house in an uncertain way, as if he were not quite sure what he was doing there.

A small rental car was parked in the driveway; the police had impounded the Volvo for evidence. Portia glanced at it, even as her mind surprised her with the certain knowledge that she would have to get a new car.

Portia fought back the sudden image of fingers curled around a young woman's throat. Ivan's fingers. Choking a little on some involuntary response that rose in her neck, she grabbed her purse, astonished by its unexpected weight.

The press, she thought dully. The reporters. They would be there too, she supposed. Hanging around like vultures at the grave, ready to pick at the carrion of Lori's life. To speculate and point their fingers and damn with half-formed innuendo. Campion. She wondered if he would be there to delight in the ruin he had caused. She wondered if he would return, like some killer to the scene of his crime.

Campion. The name echoed in her tired mind, and some part of her struggled to know the reason.

I know you—and you know me, too.

And suddenly, she did know.

She shot a glance at the antique clock that hung on the wall near the stairs. The funeral was set for eleven. It was only a little after ten. Yet she knew she could not remain there, waiting in her dark dress and makeup. She knew if she lingered, her resolve to attend the funeral would crumble by slow, agonizing degrees. And if she did not leave the house this morning, if she did not make herself attend that funeral, she knew some part of her strength would be lost forever. She plucked up her car keys from a table in the hall and headed out.

The first spatters of fitful rain fell like tears on her shoulders and the wind hit her like a slap as she crossed to the police car on the opposite side of the street. The young cop inside looked her up and down in a way that made Portia's flesh want to crawl from her bones. Thick clouds churned and rushed out of a huge whirlwind in the east. Portia set her teeth, shivering in the humid, sultry air.

"The service is at Christ Church," she said without meeting the young policeman's eyes. "On Billings Road. I'll meet you there." She turned toward her driveway, feeling his eyes on her back and legs as she crossed the street.

She could not have said when the moment came that she decided to lose the police car. She knew only that she paused at some intersection on the way to the church and slipped on her dark glasses against the strange yellow brightness of the coming storm. She glanced in the rearview mirror and saw the surveillance car. Then glanced in the mirror at her own face, the careful, sculpted mask of makeup and glasses.

And still the awful secret whispered in her mind.

I know you.

Portia McTeague was tired of being watched. And there was no protection left for her. Not anymore. She eyed the intersection and floored the accelerator, the rental car's transmission protesting. She hung a sharp left, tires squealing, turning away from her destination and back toward her office. Not daring to think, not able to feel or question, Portia wove skillfully in and out of the traffic lanes, checking the mirror. Three miles later she was sure the cop was gone. And she was greatly, absurdly relieved.

Minutes later, she pulled into the parking lot behind her office building. She took off her dark glasses and laid them on the seat. The storm was nearer now, the sky as dark as evening.

The lot was filled with the usual assortment of vehicles, sleek sedans and burly trucks; a scattering of four-wheel drives. All unaware of her own presence there. Or the ghost she had come to meet.

Her heels clicked purposefully across the asphalt as she made her way to her ground-floor corner suite. Even then she refused to believe what she knew. She pretended she'd come there for some ordinary reason—thought for a moment that she meant to leave a note on the door telling her patients she was attending a funeral, or leaving a number where she could be reached.

And still another layer of her tortured mind peeled back. Portia realized she wanted to see Lori, to find some sense of her presence left in the world, here in the place where they had known one another. She wanted to sit in her chair and remember her voice, to hear the echo of her laughter. Most of all, she wanted to beg her forgiveness for being the reason she was gone.

Such good reasons for coming, aren't they? But not the real reason. Not the real reason at all.

Portia's hands trembled as she worked the key into the stubborn lock, fidgeting and clumsy as the metal resisted and she realized suddenly that it was open, left unlocked by a careless janitor. Or perhaps, in the horror of the last time she'd been there, Portia had neglected it herself. She swung the door inward and flipped on the light. Nothing happened.

And she was blinded then, as a hundred flashbulbs strobed in her face, popping like fireworks. Wincing, she raised an arm to protect herself.

"Who is it? Who's there?"

You know.

And the room was black once more. She stumbled forward, blinded by the bright red blobs that blurred her vision. Her eyes fought to adjust. The blinds were drawn, the windows covered with something. No light. She blinked and the blobs turned blue.

Another flashbulb, closer now. More, so fast she could not count them, so many she could feel the heat on her skin. Then silence again. Then something—the whine of a camera and film.

"Please—" Her voice broke and fear traveled up through her guts like cold fire. "Who?" she croaked.

"You know who," a voice whispered from somewhere to the back of her. "I knew you'd come."

I know you and you know me.

And even then she fought the knowledge. "No!" she said. And the word hung between them like a lie.

Another flashbulb popped a warning. Her eyes streamed tears.

"No, Doctor. We have an appointment. We have to keep our appointments, don't we?"

And it seemed to her that it was a long time before she could say the name.

"Ivan?" And the knowledge turned her helpless as she spoke, joining the two of them together in the dark. "John—John Campion."

A shuffling, hulking shadow moved in the corner. She moved away, thinking it was toward the door and bumping her hip on a chair. Disoriented, she was moving away from escape, farther into the office, toward the hall.

"Very good, Doctor," he answered. "I was wondering how long it would take you. I've gotten rather impatient about it, actually."

He was moving and still she could not find him. She fingered the wall, trying to get her bearings. Some part of her wanted to run. And still she knew she could not—knew that even now there had to be some reason.

"John . . . Ivan," she whispered.

"Two forms of the same name," he announced. "You should have known that. You should have been smart enough to know that."

"You're right." Her vision was beginning to clear, she could make out the shapes of the nearest things in the dark. She placed Campion somewhere in front of her now, blocking the exit. "I should have known."

An unpleasant little laugh. "One transforms to the other, don't you see? How could you not see that? We are all transformed."

"John . . ."

And she was blind again, staring into a hideously bright continuous light that shone into her eyes. The outline of his profile shone as he watched her through the lens of a video camera. "Yes," he said softly. "This is better—this is right." His voice came at her from behind the camera, urgent and sexual and utterly bizarre.

"You're so beautiful," he murmured like a lover. "Yes, that's right. I love the look in your eyes. So lost, so afraid."

Portia began to cry, hoarse, strangled sobs rose up in her throat, and she turned her head, ashamed of the fear inside.

"DON'T YOU TURN YOUR BACK ON ME, YOU STUPID BITCH!" Campion thundered. For a moment, the terrible light jiggled crazily in his hands. His breath was coming hard. "You want to ruin it?" he demanded.

Portia stared at the light. Something dragged on her shoulder. Her purse, heavy—so heavy hanging there.

"There, that's just right. Now, reach up, very slowly. Unbutton your dress. Slowly, dammit! I want this to be perfect!"

Her shaking fingers obeyed. One button, then two. Cold tears slid down her cheeks.

"Look at the camera," Campion barked. "Look at the light!"

"I can't . . . I can't see."

Another snarl of laughter. "Ironic, isn't it? That you would be blind. So blind. All the time the truth is there and no one sees. No one believes anything. Unless it's on TV."

"John—you can't do this! They'll know. If you kill me, they'll know it was you."

A sound, a sort of snort. "Will they know, Doctor? Will they really? You were their best chance. The only real hope of catching me. And now you'll be dead. Unbutton your dress. I'm wasting tape."

She felt the damp air against her chest, smelled her own perfume. The video camera whirred on. "The tape! The tape is evidence."

"Wrong," he said. "The tape is *my* evidence. You have beautiful eyes, you know that? So green. I plan to take them with me. Souvenirs, you know."

Portia's gut tightened as vomit rose in her gorge, fueled by tears and snot and a terrible helplessness. She swallowed it back, choking. "Don't," she whispered. "John—I can help you!"

His laughter was almost gentle. The light burned a hole in the dark. "That's not how it works." His voice hung between them, strange and dreamlike. "I have to kill you first. Slowly. Very slowly. And I watch you die. That's how I learn. You become part of me and I will be healed. Because we will be the same. You see?"

The terrible light jittered. "It's called a transformation," he hissed. "Take off your dress."

And then, like a miracle, she remembered.

"I have to put my purse down. On the floor."

Her knees buckled as the strap slid down and she fumbled for it in the dark and felt it in her hand. One arm hung at her side as she rose again, hiding it in the folds of her narrow skirt. She coughed as she clicked the safety. The dress slipped from her shoulder.

Campion moved the camera, and even in her blindness Portia was sure she saw some other light, thin as a blade, flashing in the awful smothering dark.

The shadow moved. And the world blew apart as gunfire shattered the blackness, popping like fireworks through an endless night.

And someone began to scream.

EPILOGUE

Declan Dylan sat at a breakfast table laid out on the flagstone terrace in back of the house where he had been born—a rambling gray stone mansion on Colville Road. He poured his coffee from a gleaming silver service into one of his mother's Havilland china cups, stirred in too much sugar and a quantity of cream. The storm front had moved up the coast in the night, leaving the air washed brilliantly clean. The whole world smelled new to him this morning, as if it had just been made.

Flowers, the last of the season, nodded from lushly planted beds scattered over the lawns. Chrysanthemums and marigolds, the late-blooming rose arbors that were his pride. The world that morning spoke to him more of April than of August. The more than three months he had spent in England had left him homesick for this place, for he missed this house and these gardens like a person when he was gone.

His housekeeper appeared with the morning papers, warm croissants in a basket, and a dish of translucent Seville marmalade. He smiled at her briefly, not seeing the mute concern in her eyes, dropped a generous dollop of jam on a croissant, then turned to his papers, still anxious to catch up with local affairs, to pick up the threads of news he'd been missing in all his months away.

He flipped open the *Star*, and the bright world crashed around him. He blinked, once, then once more. He turned to his housekeeper, the blood drained from his face.

"Karen," he said. And though his voice was no different than it ever was, something made her place a hand on his shoulder, the soft hairs rising along the length of her arms.

"I know," she said. "I thought you'd want to see it for yourself."

He pushed himself back from the table, betraying no loss of composure. There was just that terrible pallor, the look that haunted his eyes. "See if you can find Henry, will you? Have him bring the car around."

Karen stared at him, wanting to offer some comfort and not knowing how. "The van?"

"No," Dylan answered, his eyes fixed on the mess of papers and breakfast on the table before him. "The Jaguar. Ask him if he can drive. The county jail."

Karen laced her fingers together. "I'll tell him," she said. "When?"

Dec sighed, transfixed by something she could not see. "Three minutes. I'll meet him out front."

And when she was gone, Dec removed his palm from the place on the page where he had covered the face he knew so well. He stared at it for a long moment, knowing the profile that was hidden behind the long white fingers, her hands spread in front of her face as she shrank from the cameras. He read the headline one last time as if it might be true and not some cruel joke played upon his heart.

VIDEO OF DEATH? it blared at him.

Then, beneath the headline, the crueler explanation.

Psycho Shrink on Shooting Spree?

A formal inquest into the bizarre allegations by Charlotte psychologist Portia McTeague that she shot and killed *Star* reporter John Campion in self-defense is pending authorities' investigation. Despite the psychologist's continued insistence that Campion's assault was videotaped, police sources say a viewing of the tape found at the scene revealed it was blank.

Dec read no further. He did not need to.

He stared out over the gardens, where petals dropped in little deaths, each a silent witness to his suffering.

"Oh, Pokey—" he said to no one. "What happened to you?"

DATE DUE

FEB 1 9 1999	
FEB 2 0 1999	
MAR 0 9 1999	
MA 7 1999	
APR 0 1 1999	
APR 1 5 1999	
APR 3 0 1999	
MAY 1 3 1999	
AUG 1 0 2000	
FEB 0 7 2001	
SEP 2 0 2003	
JAN 1 9 2005	